THEY ONCE WERE GODS

By Chris Petherick

ISBN: 979-8-234-01143-5

Library of Congress Control Number: 2026904992

Front cover image art: Manu
Interior art: Rizal Abdillah

First Printing: March 2026
Brandywine House
14109 Brandywine Road
P.O. Box 121
Brandywine, Maryland 20613
United States of America
https://brandywinehouse.us

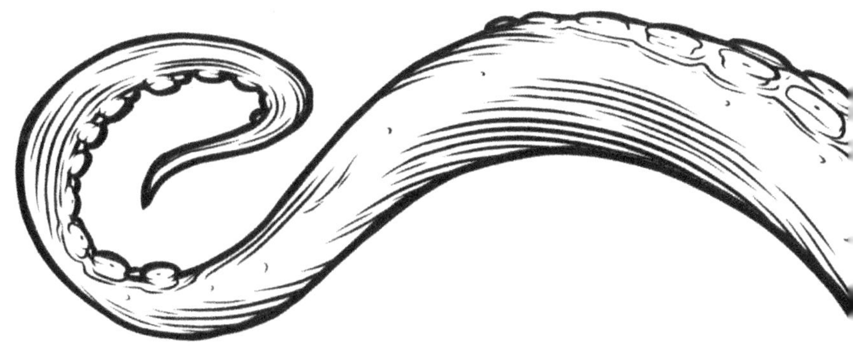

To my wife, who with extreme grace and love, mostly tolerates my many ideas, whims, and projects, and to my two children, who over the years have taught me to practice what I preach about patience and humility.

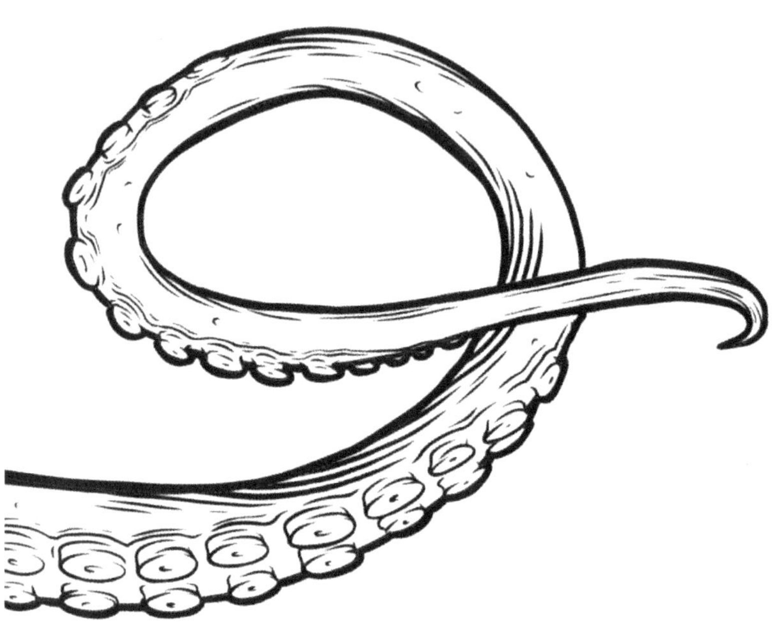

"We have been here since the beginning of time, conceived among the stars but born here on this world to live forever."

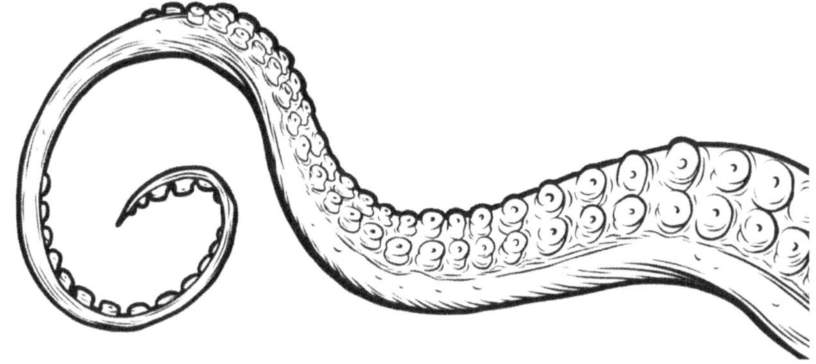

CHAPTERS ...

Prologue
Chapter 1: Chicagoland
Chapter 2: A Bitter Pill
Chapter 3: I Think I Just Met a God
Chapter 4: So Much for Talking
Chapter 5: They Just Wouldn't Listen
Chapter 6: Not That Crazy
Chapter 7: The Gods Are Insecure
Chapter 8: Who Is the Bad Guy?
Chapter 9: Bury the Secret
Chapter 10: About That Immortality
Chapter 11: You Are Not That Special
Chapter 12: Before the Plunge
Chapter 13: That Did Not Go As Planned
Epilogue

PROLOGUE

Andy Keene leaned over and tugged on his five-year-old son's seat buckle. So far, the flight had been bumpy, but it wasn't his first time flying, so he distracted himself and tried not to worry.

Ten more hours until we land in Melbourne, he told himself, then he could relax.

The pilot had come on earlier to inform the passengers that they were diverted further south than usual due to some bad weather, but he didn't anticipate any delays, which was always a good thing.

Andy closed his eyes and tried to sleep but was awakened by a loud ding followed by the flight attendant telling them to fasten their seat belts.

He reached down and tugged at his belt to make sure it was snug. He looked over at his son to see him still sleeping soundly when all of the lights in the 747 suddenly flickered and went black. He could hear people all around him loudly questioning what was going on and saw one of the flight attendants quickly making her way toward the front of the plane.

He swore out loud, wondering if the jetliner was slowing down.

The flight attendant was just in front of him when he felt the plane lurch and begin to fall. He saw her feet lift from the floor. Before he could even react, he noticed the look of fear on the woman's face. Without even thinking, he grabbed his son's hand and looked down at him. The boy was awake but was clearly confused. His eyes were wide, and he looked around as if he had just awakened from a nightmare.

As people around Andy began to scream, he looked at his son and quietly said to him, "It's gonna be okay."

One hundred twenty seconds. That was all it took for the plane to drop 10,000 meters and hit the water, crushing the massive 220-ton aluminum frame, killing everyone instantly before sinking into the dark depths of the Indian Ocean.

An hour and a half later, the 747, its fuselage and wings bent and broken into eight pieces, hit the bottom of a deep hole in the southeastern end of the Sunda Trench, throwing up dark sediment all around it. As the sand, rocks, and volcanic ash settled, light thrown off by small areas of lava flows reflected off the plane, highlighting the dozens of crushed and mangled human bodies that were now gently floating in the current. It almost looked peaceful – were it not for the violent, terrifying death these people had just endured.

At the extreme edge of that light, an old stone temple could be seen, striking amidst the bleak terrain at this depth, its thick, beige columns framing a large opening that faded into total blackness.

Four massive black tentacles undulated at the edge of the structure, reaching out into the nothingness of the deep, gripping and releasing the temple's columns in a slow, rhythmic sequence.

A moment later, in a blur of light, a lithe woman stood at the entrance to the temple, dressed in a long, flowing, cream-colored dress, her long, dark hair floating languidly around her head. A serious, hard look was etched onto her olive-complected face. She blinked once, revealing her dark eyes, and smiled, before turning and walking back into the absolute darkness inside the temple.

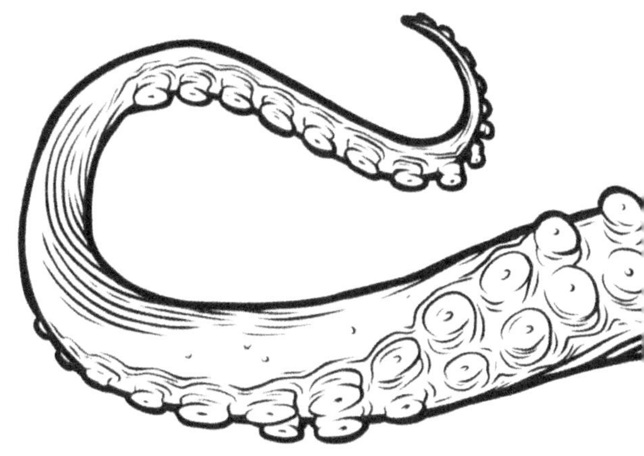

CHICAGOLAND

CHAPTER I

"Tokyo Airlines flight 992 went down over the Indian Ocean last night. We've been told that rescue boats are in the area, but poor weather and rough seas have so far made it extremely difficult to search for potential survivors."

Martin Lee paused while brushing his teeth to listen to the news report on his television.

He heard the female reporter continue, "We just received an official statement from the airline that reads, in part, 'Tokyo Airlines flight 992 was diverted south over the Indian Ocean due to bad weather. The pilot issued a 'Mayday' at 9 p.m. before the plane lost communication. We are working with local authorities in Indonesia and Australia and will provide regular updates as information becomes available. ...'"

Martin placed his toothbrush on the counter by the sink and walked to the television, standing in front of it. He watched as another television reporter discussed a graphic of a map placed on the screen. It showed the flight path of the jet as it headed further south over the Indian Ocean.

"Commercial airlines typically follow a more northern route over Indonesia when traveling southeast to Australia, but, in this case,

Tokyo Airlines flight 992 flew further down here, bringing it just south of the Sunda Trench."

The reporter pointed toward the graphic, signaling toward a red circle that indicated where the plane had likely gone down.

Martin picked up his remote and muted the TV. He walked over to his desk, sat down, slid some papers and two books off the keyboard of his computer, and rummaged around to find his mouse. When the small black mouse was located, he shook it to wake his computer before clicking on a folder on his desktop that read "Old God of the Deep." He then opened another folder labeled, "Tasman Air flight 451," and clicked on an image file. A map of the Indian Ocean popped up on his desktop with a red circle marking a spot in the southern region. A note on the map read, "Last known location of Tasman flight 451, 9:12 p.m., Aug. 21, 2000."

Martin printed out the map, opened a drawer in the wooden filing cabinet next to his desk and began to rifle through the red, blue, green, and manila folders that were inside. He stopped on one of the red folders that had "Alas Purwo" written on the tab and removed it, placing it flat on his desk. He grabbed his worn leather satchel before reaching over to the printer to take the map off it and place it inside the folder. He then slid the whole file folder into his leather case and snapped it shut.

Walking briskly to his bedroom, Martin slipped out of his pajama bottoms and white tank top and started getting dressed when his phone rang. He looked at the name that came up, threw his head back, and sighed.

"You're calling awfully early," he said into the phone. He dropped his hand, put the phone on speaker, and placed it next to him on his bed.

A man's voice came back: "I thought you said you'd be in early today."

"I'm sorry," answered Martin. "I did, but I was up late last night reading."

"What was it this time," asked the man, laughing. "Sea monsters or dragons – something like that?"

Martin felt his face flush, so he paused and took a slow breath.

"Sea monsters aren't real," he said. "That's not what I've been working on…"

The man on the phone cut him off. "Whatever. Your weird story about Bali or something. You saw that a plane went down over there last night?"

Martin was in the process of buttoning his shirt when he caught a glimpse of a news reporter, reporting live from Jakarta.

"Yeah, I saw that," he said. "Horrible story."

Martin could hear the man breathing through the phone.

Exasperated, Martin finally asked the man, "Did you just call to bug me, or was there an actual reason?"

"Yes and no," answered the man, chuckling to himself. "Paul wanted to know where you were. I told him I'd call you and give you shit for being late."

"I'll actually be there on time," he said. "I'm leaving now. See you in 25 minutes."

Martin ended the call, grabbed his shoes, and headed for the front door.

* * * * *

The thick wooden office door opened into a small entryway that turned into a short hallway. A tiny brown loveseat, matching coffee table, and tall coat rack had been wedged against the wall in a small alcove. Martin hung up his coat on the rack and paused to listen. He stared intently at a large black stain on the gray carpet. Down the hall, he could hear multiple voices laughing.

Fuck, he muttered to himself. They're not done yet – probably not even close.

Martin slowly walked down the hallway, passing two compact offices facing each other. Each office had a wooden desk and cheap office chair crammed into it. Papers were spread across the desks, half burying the black laptops in the middle.

Martin paused at a closed door on the right just after the first set of offices. An engraved nameplate on the door read, "Dr. Martin Lee, Senior Researcher."

As he reached for the doorknob, a thin man in his early 30s with short dark hair, wearing khaki pants and a blue polo shirt, came out of one of the offices at the end of the hallway and stopped.

"Martin!" shouted the man. He paused to look down at his watch, before turning to look back into the room. "Twenty-five minutes on the nose, buddy! So nice of you to join us this morning!"

Martin closed his eyes before subtly shaking his head.

"I'll be right there, Johnny," he said. "Let me drop my bag off and grab a…"

"Coffee's already in the conference room," interrupted Johnny. "Paul brought donuts, too."

Martin walked into his office, shutting the door behind him. It was larger than the first two offices, but not by much. There was just enough room for his wooden desk, his office chair, a black metal filing cabinet, and two bookshelves that were full of books.

He placed his leather satchel on the floor next to his desk, opened it, and removed the red file folder he had brought from his home. He tapped his laptop to wake it up, clicked on a browser, and opened the BBC's website. At the top of the page in large letters was a headline that read, "Australians Mourn Passengers on Downed Flight from Singapore."

A chyron ticked past that read, "Latest news: All 226 passengers presumed dead."

Martin clicked on the article and began reading it when his office door abruptly opened and Johnny stuck his head in.

"Paul said he wants you in the conference room," said Johnny. "Pronto." He overly enunciated the last word, adding an "uh" between the "P" and the "R."

Martin closed the browser window and looked down at his desk. "I'll be right there. Just have to grab a few things first."

Johnny didn't bother to respond; he slammed the door closed with more force than was necessary, leaving Martin alone for the moment.

Before he closed his laptop, he noticed an email pop up on his desktop from his friend Melissa Langsdon, one of the collections directors at Chicago's Field Museum of Natural History. The subject line read, "You Might Be Interested in This…"

Martin opened the email and began reading. It read:

Martin,

Hope you're well. Not sure if you saw, but Field just opened a new deep ocean exhibit, and I came across something you might be interested in. Call me, or, even better, stop in some time, and I'll fill you in! Don't be a stranger!

Martin began to reach for his cellphone when the door to his office opened abruptly. Johnny stuck his head in again. "Paul says he wants you in the conference room now, Martin."

Martin hit reply and quickly typed out a response: "I'll swing by this afternoon with that report we just wrapped up. Thanks for thinking of me."

He hit "send," closed his computer, stood up, and made his way down to the conference room.

*　*　*　*　*

Mercifully, the meeting only lasted an hour. As the other staffers began to funnel out the door, Martin leaned back in his chair, turned to his boss, and said, "Paul, I need to take a few days off for a trip to Washington."

"D.C., huh?" asked Paul without looking up from his laptop. "What's going on there?" He kept typing away at whatever he was writing.

"I … uh … you know … just like the city," Martin stammered.

Paul looked up at Martin and gave a wry smile.

"How's that report coming for Field?" asked Paul.

"Done. It's in Sarah's hands now for final edits. I was going to run it over there this afternoon."

Paul tapped a few more keys on his laptop.

"Why don't you let Sarah email it like a normal person?" asked Paul.

"I thought it might be better to hand deliver it and go over some of our more contentious conclusions," Martin said. "You know, give it a more personal touch."

"You got time for that?" said Paul.

"Absolutely," Martin quickly responded, adding, "Besides, what kind of anthropologist would I be if I didn't love that place?"

Paul exhaled heavily and closed his laptop with a sharp thump.

"You sure it's not about that thing you've been OCDing on?" he asked.

"I don't … I mean …" stuttered Martin, looking down and away from Paul's gaze. "What do you mean?"

"I'm not stupid," said Paul. "I've already heard about your extracurricular research. Would your interest in the Field Museum have anything to do with their new exhibit on the oceans?"

"Melissa's an old friend …"

Paul cut him off.

"More like an ex, right?" asked Paul.

"Look, I just want to hand-deliver the report to the Field, and then I'll be out for a few days. It's not like I don't have vacation time backed up."

Paul studied Martin.

"Monsters aren't real, Martin," he said. "You're just going to embarrass yourself, and, frankly, I'm a bit worried how it's going to look that one of my senior researchers is going around telling people a sea monster is bringing down planes. We have contracts with the feds."

"I just have these documents I want to give to the feds," said Martin. "I think it may help them."

Paul slid back his chair and stood up.

"I don't see this ending well, but you do you."

He paused and turned to Martin, looking him up and down. "You're a hard worker, Martin, one of the best researchers I have, so I don't say this lightly: If I even get one whiff that this is gonna blow back on this company, you're out the door. Gone. You understand?"

Martin started to respond but thought better of it and closed his mouth. He nodded his head twice before quietly sliding several papers back into a folder and feigning distraction as Paul quickly walked out of the room.

* * * * *

An hour later, Martin sat in his office, tapping away at his laptop. His edited, proofed, and finalized report on the provenance of multiple museum properties sat on his desk. Martin used the office's color printer to print out line art images of an ancient temple that, in 400 C.E., sat near what is today the Indonesian city of Malang on the southeastern side of the island of Java. He was writing some notes on the pages when his door opened and Paul walked in.

"I wanted to apologize to you for what I said earlier," said Paul.

Martin didn't say anything. He just blinked and looked up at his boss. The tall man filled up the doorway.

"I shouldn't have said that to you," he continued. "It was unprofessional and inappropriate."

Martin smiled and nodded. "Thanks."

"I also wanted to invite you to dinner at my house tonight," Paul added. "Anox is making some exotic meals for a few friends. He's throwing a little social thing, and he wanted me to invite a few people from work, so consider this a formal invitation."

This wouldn't be the first time that Martin had been to Paul's house. His husband, Anox, regularly threw parties at their brownstone in the trendy West Loop area of Chicago.

"Sure," said Martin. "I have to pack later, but I can come by after work for a drink and some dinner. Would Anox be offended if I had to leave a bit early?"

"Honestly," said Paul, "He probably wouldn't even notice."

For a brief moment, Martin saw sadness in Paul's eyes before a smile spread across his face, erasing it.

"Great," he said. "We'll see you at seven. Feel free to bring a plus-one."

"I …uh," stuttered Martin. "I don't really have a plus-one at the moment."

Paul laughed. "Totally fine. We'll see you at seven then."

Paul shut the door, leaving Martin to his work. He sat there looking down at a raft of pages of research, shuffling through them until he found the drawing of the temple. He picked up a magnifying glass that sat on the edge of his desk and held it over the page, scanning some markings that were drawn on the side of the temple. They looked like it may have been some kind of language, but, to this day, it had never been deciphered by anyone. Martin figured it had to be some form of long-dead script similar to cuneiform, which was impossible as that system of writing was from Mesopotamia, 10,000 kilometers from Java and across several oceans.

Realizing he was going to be late, Martin looked at his watch and jumped out of his chair. He grabbed the report and slid it into his leather satchel before racing out of the office and catching an Uber to the Field Museum.

Twenty minutes later, Martin stood in front of the Field Museum of Natural History. He stared up the stairs at the huge stone columns that framed the entrance. Two enormous banners hung on either side of the front entrance that read, "Field: Experience the Ocean Deep."

Martin smiled as he walked briskly up the stairs, dodging dozens of tourists on his way. Upon entering the museum, he waited in line to speak with staff at the ticket counter.

"Good afternoon," Martin told the woman behind the glass. "I'm Dr. Martin Lee. I'm here to drop this off to Melissa Langsdon. She's a collections manager."

"Yes, I see you on the list, Dr. Lee," said the woman, as she turned and pointed to a set of doors labeled, "Staff Only." She added, "Just head through those doors over there and take the elevator to the third floor."

Martin smiled and nodded. It had been a year since Martin had visited the museum, but he still remembered the way to Melissa's office on the third floor.

He was jolted from distraction by the woman yelling out to him. "Sir, you'll need this visitor badge before you head up."

Martin apologized, walked back to the counter, took the badge from the woman, and hung the lanyard around his neck. He smiled, turned, and headed through the doors.

Melissa had remained a close friend, despite their relationship ending after only three months. They were always better friends than lovers, anyway, having met five years ago at a fundraising event for the museum when they bonded over their shared interest in paleoanthropology.

Unlike so many others around him—especially the other academics—Melissa never outright dismissed Martin's theories about what may be at the bottom of the Sunda Trench. Throughout their friendship, he had shared with her much of his research on the topic, including images he had come across of strange inscriptions on a stone tablet found in southeastern Indonesia dating back almost 3,500 years. Most academics rejected the stone as a fake, considering that the earliest inscriptions in that area dated to 700 C.E. at the earliest.

In his free time, Martin had spent a decade deciphering the writings on it. He believed the tablet was genuine and that it pointed to an ancient tribe that worshiped something that lived—or maybe even had been trapped—at the bottom of an area we now know to be the Sunda Trench, a 3,000-kilometer-long chasm that runs just south of Indonesia and bottoms out at over 7,000 meters deep.

Martin knocked on Melissa's door, smiling as several staffers he recognized walked by him down the hall.

"Come in," came a voice through the door.

Martin turned the knob and stepped inside, carefully closing the door behind him.

"Hey, you!" the woman sitting behind the desk called out as she stood up.

Melissa was a small woman, standing just over a meter and a half. Despite her thick charcoal sweater, however, it was clearly apparent she was not at all delicate. Her athletic build was obvious to anyone who gave her a passing glance. Her shoulder-length curly hair bounced as she rounded the desk and spread her arms, embracing Martin tightly in a hug. He hugged her back, leaning into her. It felt good, he thought to himself, but they were only friends now, so, after a brief moment, he broke away.

"I brought you that provenance report you guys were waiting on," he said, as he watched Melissa walk back around her desk and sit down. "And I also brought you lunch from that little Vietnamese place near my office."

"Oh, I haven't been there since we split up," she said to him as she leaned in and reached out to him. "Please tell me it's a veggie banh mi."

Martin handed her the small bag along with a cup. "And an iced coffee."

"I hope you didn't think we'd share," she said to him as she opened the bag and took out the sandwich.

Melissa wasted no time opening the paper wrapper to reveal the sliced baguette with all sorts of roasted, pickled, vibrantly colored vegetables and tofu spilling out. The sweet, pungent, vinegary smell of the sandwich filled the room.

"God I've missed you," she said to the sandwich, before looking up at Martin and adding, "Oh, and you, too, of course."

Martin smiled at her and watched her eat the sandwich. After a few moments, he spoke up. "So you said in your email you had something for me?"

"Oh yeah," she said, swallowing and wiping her mouth on a white paper napkin.

She took a sip from her stainless steel mug on her desk and swallowed again.

"Right, sorry about that," she said. "I forgot all about that once you dropped that sandwich on me."

She reached down, opened one of the drawers on her desk, pulled out a green folder, and handed it to Martin. "The curator of the new ocean exhibit was talking to me about some things the group had rejected, and one item struck me," she said. "I immediately thought of you when I heard about it."

Martin opened the folder and took one of the papers out of it. He held it up to the light so he could see better.

"What am I looking at?" he asked her.

She had already taken another bite of the banh mi and had to pause for a moment to swallow.

She held her hand up to her mouth before saying, "It's a long-range sonar scan of the bottom of the Indian Ocean just south of the Sunda Trench. You know, a 'Gloria' scan. It's that place you kept talking about, so I figured you'd want to see it."

Martin held the paper up to his face, carefully scanning it.

"They apparently found something weird about it, like a hole or something that wasn't supposed to be there," she said. You can see it closely if you look right on the lower left of the page."

"Who did the scans?" asked Martin.

"An ocean research group out of Hong Kong," she said. "Some billionaire funded the whole thing. It's all in the folder."

Melissa paused to take another bite of the banh mi. She chewed for a few seconds and then put her hand in front of her mouth.

"Sandy said they thought the hole was just a glitch. 'Total bullshit,' she said to me. That's why they rejected commissioning a cast of that part of the trench's floor for the exhibit."

She wiped her mouth again and took another sip of her drink out of the mug. "Anyway, I thought you might be interested in it, so I had her print out a copy for me."

She held her palm up to him.

"Don't worry," she said. "I didn't tell her what it was for if you're worried about it."

Still looking at the paper, Martin mumbled, "Why would I worry about it?"

"Some people just think you're kind of weird," she said.

She quickly added, "I don't. I have friends who believe in bigfoot."

She picked up the banh mi, looked at it, and placed it back down on the paper.

"It's just," she said, pausing for a moment. "You know, the plane that crashed. People might get upset if they knew what you thought about all this."

Martin put the paper back into the folder.

"The only two planes in the past 20 years to go that route just happen to crash," he shot back, a hint of anger in his voice. "Don't you think it's worth investigating all possibilities?"

"Please don't get upset," she said. "I know you're not crazy. I wouldn't say you're normal, but you're not nuts. This is just kind of out there, you know? A god or monster lives in the bottom of the ocean and is bringing down planes that make the mistake of flying over it? Surely there've been boats to take that same route. Why aren't they sinking?"

"Maybe it doesn't affect them the same way?" said Martin. "Maybe it only happens every few years, and we've lost boats in that, but people assume it's bad weather? I don't know for sure. All I know is that I have evidence that needs to be pursued. I think it'll save lives, and I don't really care what people think of me."

Melissa smiled at him. "I didn't mean to get you all worked up. I just figured you'd like this scan."

Martin looked down at his shoes. "I'm sorry, Mel. I didn't mean to snap at you."

"It's okay," she said, taking another bite of the banh mi. "I don't want to piss off my sandwich connection."

She picked up her purse off the ground and began to poke through it. "What do I owe you, by the way?"

"Don't worry about it," he said, laughing. "It's on me."

"Alright, fine," she said, "but I insist on buying you drinks. What are you doing tomorrow night?"

Martin began to fidget in his seat.

"I … uh," he stammered. "I'll be in D.C."

"Oh fun," she said. "Work trip?"

"Uh … not really … no"

She caught his eyes.

"What does that mean? Why are you going to Washington, Martin?"

"I'm trying to meet with the feds," he muttered, his eyes dropping to the floor, "to drop off some of my research."

"Martin," she blurted out. "You can't be serious?"

"I don't want to hear it, Mel," he said, holding up his hands. "I've already gotten shit from Paul. This is important to me, and I want to try at least."

"I just worry about you," she said. "I don't want you to get hurt."

"I appreciate that, but I'm a big boy. I can take it."

"I know you can," she answered, smiling up to her eyes. "Whatever happens, I still think you're one of the smartest people I know. I hope those guys in D.C. realize it, too."

"Thanks, Mel. I'll call you once I'm back in town."

* * * * *

Martin paid the Uber driver and stepped out into the evening in front of Paul and Anox's four-story brownstone, a brown paper bag in his hand. He walked up the stairs and rang the doorbell. A tall man with tanned skin, blue eyes, and reddish-brown hair opened the door.

"Martin," said Anox. "So glad you could make it. Paul said you may be coming. Please come in."

Martin stepped across the threshold and handed Anox the bag. "I brought some wine."

Anox peered inside the bag and looked up at Martin.

"Thank you, Martin," he said, handing the bottle to a woman standing behind him in the hallway. Martin watched as she took the bottle, walked down the hall, and disappeared into a side room. He could hear talking coming from a room at the end of the hall.

"Everyone is down the hall," said Anox. "Feel free to join them. Dinner will be served at 1930 sharp. In the meantime, please enjoy a cocktail, or two, and a light mezze before that."

Martin followed Anox down the hall into a larger living room that opened up into a dining room. There, a long table was already set with what looked like expensive dinnerware. The young woman who had greeted him earlier was in the room, picking up glasses and small plates, while a man, who looked to be barely 21, stood by a waist-high table, mixing drinks.

This wasn't the first time Martin had been to his boss's home. He knew how much Paul's firm made every year, and it still surprised him how nice his house was. Located in the hip, young part of the city, Paul's brownstone had to be worth several million dollars. There always seemed to be at least two staffers around, cooking and cleaning. What were they called? Butlers? Hired help? That was way above Martin's pay grade. As far as he knew, Anox just dabbled in things. He wasn't some high-priced attorney or finance guy. One of them had to be from pretty extreme wealth to afford all of this.

To a paleoanthropologist, Paul's house was a goldmine. All sorts of artwork and artifacts were prominently displayed all around the room, some of which Martin knew to be thousands of years old.

Martin caught Paul's eye, who rushed over to greet him.

"You made it," said his boss from across the room. "Everyone, this is one of my lead researchers at the firm, Dr. Martin Lee. He's truly brilliant, so if you ever need anyone to figure out the history of something or where it came from, he's your guy."

Paul laughed before adding, "Well, he's my guy, so you'll have to pay me first before you can hire him."

Martin looked around the room. There were about a dozen men and women, all dressed very well compared to his casual appearance. He recognized two people from the office and smiled and casually waved to them before making his way to the bartender. The young man nodded to Martin and then mixed an old fashioned for him. Before he could turn around, he heard Paul behind him.

"Martin, I wanted to apologize again to you," said Paul. "I was out of line. I just want you to know how much I value you at the firm. I know they say graveyards are full of indispensable people, but you're about as close to indispensable as they come."

"Thank you, Paul," said Martin, smiling. "I didn't take it personally. I understood that you're just trying to protect what you've worked hard to build."

Paul looked around the room and then leaned in close to Martin. "Can I tell you something? I've actually been thinking about retiring and selling the business. "

It was shocking to hear, considering that Paul was pretty much always at work. When working on projects with deadlines, Martin had regularly seen Paul there on Saturdays and Sundays.

"What would you do with yourself if you sold the firm?" asked Martin.

"That's a great question. Probably travel more. Visit my distant relatives. Relax. Enjoy myself for a while before I start something else."

"You act like you're getting old," said Martin, laughing. "You can't even be 50."

Paul put his hand on Martin's arm and gave him a serious look. "We don't talk about age around here," he said, smiling.

"I hope you'll keep this in confidence," said Paul. "If you're at all interested in taking over the firm, I can make you a very good deal."

Martin watched Paul look around the room and stop his gaze on Anox.

"Anox has been complaining that I'm never around," he said, "And, when I am here, I'm always distracted, so think about it. I know you'd do well by the firm."

Paul squeezed Martin's arm before turning toward a middle-aged woman who was in the process of ordering a cocktail.

"Mandy," said Paul. "You're looking so good. Tell me all about your trip to Paris. It's been forever since I was there."

Martin stood, sipping his old fashioned. He then walked over to an antique wooden mask and began studying it.

Martin heard Anox behind him say, "Seventh century Javanese mask. Paul told me that that's your wheelhouse, right?"

"It is," said Martin, still focused on the mask.

"Please tell me it's real," said Anox, laughing. "I paid a lot for that piece."

"It looks authentic," said Martin. "I'd guess it's actually an eighth century ceremonial mask for rituals honoring the ancestors."

Martin turned to face Anox. "But it's not from Java. It would be from Bali."

He studied Anox. "But you knew that."

"I'm not sure what you mean, Martin," answered Anox, taking a step forward to look at the mask more closely. "I bought this on a trip to Jakarta years ago. I was told it was from the southeastern end of the island."

"Balinese masks are more elaborate," said Martin, "Compared to the ones from Java, of course. It's not really that subtle. Whoever told you it's from Java either lied to you or didn't know his stuff."

Martin met Anox's eyes. "You knew that it was from Bali, not Java."

"Paul said you're very good at what you do, Martin," answered Anox before taking a sip from his wine glass. "He was right."

"Wait, was this some kind of test?"

"Paul has been looking to get out of the work grind for some time now," said Anox. "He's looking for someone to take over his firm. We've invested a great deal of money and time into it, so we want to be sure whomever takes it over knows what they're doing. We don't want to turn it over to someone who will just fleece it and run it into the ground."

"Paul mentioned that, but I'm not sure I'm cut out for running a business," said Martin. "I find my work enjoyable except for all the other people."

He stammered slightly when he added, "I … uh … also don't really have any money."

"Well, you have a lot to consider, Martin," said Anox, "Just know this would be an amazing opportunity for you, and I'm sure we could arrange something that benefits us at little out-of-pocket cost to you. Look around this room. I know plenty of very wealthy people who are always looking for places to invest their money."

Martin turned back toward the mask to avoid what was looking to be an awkward moment of silence before he heard Anox announce, "Oh, look, dinner is served." Anox turned and faced the others in the group, who were all spread around the room, talking. "If I could have everyone's attention," Anox shouted over the din of the conversations. "Dinner is now being served. Please, everyone, grab a seat around the table wherever you want. I ask you only leave the head and the foot of the table for myself and Paul."

Martin watched Anox turn toward Paul and smile warmly.

Anox walked over to the table and sat at the far end. Paul took his spot at the end closest to the guests. Martin grabbed a seat between an older woman in a black dress and a man in an expensive suit with a neatly trimmed white beard. He ate his dinner quietly, listening to the others at the table talk about politics, investments, the theater, and some new art shows. After he was done, he quietly made his way to the front door, pulling up Uber's app and calling himself a ride. On his way out, he heard Paul call out to him. "Good night, Martin. Thank you for coming."

Martin turned toward him, nodded his head, and said, "No, thank you, Paul."

A few of the other guests turned toward him.

"Don't forget I'll be in D.C. for a week," he said. "I'll see you next Wednesday."

And he turned and walked out the door.

*   *   *   *   *

Later that night, Martin was rifling through a stack of papers on his desk in his apartment when his cellphone buzzed. He looked down at it and saw that his friend, Mikel Anderson, was calling him. He picked up the phone and answered it.

"Hey Mikel," he said. "I'm really busy right now. I can't really talk."

"I haven't heard from you in weeks," said Mikel. "Work really been that busy lately?"

Martin dropped one of the papers onto the floor and cursed audibly.

"We've been friends for years," added Mikel. "I don't think I'm telling you anything you don't already know when I say I'm probably your only friend." He paused for a moment before adding, "So what's going on?"

"Nothing," interjected Martin. "Honestly, I'm just really busy. I'm going to Washington, D.C. tomorrow, and I have to pack."

"So it is work," said Mikel. "I hope Paul is …"

Martin cut him off. "It's not work-related."

"You going by yourself, or taking someone?" asked Mikel. "And why D.C. of all places? That city sucks."

"I'm going by myself," said Martin, "but it's not for work."

He paused for a moment, before mumbling, "It's for this thing I've been working on. You know, the one about the plane crashes. I want to give my research to the feds. Hopefully it'll help prevent future accidents."

"Oh yeah," remarked Mikel. "I saw there was a second crash in that area you've been looking at."

Martin knew what was coming next, and he unconsciously tensed his body.

"Come on," said Mikel. "You really believe in that nonsense?"

"It's not nonsense," Martin countered angrily.

"Alright, alright" Mikel said. "I didn't mean to piss you off. It's just weird someone like you believes in that stuff and that you'd be willing to fly all the way to D.C. They're gonna laugh you out of the city."

"I don't care about that," said Martin. "I'm just going to give them what I've found. What they do with it from there is up to them."

"You're wasting your time, Martin."

"Maybe, I don't know." Martin paused for a moment before asking, "Do you know anything about some billionaire from Hong Kong named Li Haoyu?"

"Who hasn't?" said Mikel. "He's really well known in my field. He funds a lot of climate research and projects. Why?"

"Nothing really," said Martin. "His name came up in a conversation with Melissa earlier today. I didn't know anything about him."

"You saw Melissa? That's good to hear. You guys were good together."

Martin paused for a moment to think. He was never very good at relationships, but maybe Mikel was right. Maybe Mikel realized something Martin was never that aware of to acknowledge. Melissa was good for him, but, unfortunately, that ship had sailed. She had made it clear she was no longer interested in Martin, at least when it came to a long-term relationship, anyway.

"It's not like that anymore," lamented Martin. "We're just friends. Nothing else is ever going to happen."

Martin could hear Mikel breathing heavily on the other end of the line. They had all run together in the past, hitting the bar scene in Chicago. Mikel had settled down, eventually marrying his wife and having kids. Martin was happy for him. Slightly envious of the certainties that come with marriage, kids, and a mortgage. He just could not wrap his brain around how he could do that himself. Melissa was great, and she would have made a great wife. Just not to him. They just were not meant to be.

After a few moments of awkward silence, Mikel asked him, "So you're really going to D.C. tomorrow?"

Martin sighed. He really didn't want to have this conversation, so he figured he might as well end it. Mikel was an old friend. He would get over it.

"Mikel, I really appreciate you calling to check up on me, but I have a lot of packing to do. I'll call you when I'm back in town."

The two men exchanged good-byes, and Martin ended the call.

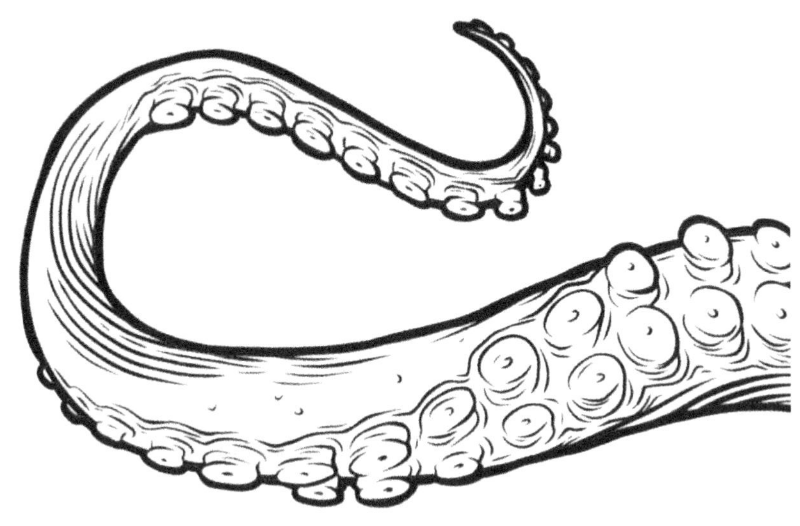

A Bitter Pill

Chapter 2

The flight from Chicago to Washington, D.C, was uneventful, except for some mild turbulence.

Martin spent the first half of the two-hour flight reading a profile puff piece on Li Haoyu in a recent issue of *Climate* magazine that had been featured on the media outlet's website.

Mikel was right. Haoyu was somewhat of a celebrity among scientists who worked in climate-related fields. He funded projects all around the world to sequester carbon, clean up the oceans, and combat rising temperatures. Based in Hong Kong, Haoyu worked on myriad programs from China to New York City.

The profile focused on Haoyu's latest venture, a giant, 300-foot-tall air purifier in Beijing that was designed to filter smog and spit out fresh, clean air. On bad days, Haoyu's air purifier was able to cut pollution by an astounding 15%. It had been such a success that the Chinese were planning to build these in multiple cities around the country.

What interested Martin was the fact that Haoyu's passion project seemed to be his work using deep-submergence drones and long-range sonar to scan the deepest parts of the oceans to study how pollution is affecting them. Last year, Haoyu spent six weeks on a ship over the Sunda Trench, taking water samples and even picking up trash 7,000 meters below the surface along 1,000 kilometers of the southeast portion of the trench. Haoyu said they collected all sorts of garbage like plastic bags, fishing nets, and even a pair of flip flops that weren't even the same size or color.

Surely, he must have seen something down there, thought Martin. The inscriptions on the stone tablet he had studied referred to a temple deep under the surface that stood out. Martin was never really able to translate one of the key words in the text. It could have meant "home" or even "living space," but it also seemed to imply "prison" or "trap" or some kind of closed, confined, protected pocket of space and time.

Martin put his head back against the seat rest and closed his eyes, envisioning the stone tablet in his mind. He had spent hours staring at the picture, trying to decipher what it all meant. Unlike other academics, who pooh-poohed it as a well-crafted fake, Martin had spent enough time studying it to believe it was real, and that is what worried him.

Reagan National Airport, the closest airport to Washington, D.C., is located on the outskirts of the city, just across the Potomac River in Alexandria, Va. Ever since the Sept. 11 attacks in 2001, commercial airlines have changed how they fly in and out of Reagan National due to security concerns. With the Pentagon and multiple federal buildings, including the U.S. Capitol and the White House, in close proximity, commercial airliners don't linger in the air as they approach Reagan National, often descending at an uncomfortable speed.

The descent into Reagan was made that much worse by the fact that, for the second half of the flight, Martin had been lost in reading about the two plane crashes in the Indian Ocean. That explains why he received angry glares from neighboring passengers after he blurted out "motherfucker" as the plane abruptly dropped a few meters on its final approach.

After regaining his composure, Martin apologized to no one in particular. He then slipped several documents spread across the tray-table back into his leather satchel before leaning back in his seat in preparation for landing.

After touchdown, the pilot's voice came over the public address system, welcoming everyone to the nation's capital and letting them all know the baggage terminal number where they could pick up their luggage. Martin stood up, grabbed his small carry-on suitcase from the overhead compartment and stepped into the line to depart the plane. As he exited the boarding bridge, he caught a conversation between two older men.

"Yes, senator," said the one man. "I'll let them know you're on your way back…"

Martin recognized the second man as Thomas Peterson, one of the two Democrat senators from Illinois. It was clear to anyone watching that Peterson was already in a bad mood, but Martin didn't care. This is serendipity, he thought to himself. If he could convince a U.S. senator that something in the ocean was bringing down planes, he could have a powerful ally.

Unfortunately, as soon as Martin opened his mouth, he quickly realized that, often, even the best of plans don't work out like they do in your head.

Martin pushed his way through the crowd so he could get closer to the older man.

"Uh .. Senator Peterson," Martin said.

The man ignored him.

"Senator Peterson," repeated Martin. "Do you have a moment to speak with me about something very important?"

The other man quickly stepped between Martin and the senator.

"The senator isn't doing interviews right now," said the man, placing himself physically between the two of them.

"It's very important, sir," said Martin, speaking over the shoulder of the man. "It's about that plane that went down over the Indian Ocean the other day."

The senator looked up, before saying, "It's ok, John. Let him through."

Martin walked around the man quickly. He saw he had also

gotten the attention of multiple people by the other gates. Great, he thought, now I have an audience as I try to explain to this senator that some kind of supernatural entity in the ocean is crashing planes.

"I'm Dr. Martin Lee," said Martin as he walked up to Peterson. "I'm a researcher from Chicago."

"The senator is very busy," said the man, who was now standing behind Martin.

"It's okay, John, let him speak," remarked Peterson, a smile spreading across his face. "I'm always happy to talk to my constituents."

"Right," said Martin, as he looked down and began to rifle through his satchel. "Yes, well, I … uh … here it is."

He looked up at Peterson, who was watching Martin's hand intently.

"I have this map that shows where the flight from a few days ago and one from 20 years ago both went down," he said. He handed the paper to Peterson, who looked at it intently.

"Am I supposed to see something here," said the senator looking back up at Martin.

"Well, uh, no, not really," he stammered, "except for the fact that it's the same area."

Out of the corner of his eye, Martin caught the man behind him moving closer to him.

"Senator, I don't want to rush you, but …" he started to say, but Peterson cut him off.

"Let him finish, John," he said.

Just say it, Martin said to himself. Tell the senator what is going on. "So I've been studying this part of the world for years. And I've found writings that show people here worshiped – no, I'd say more like acknowledged, maybe revered – something that lived deep in the ocean in this region."

Martin caught the senator shooting a furtive glance at the man, who was now standing just to the side of him.

"I know," said Martin quickly. "It sounds crazy, but there are these inscriptions I've …"

Peterson interrupted him. "Are you trying to tell me a sea monster is responsible for these plane crashes?"

Martin watched as Peterson and the other man traded looks. He noticed the smile was now gone from the senator's face.

"Ok, sir, we really have to go," said the other man as he reached for Peterson's arm and gently pulled him away from Martin. You'll be late for your meeting."

"Thank you for the information …" said the senator, as he turned away from Martin.

He paused before pivoting back, asking, "What was your name again?"

"Dr. Martin Lee," he answered. "This is really important. I wanted to know if you could help me get these documents to the people who investigate plane crashes at the FAA…"

Peterson cut him off.

"Ok, Dr. Lee," he said, as he began to walk away. "Get those documents to my office. We'll see what we can do."

"Thank you," said Martin. "I really appreciate any help you can give me."

The two men picked up their pace down the long walkway toward the exit to the gate entrance. Martin couldn't help but look at the crowd that had formed around him and the senator when they were speaking. As he turned his head, he saw that people abruptly looked away, lowering their eyes to the floor. Martin felt his face flush. He nodded his head and smiled, but it was obvious they all thought he was bonkers.

This wasn't the first time Martin noticed people around him think his theory on these plane crashes is crazy. Over the years, he easily told a half dozen people about it, including his boss. One of the junior researchers, Johnny, mocked him mercilessly over it, calling him names like "Ahab" or "the kraken hunter." Once, at a conference, Johnny pranked him by telling the organizers that Martin's name was "Jeremy Wade," the television fisherman, famous for catching large fish – river monsters, as Wade calls them – all around the world. Martin remembered how he stood at the reception table for a few minutes wondering what was going on as the two nice older ladies tried to find his name on the list of attendees. After some time, he got the reference and had to explain to them that his company's representative had a bad sense of humor and that this was his idea of a pathetic joke. He could laugh about it now, but it was embarrassing at the time. For the entirety of the conference, word had gotten out about the prank and other professionals he had known for years took to calling him Jeremy or, even worse, the monster hunter.

It still stung a little to this day, but Martin was used to the rejection by now, so he shrugged it off and made his way to the airport's exit himself.

*   *   *   *   *

"You don't understand," shouted Martin. "It's going to happen again. I have documents to prove it. I just have to meet with someone on the administrator's staff."

The tall security guard behind the front desk sighed and stood up. Martin glanced up at the large plaque above the man's head that read, "Federal Aviation Administration."

"Sir, if you don't have an appointment, I can't let you upstairs," the guard said.

He pointed toward a sign on the desk that said visitors had to be sponsored by an FAA employee. Martin wasn't even looking at the guard. He was too busy rifling through his leather briefcase for a file folder.

"It's right here," mumbled Martin.

He looked at the guard before adding, "I'm Dr. Martin Lee. I'm an anthropologist. I can show you what I have, and you can tell them I'm not some crank."

The security guard took a step to the side of the desk and looked over at the two other guards positioned near the elevators.

"Sir, if you don't leave, I'm going to have to arrest you," the guard said.

"That ... that won't be necessary," stuttered Martin as he wrestled with a piece of paper in a file folder in his bag, before inadvertently spilling multiple manila folders and documents all over the white tile floor.

"Damn it," cried out Martin.

The guard let out a slow sigh and waved off the two other guards, who were approaching to see what the commotion was. Martin looked up as the man bent over and began helping him pick up the documents.

"Look, I can't let you just walk upstairs," said the guard. "You have to make an appointment, and you have to have someone escort you."

"Can I just talk to the incident report team?" pleaded Martin.

"I don't make the rules," interrupted the guard, as he handed a handful of papers back to Martin.

"Will you just give the incident team this paper?" asked Martin. "Please. It's very important. That plane crash in the Indian Ocean that just happened – it's going to happen again. Just give them this. My contact is on it."

The guard stood up.

"Alright," he said. "I'll make sure they get it. Now you have to leave, or we'll arrest you."

This was the second stop Martin had made that day. The first involved a visit, which didn't go as planned, to the Dirksen Senate Office Building on Capitol Hill, where Senator Peterson had an office. A young woman sat at the front desk. She looked about 19 and was likely just an intern on summer break from college. Martin had handed her copies of multiple documents.

"Please make sure the senator gets these," he said as he watched her place them in a tray on the front desk that was simply labeled, "Incoming."

"Do you have a card you can leave with these?" she asked him. "If not, you can fill out that form." She pointed to a stack of papers on the counter.

"Is the senator in today?" asked Martin. "I'd like to meet with him as soon as possible."

"I'm sorry, sir," she said. "He's very busy today, but you can fill out that form if you'd like to request a meeting." She pointed to another stack of papers on the counter right next to the other forms

Martin sighed and reached for one of the forms. Just then, he caught sight of the senator walking down the hallway in the back of the office.

"Oh," said Martin, "there he is. I can just …"

Martin started to walk toward Peterson.

"Sir, you can't just walk back there," she said, raising her voice. "I'm going to call security if you don't stop."

One of the aides in the hallway stopped and turned to Martin, raising his hand and blocking Martin's way.

"Senator," Martin shouted. "It's me, Dr. Martin Lee. We met at the airport yesterday. Could I just talk to …"

He reached into his satchel and pulled out multiple documents, waving them in the air.

"You're going to have to leave," said the aide, who had stepped in front of Martin. "Now."

Martin watched as the senator peeked over at the brewing commotion. A look of recognition washed across the senator's face before he turned and quickly stepped into an office.

"The police are on their way," said the man. "Do you want to be arrested? You have to leave now."

"I just needed to sit down and discuss these with the senator," said Martin, dropping his shoulders and turning back toward the entrance. "I can't emphasize enough how important this is."

"You have to request a meeting," said the man. "You can't just walk in here like that."

"I'm really sorry," said Martin. He reached into his bag, took out a business card, and handed it to the young woman at the front desk. Just as he did, two Capitol Hill police officers opened the front door and stepped into the office.

"It's okay," said the aide, who had stopped Martin. "Just a bit of a misunderstanding. This man is leaving."

Martin apologized and raised both of his hands, adding, "I don't want any trouble. I was just leaving."

The two officers quickly stepped beside Martin.

"We'll escort you out, sir," said one of the officers.

He looked back and forth at the two of them, smiled sheepishly, and then offered yet another apology.

*   *   *   *   *

Zoe Sullivan stood outside her ex-husband's office on the seventh floor of the Federal Aviation Administration building in Northwest Washington, D.C., the FAA as it's known colloquially. The building stood just across Independence Avenue from the Smithsonian museums, so there was always a steady stream of tourists walking by it.

She had already said her hellos to a half dozen of his coworkers. She took a deep breath, let it out, knocked on the open door to Bret's office, and walked in.

"I just thought I'd personally bring by the last of the paperwork you need to sign."

Bret looked up from his messy desk that was scattered with papers.

"Thanks," he said, feigning a smile. "I … uh …"

The phone rang and he glanced down at it.

"I got to take this," he said to her. "Have a seat. I shouldn't be long."

He picked up the receiver and said, "Bret Sullivan."

Zoe could only hear his end of the conversation.

"Yes … We're going over it now … Yes … Uh huh … Working on it … Hoping to have some findings in a couple days … Yeah … Nothing definitive … Yeah, it's so remote there … Just a few ships, and an Air Force flyover … Okay … I'll let you know when we have anything … Bye …"

Bret hung up the phone and sighed heavily. Zoe met his eyes.

"That plane crash?" she asked.

"Yeah," he responded. "It's got everyone all worked up."

Zoe could see he was agitated, and she didn't want to get too involved. He was always a prick when he was stressed out.

"That wasn't even a U.S. flight," she said, looking down at her shoes. "Why do you guys care what happened?"

"Some Americans were on the flight, a couple families," he said. "Also, U.S. flights fly that route sometimes. The administrator just wants our bases covered. It looks like it was really bad weather, so we should be fine."

Zoe smiled at him. She watched him frown and look back down at his desk.

"So the paperwork?" she asked him, leaning forward to place it at the edge of his desk. "Once you sign this, we're done. That's it. No more bothering you."

She smiled again as he looked up at her. This time he at least faked a quick smile.

"You can leave it right there," he said. "I'll get to it tonight."

"All you have to do is sign, Bret."

"Obviously I have to read it first, and – look at me – I'm drowning in paperwork." He gestured around his desk.

"Fine," she said and stood up. "Just don't take too long. You can have it couriered over to my apartment. Classes don't start until next month, so I'll be home."

Zoe turned and walked out the door. She heard Bretl exhale loudly and start shuffling papers, so she didn't bother to say goodbye.

As she walked down the hall toward the elevators, she heard a familiar voice.

"Hey stranger!"

She turned and saw a woman in her early 30s, tall, thin, dark hair with short bangs walking up to her. Mary was one of Bret's friends. She was always amiable and warm, probably too friendly to be honest. Zoe figured she had been fucking Bret all this time, but he was too calculating ever to get caught.

"Hey Mary. How are you?"

"Oh, I'm great."

Zoe smiled through the awkward pause.

"It's been too long," said Mary. "Sorry to hear about you and Bret. You guys were good together."

She wasn't actually sorry, thought Zoe. It was etched on her freckleless, wrinkle-free, skinny face.

"Yeah, you know," said Zoe, "We were always better friends."

That wasn't true, though. They were never good friends before they got married. It just sort of happened after they dated for six months. Dating isn't easy anywhere. It's especially bad in a city like Washington, D.C., where you always feel like the person across the table is more focused on your career and if you'll be a 401k millionaire by the time you're 50 than hearing about your dreams or anything like that. With Bret, it always felt like he had a target in mind – date for the requisite six months, get married, buy a house in north Arlington, pop out a girl and a boy, send them to decent colleges, retire, and gloat. It didn't matter if you were miserable so long as you put on a good show. Honestly, Zoe felt like she would have rather drown in the filthiest part of the Anacostia River than complete Bret's exacting blueprint for a model marriage.

"I totally get that," said Mary. "I just hope you're taking care of yourself."

"I'm doing okay, Mary," said Zoe, feigning a smile. "Thanks for that."

"Good for you," said Mary. She looked over Zoe's shoulder and raised one of her hands. "Oh, I have to go grab Mike before he gets away. Work stuff."

She paused and smiled again at Zoe. "It was great seeing you!"

Mary walked right past Zoe, waving with one hand as she went. Mercifully the elevator dinged and the door opened just as Mary left. Zoe looked around to see a man, who couldn't have been more than 25, standing nearby and staring at her. He raised his left hand slightly in a half-hearted wave and took a loud slurp from his soda. Zoe smiled back at him, walked into the elevator, and pressed the button for the lobby. The young man entered as well.

"Can you press three?" he asked.

Zoe nodded and pressed the button. She looked up and watched the countdown above the doors going painfully slowly.

"Your Bret's wife," said the young man. "Sorry to hear about you guys breaking up."

Zoe shot him a quick glance, smiled, and nodded. "Thanks." She looked back up at the countdown again.

"He's a great guy," said the man. "I really like working for him. Everybody loves him."

Zoe didn't even bother to look at the guy this time. "He is."

The man took another loud slurp of his soda. It echoed in the elevator.

It's not that Bret was abusive or even a bad guy, Zoe thought. He'd probably make some woman with the same everyday, methodical goals a great husband, but that wasn't her. She was more interested in hearing about your side project or research trip to a remote location than a formula for retirement contributions that will make you a million dollars before you quit your job. What a sad way to structure your life, she thought, but it works for some people.

The elevator stopped, and the doors opened. Zoe had almost forgotten about the other man standing next to her.

"Okay," said the man, "This is me."

She again smiled at him and nodded as he walked past her. Two more people got on just as he left, and, thankfully, they had no desire to make small talk.

The elevator finally opened on the ground floor and Zoe stepped out into the lobby right in the middle of a small commotion. A man in his thirties, dressed in a brown suit, was arguing with a security guard at the front desk. Whatever the issue, it didn't look like it was going well for him. Somebody else was having a bad day, too, she thought to herself, and slowed down as she walked by, just enough to get the gist of what was going on. She paused right before the exit to listen to the man. He was clearly upset, but he didn't sound like a nut. She pushed the door open and walked outside into the heat, looking around at the tourists milling about, checking maps and discussing what museum they should hit next.

As she stood there for a minute, contemplating what she'd like to do with the rest of her free day, she noticed the man, still frazzled, leaving the building. He clearly didn't look like he lived anywhere near the city or was familiar with it, so she made one of those split-second decisions and decided to ask him if he needed any help.

*   *   *   *   *

Martin stood outside the large stone and glass FAA building on the sidewalk. It was hot, and he could feel sweat running down his back. He ran his hands through his hair and pushed his glasses back onto his nose. He reached for his phone and held it to his face. When he heard a woman's voice, he began to type into it with his free hand.

"Excuse me," said the woman. "I couldn't help but overhear you in there."

Martin looked up from his phone to see a woman in her late thirties with dark hair in jeans. She was wearing a white T-shirt with a sloth lying prone across the Nike swoosh and the words "Just Do It Later" emblazoned across it.

"I'm probably going to regret this, but you don't look like a nut. Why did you say there was going to be another crash?"

Martin blinked and put his phone back into his pocket.

"Uh … I … uh … who are you?" asked Martin.

"Oh, right," answered the woman. "I'm Zoe Sullivan. I teach environmental science at American University."

Martin stretched his hand out to her.

"Martin Lee," he said as he shook Zoe's hand. "I'm an anthropologist. I work for a nonprofit research firm in Chicago, but I came here to Washington on my own after I read about that plane crash last week over the Indian Ocean. I've been studying that area for over a decade, and I think I know why it happened."

Matin watched as Zoe broke eye contact and looked down at her shoes.

"I know," he said. "I sound crazy, but I swear it wasn't an accident. There's something else going on here."

Zoe looked up at the sky and then back at Martin. She exhaled. "It's really hot out here. There's a cafe right around the corner. We can probably talk there, and you can tell me all about your theories."

* * * * *

Martin placed his coffee down at the table, sat down in a chair, and started rifling through his satchel.

"I brought multiple copies of these documents," he said as he rifled through his papers. "I really thought at least someone would want to hear what I have to say."

"My husband – I mean, my ex-husband – works there," said Zoe before looking down at her coffee cup. "They get all kinds of kooks and nuts, so, yeah, no one gets past the guards without prior authorization. Even I can't just waltz in and walk up to see my ex. I have to wait for an escort to take me up to him."

"If he's your ex, why were you there?"

Martin watched Zoe tense up. She opened her mouth, as if she were about to say something, but promptly closed it. She looked like she was about to tell him to fuck off but thought better of it.

"I'm sorry," he said. "That's really none of my business."

"No, it's okay," she said, her eyes going to her mug. "I had the final paperwork for our divorce ready to go, and I wanted to hand them off to him to sign. He said he would, and that was that. It's officially over."

She raised her hands a bit off the table and shook them back and forth.

"Yay," she said, her voice dripping with sarcasm.

Martin studied her. He watched her trace her finger over a rough spot on her coffee mug.

"Our marriage wasn't bad," she said. "We just decided we weren't in love, you know? He's a great guy. I think I'm a decent person. It just ended, so we decided we'd be better off apart than together. So I moved into an apartment in the city, and he kept the house in Arlington and paid me out for my share. We're still on good enough terms that I can see him from time to time without it being an issue. I think he's got a girlfriend now. I really wish him the best."

She paused for a moment, before adding, "That's a lie. He's kind of a prick. He's really charming and can be likable, but, deep down, when you get to know him, he's just a selfish jerk. I guess I got sucked in at the beginning, and I liked being in a relationship. I realized pretty early on that he's arrogant and pretty self-centered, but then I had a ring on my finger, so I thought I should be happy. It's better than being alone, right?"

"My last relationship ended like that," Martin said to her. "We decided we were better off as friends, and we are. I just met her for lunch yesterday as a matter of fact."

Zoe looked up at Martin and smiled, but he could see the sadness in her eyes.

"I tell people we're better off friends because it sounds good," she said. "It's what you're supposed to say, but, the truth is, we're not good friends. Our relationship always felt transactional, like this is what you're supposed to do. You know, start dating, get engaged, get married, buy a house, have a kid or two, send them to a good college, brag about what they're studying, retire on the individual retirement account you've been hoarding."

She ran her finger along her mug again.

"I always wondered, when was it supposed to be fun?" she asked. "When would I start enjoying my life? It wasn't imposter syndrome. I literally was an imposter. It wasn't supposed to be my life. He would probably make someone else a great husband. They'd have a great house in the suburbs and a comfortable life if they could just ignore Mr. Know-it-all and his side piece. I just wasn't that person. Does that make sense?"

"Yeah," said Martin, "It makes total sense to me."

"I guess I figured I'd rather be alone than live that life," she said.

After a few moments of quiet, Zoe lifted her head. Martin met her eyes.

"Look at me," she said, laughing. The sadness was still evident in her eyes. "I swear I didn't lure you here to vent about my ex and my blessed life."

Martin laughed. "Yes, well, anyway," he said, shuffling in his chair. "Let me show you what my research has uncovered."

He paused before adding, "Please just try to keep an open mind. Everyone says I'm nuts, but I really think there's something here.

Otherwise, why would I take this risk?"

Martin pulled a folder from his briefcase and opened it on the table.

"Right," he said without looking up, "I think you'll find this very interesting."

Martin explained how he had been studying a small religious sect, called the Qarine, that grew to prominence on Java around 1,000 B.C.E. They worshiped a god, or honored something – maybe acknowledged it with some form of reverence – Martin wasn't exactly sure. They believed it lived, was imprisoned, or was trapped for some reason on the bottom of the Indian Ocean in the deepest part.

"I recently came upon some evidence – some deep water sonar scans – that give credence to my theory about a deep hole at the bottom of the Sunda Trench, just south of Indonesia," he said.

Martin watched Zoe leaf through some of his documents. She picked up the paper that had the sonar readings on it and looked closely at it.

"It appears that their main temple was destroyed by logging in the early 19th century," he said, "but the Indonesian government stopped that and managed to preserve some of their ancient artwork."

Martin pointed to an image on the paper, running his finger along it.

"See here," he said. "I think this is a map."

He reached for another paper and slid it in front of Zoe.

"The Qarine believed this area right here was sacred to them," he said looking up at Zoe. "It corresponds perfectly with an area at the southern end of the Sunda Trench, the deepest part of the Indian Ocean – the exact spot where last week's plane crash occurred and the same spot where another plane went down 20 years ago."

Zoe looked up at him and their eyes met.

"Hundreds of planes travel that route every year," said Zoe, leaning back in her chair and turning her head to look out the front window. "It's just coincidence, terrible luck."

"But planes don't go that route," huffed Martin. "There have only been two planes that took that flight path in the last 20 years, and both of them crashed."

Martin leaned across the table, opened another file folder and took out a piece of paper.

"I've charted all the flights for the past two decades," he said. "All of the planes follow this northern path. Only two planes – last week's flight and Tasman Air's flight 451 – followed this southern path due to bad weather over the Indian Ocean. Just like last week's crash, Tasman Air's flight 451 went down on Aug. 21, 2000, but the wreckage was never found because of how remote the area is and how deep the water is there."

"There could just be some unusual weather patterns there that led to the two crashes," answered Zoe as she leaned in to get a better look at the papers. "It's definitely remote there, and we know the weather was bad."

Martin tensed and balled up his fists.

"It's not a coincidence!" he blurted out.

Zoe sat back somewhat abruptly.

Martin did his best to soften his demeanor.

"Look," he said. "You can do the math. Only two planes fly over this area in the past two decades, and both of them crashed."

He paused for a moment and then reached into his bag again.

"Wait," he said, "there was a cargo ship that disappeared in 2011 after it took a southern route to avoid a cyclone. It went right through the same spot as the planes."

Martin handed Zoe a piece of paper with a photocopy of a newspaper article on it.

"It says right here that it's believed this Chinese cargo ship sank somewhere south of Java and was never found after it was diverted south to avoid a large storm."

Zoe looked closely at Martin before her eyes dropped to the paper in her hand.

"If what you're saying is true – and that's a huge 'if,' " said Zoe, sitting back in her chair and pausing to take a sip of her coffee. "What do you think is happening there? You can't really think some ancient god is crashing planes and boats."

"I don't know," said Martin as he let out a long, deep audible breath and sat back. "Maybe there's some kind of disturbance there. The oceans are warming. Maybe it's methane. I have no idea. All I know is that, even in ancient times, people knew this area was bad news."

He threw up his hands and dropped them on the arms of his chair.

"I know there's a pattern here," he said. "And more people are going to die if no one speaks up about it because they're afraid they'll look crazy."

Martin watched as Zoe looked around before making eye contact with him again.

"Tell you what," she said. "Give me your evidence. I'll take a look at it closely and make a few calls. If I think there's anything there, I'll give them to my ex so he can get them to whomever should have them at the FAA."

Martin looked up at the ceiling, closed his eyes, and exhaled loudly.

"That's all I wanted," he said.

*   *   *   *   *

Zoe's cellphone vibrated on the coffee table in front of her. She looked down and saw that the caller's name was "Bret." She picked it up and pressed the answer button.

"Hey," she said. "Thanks for calling me back."

"I signed the papers and sent them back to your attorney like I said I would," said the man on the other end of the line. "I guess that's finally it, huh?"

"Yeah," she mumbled. "I guess so."

"I figured you'd be happy about it," he said. She could hear the irritation in his voice. "Isn't this what we both wanted?"

"I want to try to still be friends," she said, interrupting him. "I think we can."

"I'm fine with being friendly to each other," he answered, "but it doesn't work like that. You can't just be friends after your marriage ends. You can't meet up for beers and barbeque. No one does that."

"People do it all the time," she said, trying hard not to raise her voice. She knew that he could tell she was trying to force the issue.

"That didn't work for John and Margie," he added.

"We're not them," she blurted out. "Let's just try, okay? I don't want this to be ugly. I want us to be friendly when we meet up again. It's going to happen. We have all the same friends."

"You sure you're going to be okay if I show up to Clay and Angie's Christmas party with a new girlfriend?"

"I promise you I'll be fine with it," she said, her voice taking on a more cheerful timbre. "I hope you find love with whomever that is."

"Right," he said curtly. There was a brief pause before he continued "So what's up with these other documents you sent up?"

"That's why I texted you," she said. "I met this guy who was trying to get some documents to the crash investigators. He says he thinks something strange is causing these crashes. In 20 years, both the planes that took that specific route over the Indian Ocean crashed. I know it sounds weird, but he doesn't seem like a nut."

"I took a quick look at them," said Bret. "It looks like he's claiming something supernatural in the water is bringing down planes?"

"I'm not sure that's exactly what he's saying," she muttered. "I think he's just saying something weird is happening there, and people have known about that area for a few thousand years, and ..."

"Zoe, I can't give these documents to the investigators," Bret said, cutting her off. "You can't really expect me to take this seriously? They already know bad weather took the plane down."

"What about the plane from 20 years ago?" she asked him, raising her voice.

"Probably the same thing," he answered. "Look, who even is this guy? Is he a friend of yours or something? Is there something else I need to know?"

"No," she said angrily. "He's just a guy that I know. That's all."

The line went silent for a moment, before Bret spoke up.

"I got to go, Zoe," he said coolly. "I got a meeting I need to prep for."

Zoe ended the call and placed the phone back on the coffee table. She stared out the window at the office building across the road. A cat jumped up on the sofa and began to rub itself against her side, purring. She absentmindedly petted its head before smiling down at it.

"Milo, what the fuck am I doing?" she said to the cat.

She thought, "Am I really that hard up that I offered to help some rando I met on the street?"

Zoe picked up her computer off the coffee table and placed it on her lap. She opened a browser window and typed "Dr. Martin Lee Chicago" into it.

A long string of links popped up, including one that took her directly to the staff at a company by the name of Anderson & MacMillen International. She glanced over his bio. He was listed as one of the company's senior researchers. He got a Ph.D. in archaeology with a concentration in paleoanthropology from Boston University. He had authored three books, one of which focused on ancient religions in southeast Asia. She scrolled back and saw a dozen links to reports he had either authored or been given credit for working on.

This guy's no weird dummy, she thought. Maybe stress got to him, and he's having a breakdown? If that's the case, he could be dangerous. He certainly doesn't seem like that, though. He was mostly soft-spoken and polite and was just passionate about what he thought. She had met plenty of academics like Martin. Maybe that's what she liked about him. Sure, a couple of the professors at American had hit on her – one of whom was married – but she had a firm rule that she had stuck to over the years: Don't fuck where you eat. It had worked out for her, and she largely avoided a lot of the drama that ensnared a few other colleagues.

"Ok," she said out loud to the cat. "I swear, the next time I talk to this guy I'm just going to tell him I can't help him anymore, and that's it. I'm done. I can't do this."

She sat back hard on the sofa, causing the cat to jump down and scurry to the bedroom.

"Oh no, I'm sorry, Milo," she said toward the direction the cat had run off. "I didn't mean to scare you."

She told herself, "I need to call this guy and get it over with." Be firm. Don't let him talk you into anything. What he believes is absolutely crazy.

"You just have to tell him that," she said.

* * * * *

"They don't believe you."

Martin felt his face get hot. As he paced the floor, he caught a glance of himself in the mirror on the wall in his hotel room. Take a breath, he thought to himself. Don't react. The only control you have is how you react to bad news.

"Did you hear what I said?" came the woman's voice over the phone. "I gave your documents to my ex, like you asked, and he got back to me a few minutes ago. They think it's nonsense, I'm sorry to say."

Martin's arm fell to his side. He wrinkled his nose and forehead, raised his head to the ceiling, and mouthed the word, "fuck."

"Hello?" came the voice again. "Are you still there?"

Martin lifted the phone to his ear again. "Yes, I'm here. Just let down. That's all."

"I can't say I really blame them, honestly," she said. "In the past 24 hours I've been waffling between 'this guy is pretty smart and interesting' and 'this guy is waving more red flags than a Soviet military parade.' "

Martin laughed. He couldn't fault Zoe. She did what he asked her to do: get his documents to the FAA. She had just met him, and they only talked for an hour at a coffee shop. He didn't think their conversation went particularly well, either. It's a miracle she didn't throw the documents in the trash and lose his number after they parted ways earlier that day.

The past few days had been weighing heavily on him. He had to admit his theory was bizarre. He probably wouldn't believe it had someone come off the streets with a bunch of maps and drawings that purport to show something deep under the ocean influencing currents, temperatures, wind, and was, ultimately, affecting whatever traveled above it.

It sounded insane, really, but he felt like, when he had the time to present all his evidence, it made sense. Zoe evidently believed him, and he had just met her. Why wouldn't the feds agree to meet with him?

"I get it," said Zoe, softening her voice as she spoke. "This isn't what you wanted, but can you blame them? You're asking them to believe some malevolent supernatural force is bringing down airplanes."

Martin let out a heavy sigh and took a deep breath, doing his best to calm his nerves.

"I'm sorry," he said to her. "I've just been doing this for a long time now, and it's frustrating that no one wants to have a serious conversation with me about it. They either want to dismiss it outright or mock me."

"Can you really blame them?" she cut him off.

"I mean, No," he answered. "Not really."

He paused for a moment, before adding, "but you believe me."

Martin waited for a response. When none came, he felt his face flush again. "You believe me, right?"

"I said you had evidence," she shot back. "I didn't say I believed you about everything."

Martin dropped his shoulders and tried to relax. "That's fair."

He sighed again.

"I got to go," he told her, lying, "I got to take this call."

"Okay, I'll call you tomorrow if I hear anything else."

After they exchanged their goodbyes, Martin ended the call and slammed his cellphone onto the desk. He slumped into the office chair in front of his desk where his laptop sat open. After a moment, he closed his laptop, sat up, and leaned back into the chair.

I've done everything I could, he thought to himself. If there's another accident in that part of the world, at this point, it's on them. I can't make them all believe me, and if I push anymore I'll probably just end up in jail. I'm not going to destroy my own life over this. He shut off the desk light, stood up, stripped off his clothes, and headed to the bathroom to take a long, hot bath.

* * * * *

Martin rubbed his eyes and rolled over in the hotel bed to reach his cellphone. The haptic was causing the phone to vibrate annoyingly on the nightstand. He picked up the phone and saw that Zoe was calling him. He sat up and tapped the accept call button before putting the phone to his ear.

He had slept fitfully the whole night, tossing around in his hotel bed. He couldn't get it out of his head that, maybe, everyone was right. Maybe this was all coincidence. Maybe there really was nothing to the story other than bad weather taking down two planes. But Martin had to concede that the odds of this just being a coincidence were slim. Only two planes had taken that route in the past 20 years, and both planes went down. Planes divert to avoid making passengers scared and uncomfortable. Modern airplanes are amazingly resilient and can fly in almost all weather, especially behemoths like 747s.

No, the inscriptions were prescient, and the feds have to be made aware of the dangers. Even if it were something more mundane, they had to know this isn't just bad luck.

"Hello," he said, his voice sounding weak and hoarse.

"Hey, sorry for calling you so early," responded Zoe. "I didn't like how things ended last night, so I wanted to make sure you're okay."

Martin leaned back against the headboard with a thump. It was not as soft as it looked.

"Hey, Martin, are you okay?" Zoe asked him rather abruptly.

"I'm fine," he groaned. "I just … I didn't sleep great. That's all."

After a few moments, Zoe broke the awkward silence, asking,

"Can we meet somewhere for coffee this morning so we can talk? I'd really appreciate it if we could."

Martin rubbed the back of his head with his free hand.

"I really don't know what else there is to talk about," he said softly. "I …"

She cut him off.

"I know you're heading back home soon, so let's just meet one last time and talk," she said. "I felt like I was unnecessarily mean to you, and it doesn't sit well with me. Maybe we can talk and come up with a new plan or something."

"How about that same coffee shop we were at yesterday?"

"That sounds perfect," she said. "I can be there in an hour."

Martin looked at his phone. It was 8 a.m.. He could see light beaming in around the edges of the hotel curtains.

"Ok," he said. "I'll see you then."

He ended the call after saying good-bye. Before he could put his phone down, he saw an email from Melissa in his inbox. He opened it and started reading.

Martin,

I hope your trip to DC isn't a complete bust. I spoke to the curator again. That billionaire from Hong Kong will be coming to Chicago for a private showing of the deep ocean exhibit. You can be my +1 if you promise to be professional and not embarrass me! Love you!

Martin audibly groaned before hitting the respond button and typing out: "Sounds like a fun time. Count me in. And aren't I always the charming, consummate professional? Email me the details. I'll call when I'm back in town."

He read his email once more and then hit the send button.

This was all happening so fast, he thought to himself, and it was really starting to bother him. Either people are going to be open to what he has to say, or he's going to crash and burn – epically – likely resulting in him ruining his reputation and getting fired from the best job he ever had. He had to laugh as he usually only faced these kinds of insecurities at three o'clock in the morning, not when he should be getting ready to meet the only person in Washington, D.C. who seemed willing to talk to him about all of this.

Martin rolled out of bed, walked over to the little hotel coffeemaker, brewed himself a strong cup of coffee, and did his best to choke down all the crippling self-doubts that were swimming around in his brain.

* * * * *

The small coffee shop had just about cleared out by the time Martin saw Zoe walk through the front door. At this point, it was a few minutes after 9 a.m. and most of the customers had come and gone, and the staff were in the process of busying themselves, cleaning and preparing for lunch. Martin had taken a seat at one of the six tables that were positioned around the room. He smiled as he inhaled the rich, sweet scent of brewing coffee and hot pastries.

Martin waved to her just before taking a sip from the small white paper cup he held in his left hand. She quickly walked over to him and apologized.

"I am so sorry," she said. "A Metro train broke down, and everything was backed up."

Martin smiled back at her.

"I got your text," he said, holding up his hand. "It's fine. Don't worry about it. It's not like I have anywhere to go today. It's kind of nice. I have zero plans, you know?"

Zoe looked around the coffee shop, before saying, "I'm just gonna …"

Martin gestured toward the front counter, adding, "I would have ordered a coffee for you, but I have no idea what you drink."

Zoe smiled back at him, slid a chair out, and placed her bag on it.

"Don't go anywhere," she said to him. "I'll be right back."

He watched her walk to the young man standing behind the register and ask for a black coffee. After she paid, she walked back to the table and sat down.

"Black coffee?" he asked her with a wry smile.

"I started drinking it when I was working on my dissertation and working full-time," she said. "I was broke, but I also learned to like the taste."

Martin took a sip of his own coffee. Zoe leaned forward over his cup, waved her hand up to her nose, and sniffed.

"I smell vanilla, cinnamon," she paused for a moment. "Pumpkin spice? It's July."

"What?" questioned Martin, sheepishly. "I like the way it tastes. The more cream and sugar, the better."

Zoe huffed and wrinkled her nose.

"I'm not sure which is worse," she said, smiling. "The fact you believe a monster is messing around with airplanes, or you like pumpkin-spiced coffee."

She took a long drink from her coffee, before adding, "Please tell me you don't drink that pumpkin beer, too?"

"That, my friend," he quipped, "is a bridge too far."

He stopped and stared at her while she laughed, causing her to pause and put her hand to her cheek.

"Do I have something on my face?" she asked, rubbing her hand over her mouth and nose. "You'd tell me if something was in my teeth, right?"

Martin laughed.

"Of course," he said, "but I'd say, like, you're very pretty, but you have lettuce in your teeth."

He watched her blush and look away from him. She looked up at him again and their eyes met.

"You think I'm pretty?"

It was Martin's turn to look out of the window.

"I mean," he mumbled, "you are, but I was just saying …"

His voice trailed off, and the stillness between them lasted for a few seconds. When Zoe finally broke the silence, Martin sat up in surprise.

"I really don't want to think you're crazy," she said, pausing to study him. "Are you?"

"Isn't that the thing about being crazy? It's the people who don't think they're crazy who usually are, so I'm damned no matter what I say."

"Well, are you?" she pressed.

Martin sat back in his chair, threw back his head, and slowly ran his hand through his hair.

"I realize what I've been showing you is out there," he said. "What normal person travels halfway across the country, risks his career and reputation, to spin some tall tale about forces being responsible for plane crashes?"

He laughed.

"That sounds pretty fucking nuts to me," he said. "But I've spent years researching this. The math doesn't add up. Something is doing this, and I can't sit by and watch more people die."

Zoe finished her coffee and placed the empty mug back on the table. The sound of ceramic hitting wood filled the quiet cafe. Zoe looked around, slightly embarrassed, before their laughter broke the tension between them.

"I swear to god," she said. "If you're fucking crazy ..." She paused for effect, adding, "I have no problems making you regret it. My divorce, me giving up my house, my life all falling apart – there's no shame. I'll have no problem flying to Chicago to hunt you down and ruin you."

Martin laughed for the second time that day. It felt really good, he thought.

Zoe furrowed her brow and squinted her eyes, but a smile crept back in. They broke into laughter again.

After a few moments, he looked at her, and asked, "Ok, hear me out."

The smile left her face, and she stared at him.

"Come back to Chicago with me," he said.

He could see her tense up and move back in her chair, putting distance between herself and him.

"Just as friends," he said, putting his hands up in front of him,

"I'll pay for your flight and a hotel room for yourself. Your choice where."

He paused before adding, "Within reason, of course. I don't have a lot of money."

She started to say something, but he interjected, "There's this thing that's happening, an event with this Chinese billionaire, who's been funding all kinds of research in the oceans. Come with me to it. It's at the Field Museum."

He could tell by her face that she wasn't sold on it.

"He's the one who paid for the deep scans of the Sunda Trench, and they found that anomaly, that deep pit in there, down on the southeastern end. That's exactly where the planes went down."

Her jaw tightened and her eyebrows went up.

"I already swore to my friend who's getting me tickets that I wouldn't embarrass her," said Martin, holding his hands up. "I just want to ask him about the scans."

"Alright," she said. "I got another month before school starts again. I'll go to Chicago, but I'm serious. Any weirdness, and I will have no problem fucking you up. I'll be on the first flight back to D.C."

*　*　*　*　*

"Any chance you can get one more ticket for a friend, who's here visiting me?" said Martin as he laid the cellphone on his bed next to his travel suitcase.

"I can absolutely do that."

Before Martin could thank her, Melissa added, "You're still my plus-one, so who's this mystery person I'm getting another ticket for?"

"She's a friend I met in Washington," he said.

The sound of him unzipping his suitcase filled the silence as Martin awkwardly fumbled with his clothing.

"So it's a 'she,'" said Melissa coolly. "You sure she's just a friend?"

"I can assure you, she is very much just a friend, Mel. She's a professor at American University, and she's actually kind of interested in my theories about the Indian Ocean."

"Is she crazy?" Mel asked, laughing. "Crazy can be fun – until it's not."

"She's not crazy," he shot back quickly.

He paused for a moment to take a deep breath and regain his composure.

"Sorry about that," he said, "She doesn't believe everything, but she recognizes coincidence and bad weather can't explain what's happening."

"I'm just saying," Melissa said, "if I'm gonna be a third wheel, I should invite someone else as my plus-one."

"It's gonna be packed with colleagues and all your friends," answered Martin. "I was always deadwood at these events when we were together, sitting somewhere out of the way, nursing a cocktail. I didn't hate them. It was just awkward."

"That hurts," she said, laughing. "I always tried to include you. I can't help but think that you're just shy. And, besides, I always made it up to you."

Martin smiled.

"Fine," she added. "I'll get another ticket. Rules still stand. Don't be weird. And, please, I'm begging you. Whatever you do, don't embarrass me."

"Come on, Mel," joked Martin. "When have I ever been weird?"

"Really?"

"Fine, you have my word," said Martin. "I promise to be my best self."

"That's what I'm afraid of."

*   *   *   *   *

So many years studying plane crashes certainly had an effect on Martin. He tried to put on a confident air, but he had been fidgeting for at least an hour, before Zoe looked up from her tablet to tell him to stop squirming.

"I'm sorry," he said. "I'm just not very good on planes anymore. They make me nervous."

"It's safer than driving," she said, looking over at him. "At least that's what my ex always said."

Martin watched her smile all the way up to her eyes and felt her gently squeeze his hand resting on the armrest. He felt some of the tension leave his neck and shoulders.

"I guess I'm just getting more neurotic as I age," he said, looking down at the carpet on the floor. "It's pretty tough not to be when you've immersed yourself so much in catastrophes. You hyper-focus, which is what I do when I fly anymore."

"Ignore and override," she said, her eyes going back to what she was reading on her tablet.

"What?"

"Ignore and override," she repeated. "It's what my dad used to tell me when things stressed me out as a kid. He was in the Army. Never made it very high up, but he talked about it a lot. When I was younger, it would make me mad, because I thought he was just telling me to suppress what was bothering me, which he kind of was. Now that I'm older, though, you know, I've come to realize you can't really let things bother you all of the time. You'll go crazy. You have to figure out what's important and ignore and override all the small stuff."

"That doesn't sound very healthy," said Martin.

"Oh you'd be surprised," she answered, looking up at him again. "Think about it. If you respond to every little thing, especially things you don't really have any control over anyway, you're going to struggle in life. You'll just be a reactive raw nerve. That can't be good for your mental health."

"Ok," said Martin, nodding, "but here's the major flaw I see in that: what if you choose to ignore and override something you think is small, but, then, it turns out it's actually really important, and now it's metastasized into an even bigger issue for you?"

"That's the trick," she said. "Most of the time, the small stuff goes away. It's how you know it's trivial. The big stuff sticks around."

She paused to close her tablet. "None of this means you go crashing through life, oblivious to everything and never paying attention. People have other ways of saying this, like, choose your battles or get your priorities straight."

"Well, it just so happens that not dying in a plane crash is one of my priorities," he said, a grin spreading across his face.

"Then I'd say your priorities are misplaced. You'd be better off worrying about dying in a car crash or, for that matter, falling down an open manhole on the streets of Chicago."

"Great, now I have one more thing to worry about – open manhole covers."

He watched her as she looked down at her lap, still laughing. He felt her squeeze his hand again just as the pilot made his announcement that they would be coming in for their final approach to Chicago's O'Hare International Airport.

"I've never been to Chicago," beamed Zoe, as she leaned forward to peer around the sleeping woman in the seat next to her and catch a glimpse of the city lights as the plane passed over the shores of Lake Michigan.

The plane bounced in some light turbulence, and Martin sat back in his seat. He gripped the armrests and closed his eyes, taking a deep breath.

Ignore and override, he thought to himself. Ignore and override.

I Think I Just Met a God
Chapter 3

Aji and his brother, Harto, stood on the beach at the edge of the ancient forest. The boys were tired from fishing along the shoreline all day, casting their woven net into the waves, and decided to rest for a bit. The day had been productive so far, and they had caught a dozen fish of varying sizes. Their mother would be happy with their success.

Aji stared out into the sea as Harto lay back. He looked down at his younger brother to see him closing his eyes.

"Wake up," Aji shouted, pushing his brother. "We have work to do. You can sleep later."

"I'm tired," said Harto, his eyes still closed. "We've been fishing since first light."

"We can fish more and still get home before dark," he said to his brother.

Harto grumbled and sat up.

"Mother will be happy with our catch," said Harto. "We can rest …"

Before Harto could finish his thought, the two brothers heard a sharp cracking sound, like a peal of thunder, followed by a flash of light that seemed to be coming from far out in the water. The two boys jumped to their feet, looking around for what may have caused it.

Aji was the first to speak.

"Storm is coming," he said. "We should hurry."

Harto picked up the fishing net, spread it out, took three steps, and threw it as hard as he could into the swell. The rocks carried it 2 meters into the water with a soft splash. Harto pulled hard on the long woven tether, closing the net, and began to pull it back in. Then Aji stepped in and helped Harto pull.

The boys did this over and over again for the next hour, catching another four fish. On the last throw, Harto pulled hard on the net, just as he had done dozens of times that day, but it didn't move.

"Help me, Aji," he cried out. "It's stuck on the rocks."

The waves had been picking up in the last few minutes, and the sea had grown increasingly violent.

"You should swim out and see," Harto said to Aji.

"I swam out the last time," Aji answered.

"But I've been throwing since our rest," countered Harto.

"Maybe we can pull it free," said Aji as he reached for the long rope.

The two boys began to pull on the rope.

"Be careful, " barked Aji. "You'll tear the net."

"One more time," yelled Harto as he braced himself for another pull. "If it doesn't work, you'll have to swim to free it."

The boys planted their feet and gave the rope a hard pull, and, to their surprise, it came loose.

"Quickly," shouted Aji. "Pull."

And they did. The two boys pulled and pulled, but it seemed heavier than normal to them.

"The ocean's too rough," said Aji. "This is our last cast today."

As the boys pulled the net in, Aji noticed what looked to be a long tail coiled around it. It bobbed in the waves as they dragged it to shore.

"There's something on it," said Aji. "It looks like a serpent's tail."

Harto dropped the rope and took a step back. Seeing this, Aji yelled, "Pull, Harto," before adding, "Whatever it is, I think it's dead."

Harto ran up to Aji, grabbed the rope, and began to pull along with his brother.

It didn't take long for the two boys to pull the net halfway up the beach. Aji carefully walked up to it, ready to run in the opposite direction if whatever this was showed any signs of life.

The tail, which was wrapped around the net twice, belonged to some kind of reptile the boys didn't recognize. It had large brown, dark green, and golden scales that formed complex diamond patterns and shone brightly in the sun. Before the rest of the creature disappeared into the water, at its thickest part, it was bigger around than Aji. The strangest part about it, however, was that it appeared to be shrinking as they stood there, staring at it.

"Aji!" shouted Harto. "Don't touch it!"

"I've never seen one this big before," said Aji, who could barely be heard over the crashing waves. "Even the one the elders killed."

Aji reached for the creature but it rolled as the waves grew larger and battered the beach. He quickly jumped back, turned and ran to Harto.

The ocean dumped more and more of it onto the shore. Aji thought it was never going to end when, all of a sudden, it rapidly shrank. The two boys watched the tail uncoil from the net as it slowly grew smaller. Aji rubbed his eyes and turned to look at his brother, who seemed to be mesmerized by what was happening. When he looked back at the serpent, its tail had split and appeared to form into legs.

Harto pulled hard on the net, dragging it away from the creature. As he did so, Aji got for the first time the best view of whatever this thing was. It was now not much longer than a tall man. Arms had formed from the elongated, limbless body, and the snout on its serpentine head was shortening and distending, shaping into a crude human's head. Aji couldn't believe his eyes, but where there were once thousands of scales, tan human skin appeared all over him.

Another wave hit the creature, and it rolled over and over before stopping halfway up the beach.

At this point, the boys could see that this creature was clearly a human man, its arms and legs splayed out. Aji could see cuts and bruises all over the man's naked body as if he had just come from some terrible battle.

"Harto!" shouted Aji, pointing toward the jungle. "Go get the elders! Now!"

Before he could even finish, Harto was already running to the path that started at the jungle's edge and went straight back to the village, leaving Aji alone with the man.

"If you're still alive," said Aji. "My brother is going to get help."

The man didn't move.

It didn't take long for Harto to return with eight men and women.

"I think he's dead," said Aji. "He hasn't moved at all."

Aji followed the group as they ran to the man. One of the elders placed his hand on the man's face and turned it to him. He positioned his head so his ear was over the man's face, and he listened intently. After a short moment, the elder began to bark orders at the others, telling them to fashion a stretcher for the man.

"He's alive," said the elder. "Bring him to the dukun."

* * * * *

"He is awake, Manuk," said the dukun, "but there is something very odd about him."

Just yesterday, Manuk, the village's elder, had told the others to bring the man to the village healer. He was unconscious and had been covered in bloody wounds.

Manuk stood outside the healer's joglo. It had thick, beige mud walls and a thatched roof that rose to a peak in the middle of the house. It was quite large for the village, but that was to be expected of someone as respected as the healer.

The day before, the boys had told an incredible tale of how this strange man had washed up on the shore as a huge python before slowly changing into a man. Manuk didn't doubt the boys' story. They both told similar tales, apart from each other. He had heard stories in the past told by previous elders of huge creatures that could change their shapes at will, switching from a man or a woman into monstrous beasts. One tale that frightened him as a child spoke of a tall, angry woman, who transformed into a huge many-tentacled squid and began to murder everyone in sight. The villagers fought back, but they were no match for it. Except for a few children, who managed to run and hide in the jungle, the village was no more. Other villagers found them and raised them as their own. That is where Manuk heard the story – from one of the survivors, who spoke with great fear that this creature would someday return to kill everyone.

Manuk had no idea if this man would wake up, and, to be honest, he hoped he would not. There could be no doubt that the world would be better off with one less of these things roaming about. He had seen plenty of people who suffered far less grievous injuries never wake again, so he would not be surprised if the man died quietly in the night.

"How so?" he asked the healer, as he peered into his joglo.

"He is completely healed, Manuk," said the dukun, "I saw with my own eyes that the wounds he had yesterday were all gone this morning, and he spoke to me. He thanked me for helping him. I have never seen anything like this. He should be dead. Everyone thinks he's Antaboga."

"I shall talk with him," said Manuk before stepping around the dukun and heading inside the house.

The dukun's joglo was quite spacious inside. Manuk saw thatch cots set up all around the room. It smelled fresh inside, the outside air wafting in, carrying the scent of the jungle with it. All the cots were empty except for one near the back of the room. A tall man with dark skin and hair lay on his back, his eyes open. When Manuk entered, he saw the man's head turn toward him. He studied him closely. The man never blinked. He just stared at Manuk for a moment before saying, "Hello, friend. I am Çig'Allagosh. I owe you a debt for saving my life."

Manuk stood in the doorway, too frightened to walk up to the man.

"You may come closer," said Çig'Allagosh. "There is no need to fear me."

Everything inside Manuk told him that he should run away from whatever this thing was. He was breathing fast, and he could feel his hands tingle.

"You should have died," was the only thing Manuk could think of saying.

Çig'Allagosh paused for a moment before a smile spread across his face. It reminded Manuk of the look a snake makes before it strikes.

"Our kind heal quickly," answered Çig'Allagosh.

Manuk watched the man struggle to sit up and slide his feet off the cot and onto the floor. He continued to brace himself on the bed, wobbling slightly.

"The others believe you're the snake god," said Manuk. "They're calling you *Antaboga*."

Çig'Allagosh chuckled softly. "I am no god," he said.

"Whatever you are, you still need rest," said Manuk. "You should lie back down."

Manuk saw Çig'Allagosh look up at him, give a quick smile, before settling back down onto the cot.

"You are right," said Çig'Allagosh. "I am still weak, but do not worry. I will be gone from your village soon and never bother you again."

Manuk looked at the man closely, who was again on his back, staring up at the ceiling. He took a few steps forward so he could see him better.

Whatever this thing was, Manuk thought to himself, it was a danger to the village, and he had to put on a brave face and speak with it to learn as much as he could about it.

"I have heard stories of your kind," said Manuk.

He watched the man slowly nod his head and turn to face him. Their eyes met, and Manuk saw for the first time that they were gold with flecks of green in them and his pupils were long black slits. It unnerved Manuk that the man never blinked. He felt a cold chill run down his body. His hair stood up, and tiny bumps appeared all over his skin. He watched as the man's pupils shrank and turned into tiny black circles, and, where there was once gold, his sclera was now white and the iris was more hazel.

"Your village is in no danger from me," said Çig'Allagosh. "As I said, I am in your debt." He paused before adding, "But I cannot speak for the others."

"What are you?" Manuk blurted out, not bothering to waste anymore time with basic courtesies.

The man chuckled for a moment before grimacing in pain. Manuk watched him turn away and look back up at the ceiling.

"I am as old as this Earth," said Çig'Allagosh. "I was here before your kind, and I will live on long past you when all your children's children are gone."

Çig'Allagosh seemed to take a deep breath, adding. "I was in a great battle to save your kind. But please understand that the less you know about us, the better off you will be."

Manuk could tell the man was not interested in sharing more with him, so he said to him, "I will let you rest then. I will come back later today when the sun is high in the sky to check on you."

"Thank you," said Çig'Allagosh. "I will only bother you for one more moon, and then you will never see me again."

Manuk turned and walked out of the joglo. He saw the dukun was still standing where he had last left him.

"I told you he was odd," said the dukun.

"He is more than odd," said Manuk, looking down at the sand to avoid making eye contact with the dukun.

The two men stood staring off into the jungle. The sounds of men and women working and children playing mixed with the wind in the leaves and distant din of the ocean. Manuk heard a bird call off in the distance.

"I will be back later to check on the man," said Manuk. "Before that, I think everyone should gather when the sun is at its highest point to hear what he has told me."

Manuk took a moment to listen to the sounds all around him.

"I am worried for the village," Manuk admitted to the dukun. "Something terrible is upon us."

* * * * *

"Dr. Martin Lee plus one," said the woman at the information desk. She fumbled through a folder as Martin looked on. He smiled at Zoe, but all he could think about was how awkward he usually was at events like this.

"I have your tickets right here," beamed the woman behind the counter. "Please follow the other guests up the stairs to the reception at the deep sea exhibit on the second floor."

Martin smiled, nodded, and took the tickets. He looked around the entrance hall to the Field Museum before his eyes returned to Zoe. He could see she was taking in the sights of the museum along with all the other attendees dressed in tuxedos and black dresses. She turned her head and smiled at Martin, their eyes meeting.

"I've been to plenty of university socials," she said, "but I only once got to go to an event at the Smithsonian. It was with my ex at Air and Space, so there were a lot of military types like him. It was fun, but not my cup of tea. These are my people."

She paused to take in the museum. It had been decorated to promote the new deep ocean exhibit. A huge banner hung from the ceiling. The words, "Explore the Deep," were imposed over a still image taken of the bottom of an ocean.

"We just got here, and, already, I'm having so much fun," she said.

"Are you glad you came?" he asked.

"To Chicago?"

"Sure," said Martin, "And the museum."

"I don't usually do things like this," she said. As they walked up the stairs to the exhibit hall, Martin watched her as she looked all around the museum, her eyes wide.

"Like what?"

"You know," she said, stopping to look up at him, "Hop on a plane to fly halfway across the country with a strange man I just met who believes monsters are crashing airplanes."

Martin laughed. "Okay, you got me there."

"No really, though," she said. "This is pretty far outside my usual comfort zone, so thank you for asking me."

Zoe reached out, slid her hand into his, and gave it a gentle squeeze.

"I really mean it," she said, smiling at him.

Just as they reached the entrance to the deep sea exhibit, Martin heard a familiar voice.

"Martin!"

Martin looked up to see Melissa standing near the entrance to the exhibit, a martini glass in her hand.

"I'm so glad you could make it," she shouted to him above the clamor of the crowd. "Get over here and introduce us to your friend!"

Martin waved back to Melissa before leaning down to whisper to Zoe: "This is my old friend, Melissa. She's one of the collections directors here at the museum."

The couple made their way through the growing crowd gathered in front of the bar.

"Nice to see you made it home safely," said Melissa. She held out her free hand, palm up, in the direction of the man standing next to her. "This is my friend, Tony Wilson," she said, turning her head toward the tall man with dark hair and eyes.

She looked at Zoe and then at Martin.

"Martin, I don't believe I've met your friend," she said.

Martin watched as Melissa sized up Zoe, her eyes going from Zoe's shoes to her hair.

"You were never one for subtly," Martin said, a smile going all the way to his eyes. "This is my friend Zoe Sullivan. She's a professor at American University."

Unprompted, Melissa took a step forward and grabbed Zoe's hand, saying to her, "They charge you guys for drinks, but it's free for me since I work here. Let's go grab a cocktail and chat. What do you like?"

Zoe shot a quick glance back at Martin, who just tilted his head and shrugged, mouthing the words, "Sorry." Zoe smiled and turned to look at Melissa, who was already peppering the woman with questions about Washington, D.C., American University, and how the two met.

Martin turned to Tony and said, "I guess that leaves us by ourselves."

Tony smirked before turning toward the crowd and walking away, an empty martini glass in his hand.

"Wow," Martin said aloud to no one. "Tough crowd."

He turned in the same direction as Tony and walked into the exhibit hall, looking around him as he went.

There were already well over a hundred people walking around the museum. The displays were impressive, many of them digitally enhanced and interactive. He walked over to the area that featured the latest discoveries from the Sunda Trench when he noticed a crowd had gathered around a middle-aged Asian man in what was clearly a very expensive tuxedo. Six large men flanked him, and they constantly looked around.

Martin heard a woman say to the man, "Mr. Li, can I get a picture with you?" The man smiled and stepped toward her, taking her phone and handing it to one of his security guards. "Get a nice picture of us for the lady, please," he said as he wrapped his arm around her lower back.

Martin watched the man for a while as he walked around the exhibit, stopping ever so often to study one of the displays. After a few moments, Martin saw an opening when the man turned and started to walk toward him.

"Mr. Li," said Martin, walking up to him. "I was wondering if you had a moment to talk about your recent project in the Sunda Trench?"

Li Haoyu turned to him and smiled, adding, "Of course. What is it you want to know?"

"I actually wanted to ask you if you really believed the deep hole at the southeastern end of the Sunda Trench was just a glitch?"

Before Haoyu could reply, however, a young woman interrupted him, saying, "Excuse me, Mr. Li, but you're needed at the stage."

Haoyu nodded at her before turning back to Martin.

"That's what the experts tell me," he said, "Do you have any evidence they're wrong?"

"I actually do, and I ..."

Before Martin could finish his sentence, however, Haoyu was escorted away. As Haoyu walked away, he turned to Martin, saying, "Catch up with me later. I want to hear more."

Martin stood for a few seconds holding his drink, trying to think of some way to get Haoyu to speak with him when a woman's voice jolted him from his thoughts.

"Dr. Lee, isn't it?"

Martin turned around to see a tall, thin woman with reddish-blonde hair, pale skin, and bright blue eyes smiling at him. She was wearing a long black dress that hugged her body tightly. Martin felt his face warm as his eyes met hers.

"Do we ... uh, " he stammered. "Do we know each other?"

"We do not," she said, "but I am very aware of you and your work, Dr. Lee. My name is Catharine Barlos. If you can spare a minute of your time, we should talk."

"Sure," said Martin, looking down at his hands. "I got plenty of time right now."

Catharine looked around.

"There's a quiet spot over there by the railing," she said.

Martin followed Catharine to the other end of the entry hall, just by the stairs. Once they arrived, the noise of the bustling exhibit hall dissipated, and Catharine abruptly turned to face Martin. He immediately could tell her friendly demeanor was gone when she spun to face him.

"You have to stop your search in the Indian Ocean, Dr. Lee," she said, real anger showing in her tense jaw and behind her eyes. "You have no idea what you're doing."

"I ... uh," Martin stuttered. He felt his face flush again. "What is it exactly that you think I'm doing?"

"Don't play stupid with me, Dr. Lee," she said, taking a step toward him and lowering her voice. "You know exactly what I'm talking about, so let's just skip ahead to the part where we agree I'm not an idiot and know you're looking for something in that ocean."

Martin looked around quickly.

"Who talked to you about this?" he asked her.

"The less you know about me and my history, the better off you'll be, Dr. Lee," she answered. "So, again, I'll say to you, end your search, or else you will regret it."

"Wait," he said, taking a step back. "Are you seriously threatening me?"

"Not a threat, Dr. Lee," she said, a serpentine smile spreading across her face. "Just letting you know what will happen if you don't stop poking around things that do not concern you."

"Hundreds of people just died when a plane crashed there," he said to her. "It seems apparent that something's behind that, and I think the world should know so it doesn't happen again."

"It will happen again," she countered, "and that's the price we all have to pay to keep from something even worse happening."

"That doesn't make any sense," he said to her, pushing his glasses back up on his nose. "You can't be willing to sacrifice hundreds of people like that. We have to know what caused this and stop it. Now if you don't mind …"

Martin started to walk away but she reached up and grabbed his arm, stopping him. He tried to wrench his arm free but could not break her grip.

"You can't stop it, Dr. Lee," she said, "so let it go. You'll only get this one warning. The next time, the others will not be so charitable."

Martin watched in dismay as Catharine let go of his arm, turned, and began to walk down the stairs. Just as she reached the bottom of the stairs, Martin heard a familiar voice.

"You don't waste any time, do you?"

He turned to see the two women standing there, both holding cocktail glasses in their hands and staring at him. Mercifully it looked like Zoe was still smiling.

"What'd you say to Mr. Li?" asked Melissa, staring squarely at Martin, her arms folded.

"I just …" Martin stammered. "I … uh … Did you guys see me

talking to that strange woman?"

Zoe and Melissa traded looks. Zoe shook her head and said, "We just saw you staring down the stairs and walked over to you."

"That was really weird," he told them, rubbing his forearm. "She warned me to stop looking in the Indian Ocean. She said if I don't then 'others' will make me regret it."

He saw Zoe looking down at his arm. He was still rubbing it.

"Are you okay?" she asked him.

"She was really cryptic," he said. "I have no idea who she is."

"Do you want me to get security?" asked Melissa.

"No," he shot back. "No, that's okay. She's gone now."

"You look pretty shaken," said Zoe. "You sure you're okay?"

"I'm fine. Really."

"Right," said Melissa. "So what about Mr. Li? What did I ask you when I suggested you come to hear him speak?"

"I didn't say anything," said Martin. "I just asked him if he thought the deep hole at the bottom of the trench was a glitch. He said that's what he was told. He asked if I had any evidence to the contrary, and I said I did. Then he was pulled away."

"I thought I told you not to embarrass me?" she said, her arms still folded tightly across her chest.

"Well," said Martin, looking down at his shoes. "I, uh …"

"How about you just give him your card later and ask him if you can schedule a meeting some time in the future?" interrupted Zoe.

Melissa added, "Seriously, Martin, don't start going off about sea monsters and shit to him. I'll never hear the end of it."

Martin dropped his shoulders and frowned.

"Alright," he said. "I won't talk to him here. I'll just give him my card."

Melissa smiled and looked away quickly.

"Oh, there's John," she said. "I'll catch up with you guys later."

Martin watched her disappear into the crowd before turning to face Zoe. He could still see Melissa out of the corner of his eye when he heard Zoe say, "Oh boy, did she have a lot to say about you."

"All good things, I'm sure."

"I'd say a little of both. I didn't know you two used to date."

Martin winced.

"We were always better friends than boyfriend-girlfriend," he said. "What did she tell you?"

"You know that I know that that's bullshit." She took a breath and then added, "She said you're a good person, but you have no idea when to shut the fuck up."

"Why do I feel like there's more coming?" he asked before looking around. "I think I need a drink before we start this conversation. Where's that bar?"

Zoe took Martin by the shoulder and physically turned him toward her. He didn't resist.

"No," she said. "She likes you. She wants the best for you, but she's afraid you're losing it over this stuff in the Indian Ocean."

Martin frowned again.

"I promised her I wasn't going to talk about it anymore tonight," said Martin, turning his head to look for the bar, "but that woman a few minutes ago really freaked me out."

"She's not talking about tonight," said Zoe. "She means overall. She's worried you're losing it, that you're going to lose your job and end up homeless over this stuff."

"She invited me because that billionaire was going to be here," said Martin, turning to look at Zoe. His brow furrowed and his shoulders went up.

"I think she was hoping you'd use some discretion. You know, don't just make a run at him, all Don Quixote-like."

Martin chuckled. "You know what happens at the end of Don Quixote? He quits, and the next day he dies. Is that what she wants for me?"

"Jesus, Martin, that's not what she wants at all. She cares about you, and she's just worried. So don't be a jerk and take a bit more care of yourself."

Martin smiled. He paused for a moment to think before telling her, "If we didn't just meet, and I didn't like you as much as I do, I don't think we could be friends."

"So you do like me?" she asked, bumping him lightly with her shoulder.

"Don't you hate it when your internal monologue goes external?" he joked.

"If that's the worst of your intrusive thoughts, I guess you can't really be as bad as Melissa says."

"Yup," said Martin. "Worst mistake she ever made was dumping me. Go ahead and ask her."

"She may or may not have said something like that to me."

"Did she say that?" asked Martin, turning to face Zoe. "Now I want to know."

"Nope," she teased, "Implied confidentiality. I'm not spilling all our secrets?"

"Really?" he taunted her.

"No!" she said, shaking her head.

*   *   *   *   *

Later that night, the museum presented Haoyu with an award for his support of ocean research. He gave a brief speech, where he told the crowd that the world must do more to fight pollution and overfishing or risk the death of our oceans and the end of the world.

"Last year, I took a deep-submergence vehicle to the bottom of the Mariana Trench – 10,975 meters to the bottom," said Haoyu to the crowd. "You know what I saw down there among all those incredible sea creatures that have evolved to survive at those depths? A couple of plastic bags and a plastic shoe."

He paused for a moment to let his words sink in.

"It sounds ridiculous, but it's 100% true," he said. "We can't keep living like this. If the oceans go, humans go."

He looked around the room casually, before adding, "Thank you, and I hope you all enjoy the rest of your evening at this very impressive exhibit."

Haoyu waved to the crowd, which responded with enthusiastic applause, and stepped off the stage. He was immediately swarmed by attendees.

Zoe turned to Martin. "Great speech, but I need another drink," she said, looking down at her empty martini glass.

They had watched Haoyu's speech from the back of the crowd.

"If we hurry we can probably catch the bar before it's swamped," he said to her.

The two made their way to the entrance of the exhibit and ordered another round of drinks. There were seats available by the top of the stairs, so they worked their way over to them and sat down.

"I think this night went pretty well," said Zoe, smiling up at Martin. "How much longer do you want to stay?"

"I was ready to go about an hour ago."

"You don't know how much I needed this," she said. "I'm sad it's nearly over."

Martin leaned close to Zoe, whispering to her, "It doesn't have to end when we leave here."

"I, uh," said Zoe. "I really don't know about that, Martin. I just finalized the divorce, and I'm not sure I'm ready ..."

Martin interrupted her, waving his hand.

"Oh no," he said, laughing. "I didn't mean that. I was thinking some food, like breakfast or something."

Zoe burst out laughing.

"I'm so sorry," she said. "I just thought, you know, you were, um, you know, inviting me back to your place."

Martin looked over at her. She was smiling as she stared back at him.

"Totally fine," he said. "Let's just pretend that never happened. Ignore and override, right?"

*　*　*　*　*

Zoe opened the door to her hotel room with her keycard and walked into her room, closing the door and locking it behind her. She walked over to the wardrobe across from the bed, took off her watch and necklace and earrings and placed them on it. She sat down on the bed, slipped out of her heels, unzipped her dress and slid out of it. She stood up and carefully placed the dress on the chair by the small round table in the corner of the room. She then took off her black bra and placed that on the chair next to her dress.

She walked to the bathroom, turned on the water in the tub, adjusted the temperature, and closed the drain. She sat down on the toilet to relieve herself and rested her head in her hands, finally feeling like she could relax.

After a moment, she checked her phone. There was a text from her ex on it that came through earlier that evening. She had forgotten she had muted him a week ago when they were arguing about their divorce papers.

His text read, "Wanted to give you a heads-up that we're working with Indonesians on the crash. They got it covered, so you can tell your friend to drop it. They think it was mechanical failure in bad weather, but they're only 90% sure. Anyway, I'm just checking in. I stopped by your place and fed the cat and watered the plants like you asked. It looks like you could use a cleaning service. Have a good trip."

Zoe thought about sending him a middle finger emoji but thought better of it. She typed, "Thank you!" instead, hit send, and left it at that.

She sighed audibly before standing up and flushing the toilet. She kicked her black panties to the door and stood in front of the mirror. She put her hair up in a bun and picked at a small pimple on her face before turning to step into the tub. She could feel the goosebumps rising on her skin as she slowly slipped into the hot water, then she leaned back and closed her eyes.

A strange sensation immediately came over her. She smelled salt water, then the light in her eyes became unbearably bright. After her eyes adjusted to the change, she looked around and found herself completely surrounded by rolling waves on all sides. She could hear voices, speaking in a language she didn't understand. The gibberish soon turned into words she could comprehend. The words danced in her head, and she wasn't sure there were voices behind them or if they were just thoughts. The words came slowly but she could make them out. There were three distinct voices: two males and one female.

"You have to stop this madness," said a male voice.

"You've killed too many," came the female voice.

"The others don't support what you're doing," the second male voice answered.

"This is wrong," echoed the first male voice.

Everything went black after that, and there was searing, scorching pain all over her body like something was burning her.

Zoe's eyes shot open, and her hand went to her head. She could feel her hair was wet, but she didn't remember going under the water in the tub. She groaned as a terrible headache came on.

"What the fuck was that," she muttered out loud. "What just happened to me?"

She could still visualize the ocean waves as if she had been there and could have sworn she smelled salt water on her skin.

She leaned forward to release the drain before carefully climbing out of the tub. She grabbed one of the white towels and dried herself off. Her skin was clean and wasn't at all tacky like she had just come from swimming in saltwater. The headache slowly dissipated.

All this talk of the ocean and monsters must be getting to her, she thought. She laughed quietly as she took Motrin from her toiletry bag on the bathroom counter and swallowed two of them down with a drink of water.

She walked to the bed and checked her phone again. It was 2 a.m. She didn't even bother putting on the pajamas that lay folded on top of her suitcase. She climbed into bed, pulled the sheets and comforter over her, shut off the light, and promptly fell asleep.

*   *   *   *   *

The next morning, Martin woke with a start to the sound of his cellphone buzzing on his nightstand. He was surprised to see a message from Li Haoyu's assistant, who wanted to schedule a meeting with Haoyu later that afternoon.

Martin quickly called the number back to confirm the time. Haoyu was still in Chicago and willing to talk over the phone or meet in person. Martin jumped at the opportunity to meet Haoyu and share all his research with him.

Martin rolled on his back and sent a short text to Zoe, telling her he would be meeting with Haoyu later that afternoon just around the corner from where she was staying. Less than a minute after he hit send, his phone rang. He looked down to see Zoe's number, and he quickly answered it.

"Good morning," he said, clearing his throat.

"Just got your text. You want company at the meeting?"

"You mean a babysitter?"

Zoe sighed audibly. "You're not still grumpy about last night? How about we agree it's smart to bring another scientist along?"

"I'm serious," he said. "And I actually think it's a good idea."

"Wait. … What?"

"I think it's a great idea having someone who can read the room," he said. "We all know I'm terrible at that."

"Sounds like we have a plan," she added. "One more question: Have you thought about what happens if this guy throws you out of his office?"

Martin rolled over in bed and groaned. "Not really. The meeting's at one. I'll swing by early to get lunch, and then we can head over to his hotel, which is right down the street from you."

A few hours later, Martin met Zoe at a cafe next to her hotel, and they had a quick lunch.

"So what about this woman I met last night at the Field?" asked Martin as they walked toward Haoyu's hotel.

"What about her?"

"It was really weird," he said, stopping abruptly. It took Zoe a second to notice that Martin wasn't next to her. She stopped walking and turned to face him.

"She knew my name, what I did for a living, and my research – it was fucking unnerving."

'It's not like you've kept it a secret," she said. "You've been telling anyone who'll listen, even people who aren't and don't care about it."

"She said her name is Catherine Barlos," he said. "I searched for her on the Internet and found nothing. She looked like she had money. People like that always have a footprint. Always."

"Not always, Martin. Some people value their privacy. Maybe she's anonymous or uses alts?"

"She told me she was giving me one warning," he said, "That's it. After that, she mentioned something about 'others' and me regretting it. It was really unsettling."

He saw Zoe's eyes go wide. "You're really freaked about this."

"You're damn right I am," he said. "She was strong, too. I tried to walk away, but she grabbed my arm, and I couldn't move. I couldn't break her grip at all."

Martin rubbed his forearm and started to walk again.

"That's the place," he said, pointing up at the luxury hotel that stood out on the Gold Coast of Chicago with its classic look.

"Fancy," said Zoe, "but what do you expect from a billionaire?"

Martin and Zoe walked up to the front desk at the Waldorf Astoria and told the woman behind the counter that he had a meeting with Li Haoyu at 1 p.m. The woman picked up a phone and pressed several keys on it. Martin could hear her side of the conversation. She hung up the phone and told him someone would come down to escort him upstairs.

After a few minutes, the elevator toward the back of the lobby opened, and the assistant Martin spoke with last night stepped out along with a very large man, whom Martin assumed was security. The assistant told Martin and Zoe to follow him back up, where they would only be able to speak with Haoyu for a few minutes.

The elevator ride up seemed excruciatingly long, thought Martin, even though it was less than a minute. When the doors slid open, Martin could see there were two more security guards stationed in the hallway. They nodded to the assistant and the other man, before the whole group walked toward a room at the end of a long hallway.

When the door opened, Martin could see multiple people sitting on chairs and sofas in the large hotel suite, some typing into laptops while others talked on cellphones. Haoyu sat on a sofa toward the back of the room. He was holding a glass of water in his hand.

A security guard stepped in front of Martin and asked, "Do you mind if I check your satchel?"

Martin handed his bag to the man, who rifled through it.

"All clear," the man said before handing it back to him.

"Dr. Lee, Dr. Sullivan, so nice to see you again," said Haoyu. "I apologize for the security. You can never be too careful."

He smiled and waved his hand toward the couple. "Please, come over and take a seat."

Martin wended through the people in the room and offered a seat to Zoe near Haoyu. After she sat down, Martin took a spot next to Haoyu, placing his leather satchel on the floor.

"Thank you for agreeing to meet with me, Mr. Li," said Martin.

Haoyu smiled and placed his glass down on the coffee table. He turned to one of his assistants and asked them to bring two more glasses of water for Martin and Zoe.

"What did you want to speak with me about, Dr. Lee?" asked Haoyu.

"I recognize you don't have much time, so let me just get down to it," said Martin, before trading a glance with Zoe. "Last year, when you and your team did a deep scan of the Sunda Trench, you discovered a deep hole at the southeast end. I've been told both by you and others that some experts thought this was a glitch in the software, but I gathered from speaking briefly to you last night that you may not agree. Is that accurate?"

Haoyu looked down at his hand, turning it over to stare at his manicured fingernails.

"I was there when we ran those scans, Dr. Lee," said Haoyu, still avoiding eye contact with Martin. "We went over that area twice, and, each time, that hole showed up. I know what others say about this, but my feeling is that once may be an error, but twice? I personally don't think so."

Haoyu paused to look up and study Martin, before asking, "Why do you care about this, Dr. Lee? You're an anthropologist not a geologist."

"Right," said Martin. He looked over at Zoe and then back to

Haoyu. "That's why I'm here."

Martin reached into his bag, took out a manila folder, and spread several papers out on the coffee table. He picked one up and handed it to Haoyu.

"This is a picture of a stone tablet that dates to around 1,000 to 1,500 B.C.E.," he said. "The inscriptions are in a very old form of Javanese. It was found about 50 years ago in the far southeastern end of the island of Java in a place called the 'Alas Purwo,' which means ancient or primordial forest."

Haoyu held the image close to his face and looked intently at it.

"Do you know what it says?" he asked.

"I have studied it for a few years now, and I think I have deciphered what it says," said Martin. "It speaks of ancient creatures, huge, bigger than dinosaurs, that have inhabited the Earth since the times of creation. These creatures have been warring amongst themselves for millions of years."

Martin paused for a moment to let Haoyu focus on the inscription.

"This particular story was dictated by someone who went by the name of Manuk. He was an elder in a village near the ocean. They found one of these creatures, a huge serpent – his description sounds like it was an enormous python, 'larger than the biggest tree in the jungle' – who was near death, and took it back to their village to try to save it after Manuk said the creature had turned into a man. According to Manuk, the next day, the man was healed of all his wounds, and this man told him about these creatures and the great battle he fought with one particularly dangerous creature, what I think is a giant squid-god monster."

At this point Haoyu had placed the paper on the table and was staring at Martin.

"Manuk was told that this squid-beast saw mankind as a destructive force on the world," Martin continued, "and it wished to destroy us all. The man said there were many arguments among his kind and, finally, after much indecision, he felt he had to take action against the squid-god, to weaken it and imprison it at the bottom of the ocean for, quote, the rest of time, unquote."

Haoyu furrowed his brow and rubbed his eyes.

"That's an incredible story," he said, "and I appreciate you telling me this, but what does it have to do with me?"

"Manuk was told by the man that the squid-monster had incredible powers, and he fought it from, quote, when the moon was full in the sky until it wasn't, unquote. Or something like that."

Martin picked up the paper and pointed to it.

"See," he said, placing his finger on the inscription. "Right here. And here is where he writes, 'the bottom of the ocean.' "

Haoyu looked closely at the inscription.

"I'm sorry, Dr. Lee, but I still don't see what I have to do with any of this," he said.

"I think you've found the spot where the squid-god has been imprisoned," said Martin. "But there's more."

Martin sat back on the sofa and shot a quick look at Zoe. He took a deep breath and exhaled before turning back to Haoyu.

"In the last 20 years, only two commercial airliners have flown over this spot on the map, and both have crashed, lost forever in the depths of the Sunda Trench," said Martin. "The spot you found corresponds exactly with that spot on the map."

"You're not actually saying these creatures are real and are taking down planes, are you, Dr. Lee?" asked Haoyu.

Martin sighed. "Mr. Li, I think it's a real possibility …"

Haoyu blinked several times and looked over at Zoe. "What do you think, Dr. Sullivan?"

Zoe placed her hand on Martin's forearm.

"Dr. Lee and I have discussed this at length, Mr. Li," she said. "I think it's quite possible the creatures mentioned in these ancient writings are really just metaphors for natural events that were not well understood back then, so the people ascribed supernatural forces to them. It's possible that the deep well you found in the Sunda Trench is emitting gases from volcanic activity that affects airplanes flying overhead. It may be happening sporadically, so we don't know about it yet. Maybe it's been exacerbated by the oceans warming."

She took a breath and looked back and forth between Haoyu and Martin before continuing. "It's possible that these fumes could asphyxiate crew and passengers on the plane. If they contained a lot of hydrogen, they could bring it down. Whatever's happening, it's a phenomenon that should be studied."

Martin watched Haoyu look at Zoe and then back at him.

"I don't believe natural events can explain why these planes went …" Martin started to say but stopped short when he saw Zoe's eyes go wide and shake her head ever so slightly twice.

"The truth is, Mr. Li," said Zoe, "we just don't have any idea what's causing this. We don't believe it's just a coincidence that these two planes went down, and we think it's going to happen again unless we can figure out what's causing it."

"We've come to you because we need your help getting to the spot where these planes went down," said Martin. "With your technology, we can scan the bottom, maybe even send a drone down there. I think we can figure out what's happening and save lives."

Martin studied Haoyu but found him impossible to read. The young man, who escorted Martin and Zoe, walked over to Haoyu and whispered to him, "Your meeting starts in 10 minutes, sir."

Haoyu sat back on the sofa, took a sip from his water glass, and cleared his throat.

"Studying the ocean is my passion," he said. "It's really been a pleasure speaking to you. I can't say I'm sold on Martin's monster theory, but I was planning another trip to that area anyway. Let's do this. I'll have my assistant set it all up and email you the details.

They thanked Haoyu before being escorted back downstairs. On the way down, Haoyu's assistant said, "It may take a couple of days, but I'll get you something soon when we can squeeze in the time for this trip. Mr. Li loves this, so I'm sure he'll do his best to clear his schedule."

"We really appreciate it," said Zoe. "Please tell him that we'd be dead in the water without his help."

Martin and Zoe stepped out of the hotel into the bright, warm Chicago air. Dark clouds loomed overhead, and a peal of thunder cracked in the distance, signaling one of those drenching summer storms was on its way. Zoe smiled at Martin, but he could see the apprehension in her face.

"You're not sure about this?" he asked her as they started on their way back to her hotel.

"I don't know," she said, shaking her head. "This could be one big waste of time, and Haoyu doesn't seem like the type of guy who likes to have his time wasted."

"If I didn't believe we were onto something," countered Martin, "I wouldn't be doing this."

"It doesn't work like that," she said. "There's literally no data indicating these plane crashes were anything but terrible accidents. All we have is an ancient inscription that talks about monsters. You know as well as anyone that people back then just made things up to explain what were otherwise simply natural occurrences."

"We'll never know if we don't at least try," interrupted Martin, "and Haoyu is willing to give it a try. Worst case scenario: I get a free boat trip, and you get to play with all his high tech equipment on his ship."

Zoe stopped abruptly, forcing Martin to turn back toward her.

"I have a life, Martin," she said. "I have a career and students next semester. I can't just drop everything and take off."

"School doesn't start for another four weeks," he answered. "I just wrapped up a major project for my company, and I have a ton of leave banked. What do you say? Shall we hop on a flight early to Jakarta and take the train east as far as we can go? The museum that has the inscription is there. It's not far from where I think the village was that was mentioned in it."

Zoe thought about it for a moment.

"Well," she said. "I've never been to Indonesia before."

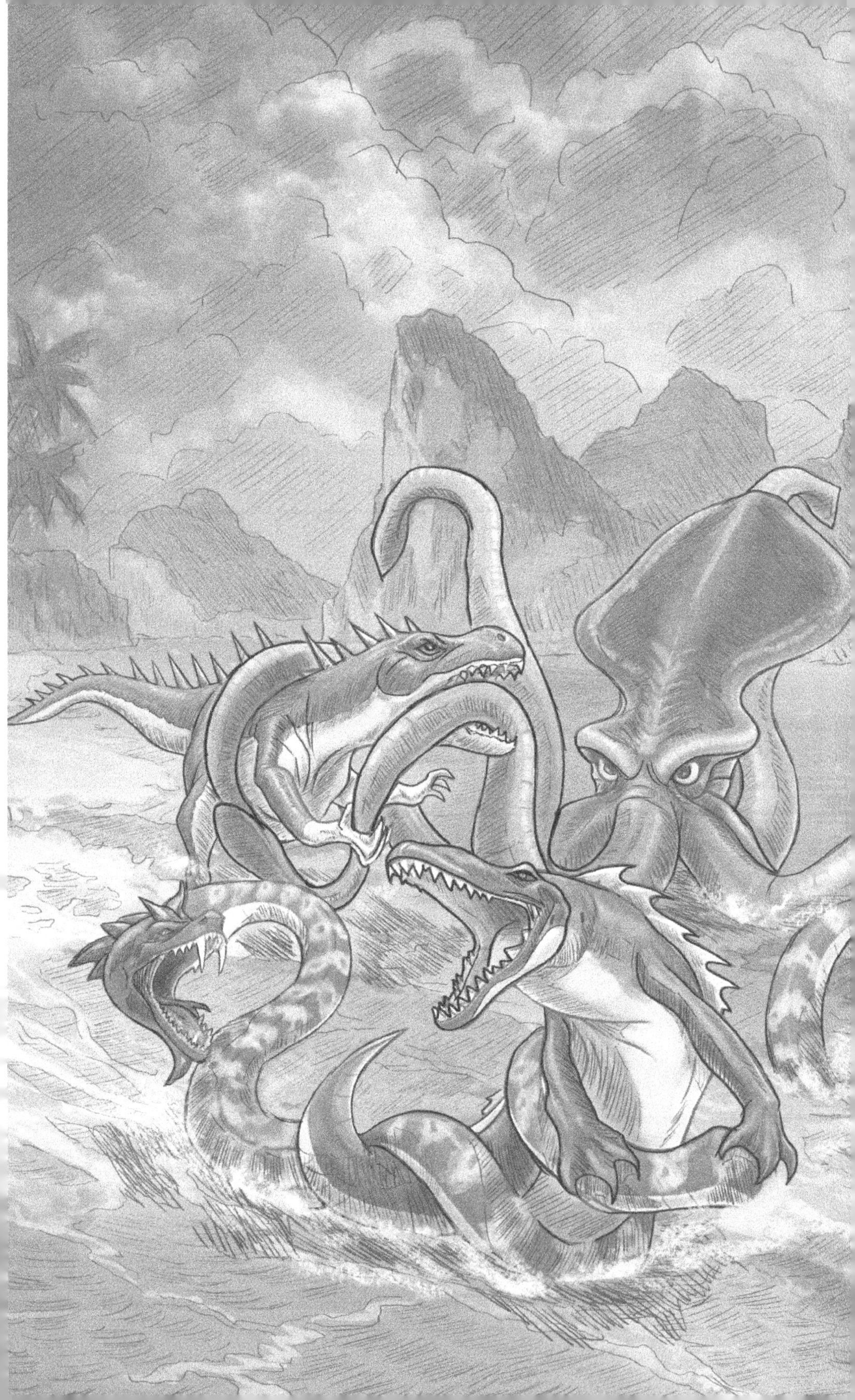

So Much for Just Talking
Chapter 4

Manuk sat at the front of his joglo as the other villagers began to file in. The breeze felt good wafting through his home in the heat of the afternoon sun. Every so often, the scent of flowers and the salty air from the sea filled his nostrils, and he smiled.

Word had gotten out that there was a stranger recovering in the dukun's joglo, who might be dangerous, so the entire village – all 114 of them – had come out, including the old and the children, and they had all taken spots on mats spread around the room.

After everyone had settled in, Manuk spoke.

"Thank you for coming out today," Manuk started. "By now, everyone knows that we have an outsider in the village. We can discuss that, but, before we do, does anyone have any important matters they wish to discuss?"

Except for some brief muttering, the room remained silent.

"Very well," said Manuk. "I have asked the dukun to attend this gathering so he can speak first to tell us about this man."

Manuk turned to the healer and said, "Dukun, if you will."

The elderly man nodded to Manuk and turned to the crowd.

"You have heard correctly that a man came to us yesterday. Aji and Harto found him on the beach, badly injured, so we brought him to my home, and I cared for him. The truth is, I didn't do much for him, thinking he would pass on soon since his wounds were so bad. I tried to make him comfortable, offering him water, which he took, and broth, which he didn't.

The dukun paused to cough and clear his throat.

"I expected that the man would die in the night, so, before I went to sleep, I said a brief prayer over him to the gods wishing him well on his journey to the next world. I woke up several times at night, but it was very quiet, so I slept until I heard the jungle wake up. Much to my surprise, however, when I went to check on the man, he was alive and well, his wounds having healed almost entirely in the night."

Loud talking interrupted the healer, and he took a moment to allow everyone to settle back down. Manuk had to intervene, so that the dukun could finish.

"I offered him more food and water, which he again refused. He did not talk much, but, when he did, it was clear he understood what I was saying to him. Manuk came shortly after I woke, and I gave them privacy so that they could speak. I did not listen, and I do not know what was said. The man is currently still in one of my cots, though I suspect he could get up and walk from this village at any time now."

The dukun adjusted himself on the floor, coughed again, and added, "That is all I know."

"Thank you, dukun," said Manuk, who then looked around the room. It was obvious that people were afraid. He could see the concern etched on his fellow villagers' faces.

"I heard he was a huge serpent when the boys found him and changed into a man," shouted one person.

"It's true," shouted a boy who sat toward the back. "Aji and I found him like that in our net."

Heads all turned toward the back of the room, and the murmuring about the room crescendoed before Manuk called the gathering to order.

"Everyone, please," said Manuk. "Harto and Aji both said this was true – that the man was a giant serpent when they found him in their net fishing yesterday. He turned into a man, and that is when they came and got me along with a few others."

Loud talking began in earnest again.

"Quiet, please," said Manuk. "Let me finish, and then you can ask questions."

"When we brought him to the dukun, he was very badly injured and didn't wake up until the next morning," said Manuk. "I was able to speak to him briefly, and he told me his name. But he really didn't tell me much of anything else out of fear for my safety and the safety of the village."

Manuk related the rest of what he knew to the others, including the story he had been told when he was a boy of the village that had been razed by some monstrous dragon-lizard.

When Manuk was finished, the others began to pepper him with questions.

"Is he a danger to us?"

"What are we going to do with him?"

"Should we let him leave?"

"Should we tell the other villages about this?"

"What about his people? Will they come for him?"

They were all good questions, and Manuk did his best to answer them, but the truth was, he really didn't know what to say.

Finally, Manuk said, "This man needed our help, and we gave it to him like we would anyone who came to us hurt. When we spoke earlier, he told me that he is in our debt. I can tell you I do not know exactly what that means, or what he and his people could do for us. If he speaks the truth, his people have lived among us forever, and, despite their incredible power, have never sought our destruction."

Manuk paused to think for a moment. He wanted to choose his words carefully, knowing that, of all things, fear can drive people to commit terrible acts.

"I plan to speak to him again," said Manuk. "He plans to leave us soon and does not wish us to know much about him or his people. I will call another meeting tomorrow to let you know everything that I have learned."

Manuk thanked everyone for coming and stood up to signal that the gathering was now over.

As the others started leaving, he could hear the concern in people's voices. He knew this man could be trouble, but they lived with danger every day from the smallest serpents that could kill with one bite to the vast ocean that swallowed entire villages in the dark of night before anyone could even get out of their beds.

After everyone had left, the dukun turned to Manuk and said, "I think that went about as well as we could have expected."

Manuk saw him smile, but it didn't do much to mask the worry clearly showing in his eyes.

"We should go to speak to him again, now," said the dukun. "I know he plans to leave before the moon shows itself."

Manuk and the dukun walked across the village to the healer's joglo. When they arrived, the dukun agreed to remain outside while Manuk went in to talk with the man.

Manuk entered, but before his eyes could even adjust to the darkness he heard the man say, "Hello again, Manuk."

The man was standing next to the bed. He had on a pair of loose-fitting pants and a short-sleeved tunic that the dukun must have given him. He was tall, almost two meters. His hair and eyes were dark, and his skin was tan. Though he carried himself like an elder, Manuk saw no freckles or wrinkles on him. He looked young, but his mouth and eyes showed a sadness that can only come from a long life.

"Hello, Çig'Allagosh," said Manuk, walking closer to him so he could show he was not afraid and get a better look at him. "Feeling better?"

"Much," was Çig'Allagosh's response. "Thank you for caring for me."

Manuk sat down on the edge of one of the cots near the man and tried to relax his body.

"Can we talk more before you go?" he asked him.

"I thought about it, and I think I owe you something," said Çig'Allagosh, smiling, "but, as I told you before, the less you know about my people, the better off you will be."

Manuk was quiet for a moment. He could hear the labored breathing of an older man, who was sleeping in a cot across the room.

"What do you call yourselves?" he asked Çig'Allagosh.

"Your people have called us many things over the years," he answered, "We have been called gods and devils. We have been worshiped, and we have been hated. Over the years, we've been called leviathan, tannin and tunnanu by some; agathodaimones and kakodaimones by others. Some call us alu and lilu, and asuras and suras. We don't really have a name for us, though, early on, when human civilizations were first forming, we took to calling ourselves Tannin, and it stuck.

He paused for a moment, adding, "In any event, we just are, and we have been here since the beginning of time, conceived among the stars but born here on this world to live forever."

Manuk watched Çig'Allagosh look up and point to the sky. He thought for a moment, before asking him, "What can you tell me of this great battle? Your wounds were severe. We didn't think you'd survive."

The man looked down at Manuk and then sat down and laid back on a cot across from him. He exhaled before saying, "I am able to tell you this much."

He went on to recount a story of a creature like him who was named Uwad'Xotl and her desire to wipe out all of Manuk's kind. She spoke of this many, many times, he added, but she never acted on it – that is, until one day, Çig'Allagosh said he had heard from others that she had taken to wiping out entire villages, often striking during storms so it would look like the destruction and chaos were done by natural disasters.

Çig'Allagosh told Manuk that he and two others of his kind decided to confront Uwad'Xotl to get her to stop this madness. If she did not listen to reason, their plan was to weaken her – since she, like the rest of their kind, cannot be killed – and trap her in one of the deepest parts of the ocean so she couldn't hurt anyone else.

Çig'Allagosh told Manuk that their plan did not go that well at all.

At first, Uwad'Xotl denied she had been attacking villages.

Eventually, she gave in and admitted to it all. She had wanted to kill all of the humans because humans are so wasteful, he told Manuk.

"Humans cut down entire forests and kill everything and anything from the smallest insect to the largest whale without any concern for their own future and how it will affect the world," said Çig'Allagosh.

"The sad thing is," he added, "She spoke the truth. Your kind is unique in that you are often mindlessly destructive.

Çig'Allagosh sat up and let out a long breath. "But that is no justification for killing so many of you. You will have to learn, or you will bring about your own end."

Manuk started to speak, but Çig'Allagosh cut him off.

"It may not be today or tomorrow," he said, "but eventually you'll destroy your world."

Manuk looked down at the floor.

"The world may be better off without us," said Manuk.

"Perhaps," said Çig'Allagosh, "but that is not for my kind to decide. That is for you to figure out for yourself. Otherwise, we're no better than the worst of you."

Çig'Allagosh slid his legs around the side of the bed and stood up. "It is time for me to leave you," he told Manuk. "I am in your debt for saving me."

"I appreciate it," said Manuk, "but you would have been fine with or without us.

"I've walked among you for many seasons," beamed Çig'Allagosh, a smile spreading across his face. "I have seen you do terrible things, but I've also seen you do too many good things to allow Uwad'Xotl to wipe you out. You will be safe so long as she remains imprisoned at the bottom of the ocean."

"What if she escapes?"

"We have taken steps to ensure that never happens," he said, "but if it did, we will do our best to make sure humans won't come to an end."

Manuk nodded his head as he watched Çig'Allagosh walk to the door and leave the joglo. Manuk sat in thought by himself, the silence disrupted by the soft moaning of an elderly villager, who was being treated by the healer. After a few minutes, the dukun entered the room and walked to Manuk.

"I watched him leave the village in the direction of the sea," said the dukun. "Several children tried to follow him but I stopped them."

"He will not hurt them," said Manuk. "He's no danger to us."

"Will we see him again?" asked the dukun. "He told me he has walked among us for many seasons."

"If he visits us again," answered Manuk, "It means terrible things are coming."

"You should tell his story, so our children's children will know about him and his people," said the healer.

"I'll go tomorrow to Nabi and tell him Çig'Allagosh's story, and he will carve it into stone."

*   *   *   *   *

In his python form, Çig'Allagosh floated on the surface of the ocean, waves crashing into him. He was stretched out lazily, the sun warming him. He thought back to a few days to a spot in the ocean not far from here where one of the greatest battles of his people took place.

He remembered that day, and how, raising his head slightly, he was able to see over the rolling sea as two forms swam toward him. He flicked his massive forked tongue and collected scents from the air. The air smelled and tasted of salt and rotting fish, but there were also noticeable traces of two of his kind: Veja'Hast and Ygg'Vilerov.

Within moments, a massive, scaly, greenish brown crocodile-like creature appeared among the waves, moving at incredible speeds toward him. Another bipedal lizard-like creature, its massive head breaking through the surface of the water, sharp canines glinting in the sun, swam just behind the crocodile.

He had been waiting in the ocean for the two others for some time, but what was time to him, a being that had been around since this planet had first cooled and turned to solid rock? He couldn't remember how many times he'd seen the sun rise or set or how many living things he'd watched disappear forever from this world.

Today, he shielded his thoughts from his allies, preventing him from hearing what they were thinking as well. He had asked them to meet him as soon as they could, as he had grave news to tell them and would need their help. When pressed for details, Çig'Allagosh deflected. "Come to me, and I will tell you everything," he thought, hiding his concern that others may hear him and confront him.

There was saltwater as far as Çig'Allagosh could see. A small deserted tropical island sat just a few yards from him. Every so often, he'd sink his head under the waves and look around at the darkness far below him as the ocean bottom fell off quickly into the deep water. With only a few passing clouds in the sky, the sun beat down on him, but it didn't bother him. After all, little in this world could harm him, so he was free to enjoy this ocean far away from most living things that would annoy him like a mosquito in the dark.

Soon enough the creatures were upon him, and they slowed so as to float near him. There were not even birds out here, only the sounds of the rolling waves breaking on the island beach and the wind. As they came close, Çig'Allagosh called out to them, using his voice.

"Shield your thoughts to keep others from listening in," he said out loud and swam to the island, changing into a man as he stepped from the water. Completely nude, his tanned, muscular body, still wet from the saltwater, reflected the bright sunlight. He ran his hand across his face and through his short dark hair, shaking the water from him. He watched as the others did the same. The massive crocodile-like creature seamlessly shifted into a skinny, towering man with olive-colored skin, green eyes, and dark hair. The monstrous bipedal lizard swam to the beach. Its huge tail splashed in the sea and elongated snout opened and closed to reveal sharp canines, each one easily the size of Çig'Allagosh in his human form. It morphed into a tall, curvy woman with long reddish-blonde hair, pale skin, and blue eyes. The new arrivals walked to Çig'Allagosh, unconcerned about the crashing waves or their apparent nudity.

After a few moments, Çig'Allagosh said to them, "Thank you for coming to meet me here so far away from anything.

He paused for a moment and then added, "I ask something of you that, for our entire lives, has been forbidden, but, I feel if I do not act, then something terrible is about to take place. It is within our power to stop this madness, but I need your help."

The other man was the first to speak.

"What is it you ask of us that requires such deception?" he said, his gentle voice in sharp contrast to his previous form.

"As you know, Uwad'Xotl has taken it upon herself to kill as many humans as she can in the hope that she can stop them from polluting this world," he said. "While I understand her reasoning, she is misguided …"

The woman interrupted Çig'Allagosh before he could finish.

"She is not wrong," she said. "I have seen humans burn jungles so they can catch and kill all the things that live in it. The sight was so awful, I nearly intervened. Our rules have prohibited that, so I had to watch as hundreds of humans burned and killed everything from the smallest insect to great beasts. Eventually, justice came to them for their idiocy when most of them starved to death, but it took a few seasons. Too long, in my opinion."

"I have seen this, too, at other times, Ygg'Vilerov," Çig'Allagosh told her. "It is sad to witness."

"So why then should I care if Uwad'Xotl stops this from happening by killing the cause of this destruction?" she asked him, her hands balling into fists. "No other living thing on this planet causes such devastation as humans."

Çig'Allagosh raised his hand and pointed a finger at the woman, but she didn't flinch. "Because that is our way. We don't get involved. We have never interfered. With the great power we have, we cannot."

"Did you bring us all this way to tell us what we already know?" asked the man.

"I asked you to come, Veja'Hast, because I want you to help me stop Uwad'Xotl. I cannot do it alone"

"She cannot be killed," said the woman, "and I know that would be the only way she would ever stop – if she is killed. She believes so strongly in this."

"I have another plan," said Çig'Allagosh, "but we need to speak with her first."

Thunder sounded in the distance. Çig'Allagosh looked out over the waves to the horizon. Dark clouds were heading in their direction.

"She needs to be stopped," said Veja'Hast. "I have no problem killing, but it makes no sense to kill all of the humans to stop a few of them. It is needlessly cruel."

Ygg'Vilerov turned her head and stared out over the darkening sky and growing waves. "I'm willing to try to reason with her," she said. "But if she doesn't listen to us, if she won't stop the killing, what do we do then?"

"We imprison her at the bottom of the ocean," said Çig'Allagosh. "And I know how to do it."

* * * * *

The three Tanninim, now in their monstrous forms, swam away from the island toward the open ocean. Neither the stormy sky nor the angry sea seemed to concern them in the slightest.

It did not take long but eventually Çig'Allagosh paused his immense serpentine body floating in the deep water which was increasingly changing from blue to green with huge white caps breaking at the top of the waves.

"We are here," he said, his voice coming somewhere from inside the huge python's head. "The temple is below us, deep down in the darkness where only a few creatures can survive. Uwad'Xotl will be safe down there."

"We cannot do this," came a man's voice from the massive crocodile-like beast, its jaws clamping shut with a deafening sound. "It would be less cruel to kill her rather than lock her away for an eternity. She will go mad."

"We cannot die," thought Ygg'Vilerov. "If this is what you wish to do, then we have no choice but to lock her away until she comes to her senses."

Çig'Allagosh could feel the pain in her thoughts as she struggled with what they were about to do.

"I will visit her often," said Çig'Allagosh. "I am willing to keep her company."

"How will this be done?" asked Veja'Hast, who turned from Ygg'Vilerov to study Çig'Allagosh.

"The temple I have constructed is below this spot," he said. "It is in the deepest part of this ocean, in a hole at the bottom of the great chasm. I will call Uwad'Xotl to us. We will try to reason with her. If she refuses to hear us out or heed our words, we will be left with no choice but to fight her. We will have to weaken her before I can speak the words that will imprison her until she sees her madness. Otherwise, she will be locked away for as long as we live on this world."

"The others will not support this," said Ygg'Vilerov. "They will not allow her to be trapped forever."

"Once it is done," said Çig'Allagosh, "there will be nothing they can do except free her themselves, which they will not do. They are cowards and refuse to act."

"When do you plan on luring her here to speak with her?" asked Veja'Hast.

"I have already asked her," said Çig'Allagosh. "She is nearby and will be here shortly."

The day was getting on, and the sun was sinking lower and lower on the horizon. Suddenly, violent bubbling came from beneath him, and Çig'Allagosh traded sharp looks with Veja'Hast and Ygg'Vilerov.

"She is here," thought Çig'Allagosh as he swam back to make room for Uwad'Xotl's arrival.

At first, they saw only two long black tentacles break the surface, writhing in the air bubbles that came from below. Then, a monstrous black form, its skin slick and wet from the sea, floated up, two huge eyes blinking directly at them. It rolled in the waves, revealing a massive beak that slowly opened and closed as if it were taking in long breaths of air over and over again.

After a few moments, the enormous squid-like creature spoke to them.

"It is nice to see you all again after so long," came its thoughts, sensual and purring. "What is it you seek of me?"

Çig'Allagosh was the first to respond.

"We wish to speak of your evil, murderous acts," he said. "You must stop killing humans."

The immense squid rolled in the waves before emitting a noise that sounded something like a cross between a hiss and a laugh.

"Why I have no idea what you're referring to, Çig'Allagosh," she said to the three of them, her two eyes blinking slowly as her body turned in the water to face each one of them.

"There is no need for lies," answered Çig'Allagosh. "We know it is you."

Veja'Hast and Ygg'Vilerov looked on quietly as the huge serpent and the squid began to circle each other.

"I don't need to listen to you," she said as a particularly large wave broke over her body, causing her to roll. "You don't speak for the others."

As the two creatures circled each other in the roiling sea, a bolt of lighting lit up the sky above them in the dark clouds, followed almost immediately by a massive peal of thunder. The color of the sea changed noticeably from a bright, deep blue to a light green, as waves as tall as three-story buildings broke over the four immense beings.

Çig'Allagosh saw his opening, and he swam forward as fast as he could, wrapping his long, lithe serpentine body around Uwad'Xotl and began to squeeze. Veja'Hast and Ygg'Vilerov rushed forward as well, but their reactions were considerably slower, giving Uwad'Xotl seconds to react. She lashed out with two of her eight thick arms wrapping them around Çig'Allagosh's head, preventing him from opening his mouth and sinking his sharp curved teeth into her. Her two long tentacles shot out, one grabbing onto Veja'Hast's snout while the other took hold of Ygg'Vilerov by the neck, preventing them from getting any closer to her.

Uwad'Xotl's beak opened and clamped shut, trying futilely to tear Çig'Allagosh in half, but he moved too swiftly for her, dodging each attempted bite. Uwad'Xotl's six remaining arms, however, were free to pummel Çig'Allagosh's body, tearing away his scales with the spiked suction cups on them and leaving him bruised and bloody.

While Ygg'Vilerov continued to struggle in Uwad'Xotl's grip, Veja'Hast rolled several times and managed to break free from the giant tentacle that was wrapped around his mouth, swimming as fast as he could toward her, his massive tail driving him forward. He slammed into the body of the giant squid, his huge mouth snapping shut on her. An ear-splitting scream that sounded far too human emanated from the giant squid. Uwad'Xotl tried to sink below the surface, her free tentacles pumping in the water, but she was held fast by the huge python and the immense crocodile.

"I do not wish to hurt you, Uwad'Xotl," grunted Çig'Allagosh in his thoughts, "but you've left us with no choice."

Uwad'Xotl's only response was to continue to bludgeon Çig'Allagosh even more with her tentacles, hitting him in the face as well as his body which remained tightly wound around her. One of Uwad'Xotl's long tentacles was wrapped around Veja'Hast's neck, but it didn't seem to be having much of an effect on him. His mouth remained clamped shut on one of her fins, and he held her fast above the water, preventing her from moving.

Even though Ygg'Vilerov remained at a disadvantage compared to the other water-bound creatures, she had been slowly moving closer to Uwad'Xotl. The tentacle was still wrapped around her neck, but the damage inflicted by the other two seemed to be weakening Uwad'Xotl so much so that Ygg'Vilerov was able to swim toward right up to her.

Çig'Allagosh also noticed that Uwad'Xotl seemed to be weakening. He threw his head back, breaking free of one of her arms, the spiked suction cups tearing away scales on his head and leaving a huge gash that bled bright red blood profusely into the sea. He ignored the terrible pain, opened his huge maw, and struck her in the side so quickly that his head was almost a blur. He again heard the human scream come from the squid's beak, as he tightened his grip on her, squeezing with all his might.

Even more lightning lit up the sky, illuminating the sea around them followed by a thunderous crack.

Çig'Allagosh could taste Uwad'Xotl's blood, his sharp teeth sunk into her fleshy side. It was metallic and slightly bitter though diluted from the saltwater that rushed in. He released her for a moment to think, "Pull her down," before sinking his teeth into her again for an even better grip.

By now, Ygg'Vilerov had made it to the side of the squid. She climbed on top of the squid, opened her huge mouth, and clamped it down hard on the other fin, keeping Uwad'Xotl still.

Veja'Hast's mouth was still firmly closed on the giant squid but he moved over her and began to lash out with his tail, forcing them all under the water. Uwad'Xotl's tentacle was still wrapped around Veja'Hast and the serrated suckers on the end of it had been cutting into him, causing his blood to spill into the water.

By now, dozens of curious tiger, blue tip and hammerhead sharks had arrived to see what the commotion was all about, drawn by the smell of the blood in the water. Seeing what they faced, none of the sharks dared venture close to the four titans, who were thrashing about in the water, sinking slowly into the inky blackness below.

Uwad'Xotl's beak lashed out again, biting deeply into Çig'Allagosh's side, ripping a huge chunk of flesh off of him. She spit it out and, as it slowly rose to the top, the now dozens of sharks swarming around them rushed the piece of meat that was the size of a car, tearing it apart before it floated to the surface.

Çig'Allagosh cried out in pain, but he didn't let go of the squid, the back half of his long body writhing and twisting, trying to force them further into the deep.

Soon enough, blackness engulfed the four Tanninim. Blood continued to spill from open wounds on each of them, including Ygg'Vilerov's neck, which was worn bloody and raw from Uwad'Xotl's tentacle wrapped around it. They had left the sharks behind hundreds of meters above them, leaving them to the darkness that was only disturbed by the sound of their fighting and their agonized cries.

Çig'Allagosh pushed on, forcing them down even further. Out of the corner of his eye, he could see Veja'Hast's tail moving side to side with great thrusts, his arms and legs pressed tightly against his body.

He could tell that Uwad'Xotl had tired. She was not fighting back so hard at this point, making it easier to bring her down to the bottom.

"I called out to the others," said Uwad'Xotl, her speech labored and broken by her constant struggle to break free. "They will come for me, and you will be punished."

"They are cowards," said Çig'Allagosh. "They want to stop you as much as we do. They've just grown lazy and don't have the strength or desire to do it."

"The humans are destroying this world," she shot back at him. "It won't be long before they've done it. Maybe a few generations – but that's no time to us."

She screamed as Veja'Hast adjusted his grip on her, sinking his teeth deeper into her side. Çig'Allagosh saw even more of her blood flow out, but this time it didn't rise up. It floated in the current and began to sink, telling him they were getting close to the bottom.

"What are you doing?" screamed Uwad'Xotl. "Release me now, or you will all pay."

Çig'Allagosh shouted back in his mind, "Do not let go. We are almost there!"He clamped his mouth hard on her, driving his teeth further into her thick skin.

Within minutes, the ocean floor came into view, partially illuminated by active hydrothermal vents that were leaking lava and lit up a sizable portion of the dark chasm they were in. A massive stone edifice with huge, beige columns rose up from below them. Ygg'Vilerov actually let go of Uwad'Xotl for a moment, apparently in awe of the structure that had just now come into focus.

Çig'Allagosh saw Uwad'Xotl's eye go wide as it danced up and down from him to the structure below and then back to him again.

"What are you doing to me?" Uwad'Xotl cried out in her head. She began to struggle even more now, flailing around, but it was short-lived as she had been weakened already from the long fight.

She continued to thrash as the four behemoths hit the bottom of the hole in the deep trench. Çig'Allagosh began to drag her toward the temple. The other two caught on quickly. Now able to sink her feet into the rocky floor, Ygg'Vilerov latched onto one of the fins on the squid's body and pulled it toward the temple, her muscular legs giving her more leverage.

As the four creatures moved closer to the temple, they could see clearly that this was not some elaborate reverential site. Instead it quickly became clear that this had more of the appearance of a jail than a place of worship. Massive stone blocks had been roughly carved, shaped, and stacked into place to form a tall square building. Eight columns rose up from the foundation to form a covered stone entryway. At the base of the building, at the front, was a simple entrance, but there were no elaborate doors. Instead, a hole in the front wall disappeared into a void of empty darkness.

Veja'Hast continued to push Uwad'Xotl toward the front of the temple as Çig'Allagosh and Ygg'Vilerov pulled her. When they were close, Çig'Allagosh spoke up.

"Hold her fast," he shouted in his head as he released her from his grip. The ringing in his ears was almost unbearable, and he felt sick, like he was going to pass out, but he tried to calm himself and remember the words from the long-dead language that they spoke in to lock Uwad'Xotl away for eternity in the prison that he had constructed just for her.

As Çig'Allagosh swam toward the temple, his shape blurred and he changed back into the form of a man. He swam to the entrance of the temple, picked up a large, ornamental double-edged dagger, and rode the current back to Uwad'Xotl, who was now pinned to the floor of the deep trench by the two monstrous beasts. Çig'Allagosh was dwarfed by the Tanninim, but that didn't stop him from swimming up to Uwad'Xotl and stating, "I am sorry to do this, but you refused our entreaties and would not stop your madness, leaving us no choice."

"What are you doing to me!" Uwad'Xotl's screams rang in their heads. "Please let me go!"

It took almost all of the strength Çig'Allagosh had left, but he slowly began to carve lines that circled, intersected, and twisted along the body of the giant squid, forming symbols and what looked like they may even be words. As he did this, he repeated lines from an ancient language that his kind used long before humans walked the Earth.

"Lag'vachem erg anum mai, Uwad'Xotl," chanted Çig'Allagosh. *"Una mas, una mal."*

"What are you doing to me!" bellowed Uwad'Xotl again. "You can't do this to me! Stop! Please!"

Çig'Allagosh repeated the words over and over as he continued to carve lines into Uwad'Xotl's body. Blood pooled around them, and Çig'Allagosh once again was able to taste metal and saltwater on his lips.

The ritual seemed to last forever, but eventually, Uwad'Xotl's monstrous form deflated, and she turned back into a tall, thin woman covered in bloody wounds. For a brief moment, her long black hair floated in the current. She paused to look around before an unseen force yanked her violently into the void at the entrance to the temple, a look of shock and surprise on her face.

Çig'Allagosh was exhausted by the time it was over. Still in his human form, he floated limply in the water, blood still flowing from wounds all over his body. The forms of the other two blurred, and they also shifted back to their human forms. Battered and bloody, they all just stared in silence at the black entrance to the temple.

"It's over," said Çig'Allagosh. "It worked."

"Well, that went as badly as I thought," said Ygg'Vilerov, looking away into the darkness. "If we're done, I'm leaving now."

Çig'Allagosh stared at the temple. "You can both go. I'll stick around to make sure she stays put."

Veja'Hast and Ygg'Vilerov did not linger. They both pushed off the rocky ground and began to swim toward the surface. Çig'Allagosh floated just above the floor and continued to look in the direction of the entrance to the stone temple. "If you can hear me, I am sorry."

The eerie silence unnerved Çig'Allagosh. He could hear the occasional crack of thunder from the surface as well as the distant whistles and calls of humpback whales that were passing overhead. He was so tired, he felt like he could close his eyes and go to sleep even at this depth. He was unsure whether Uwad'Xotl could even hear him, but he figured he'd try to reach out to her anyway.

"I'm going to rest now, but I'll be back. I promise."

Çig'Allagosh could have sworn he heard weeping, but it could have been the sounds of the whales passing by him. He pushed off from the bottom, stirring up small rocks and sediment, and started to swim to the surface, but he barely made it halfway up before he shifted back to his great serpent form. Exhausted, he closed his dark eyes and passed out.

They Just Would not Listen

Chapter 5

Martin left Zoe at the hotel so he could walk around to clear his head. After a few minutes of wandering, he found himself walking down an outdoor market with small retail shops, craftsmen and women plying their trades, and food as far as the eye could see. He stopped to take a closer look at one stall that offered traditional foods when he noticed a tall, thin man with olive-colored skin, green eyes, and dark hair staring at him.

He turned to the man and said, "Can I help you?"

The man blinked at him before turning away and walking past him. That was pretty strange, Martin thought to himself. The guy was obviously not Indonesian, but that didn't mean much since Jakarta is a bustling international city, and people from all over the world are wandering its streets. He watched the man as he walked through the crowd until the man was lost among all the people.

Two hours later, Martin was done windowshopping and decided to walk back to the hotel. As he turned a corner onto an empty street that would cut right to the main road, the man who confronted him earlier stepped out from a doorway.

"My name is Veja'Hast," said the man. "You've been warned to stop poking around, yet here you are."

Martin threw up his hands in front of him. "I don't want any trouble."

"Then you should have stopped your incessant snooping into affairs that are not your business."

The man moved so quickly that Martin didn't even have time to lower his hands before he was on him, grabbing Martin's forearms. Martin looked up and saw anger in the man's green eyes as he threw Martin like he was tossing a doll. Martin slammed into the brick wall, and he fell hard onto the pavement. He was dazed, but he had enough wherewithal to look up slightly and see the tall man slowly walking toward him, evidently taking his time. He tried to get up, but the world spun around him and his legs gave out. He fell again to the sidewalk and could taste blood in his mouth. He coughed, and pain tore through his side. He rolled onto his back, turned his head, and spit blood out onto the street.

Martin saw that the man was now at his side, and he could do nothing as the man raised his brown-sandal-clad foot over Martin's face.

This is it, Martin thought. This is the end. He closed his eyes and prepared for the worst, when, suddenly, not far away, he heard another man yell, "Stop!"

Martin heard the first man bellow, "This isn't your concern, Çig'Allagosh. Let me be."

"We don't do this," said the second man, who must have walked closer to Martin at this point.

Martin tried to roll over so he could see the two men, but the pain in his side was unbearable. It hurt to even breathe.

"He already knows too much," Martin heard the first man say. "He cannot live."

"We don't kill humans," said the second man. "I will not let you hurt him anymore."

"Ygg'Vilerov warned him once, but he didn't listen, and now he is here."

Martin tried to keep listening, but he was so tired it was

impossible to keep his eyes open.

"I will handle it, Veja'Hast," said the second man. "I'm telling you, leave him to ..."

That was all Martin heard before everything went black.

*   *   *   *   *

Martin woke with a start, his eyes darting around the room. He tried to sit up, but his head swam and he immediately laid back down.

"Careful," he heard someone say from across the room. "You've been unconscious for a few hours. You're in the hospital."

Martin groaned. The voice sounded familiar to him, but he wasn't sure he recognized it.

"You know my voice," said the man. "I was there in the alley when you were attacked. I stopped the other man from killing you."

"I knew I heard you before," said Martin, his voice raspy. He was still in pain, and it hurt to talk, but he continued anyway. "You know the man who attacked me."

"I do. He is an old friend."

"He ..." Martin stammered. "He wasn't human."

"That is a very long story for another time, Dr. Martin Lee," said the man, "But, for now, we should talk about why you're here in Jakarta."

"The other guy seemed to think he knows why I'm here," said Martin. He paused before adding, "I'm really thirsty. Can you hand me that cup?"

The man stood up from the hospital chair, walked over to Martin, picked up the plastic cup, and directed the straw into Martin's mouth. Martin drank from the cup, sighed, and leaned his head back onto his pillow. The man placed the cup back on the tray table, walked back to his chair, and sat back down. He crossed his legs, leaned back, dropped his shoulders, took a deep breath, and visibly relaxed.

"I think I remember what happened," said Martin. "You told the other guy you don't kill humans. Does that mean you're not human?"

"We are not," said the man, "but you're getting ahead of yourself. My name is Çig'Allagosh, and the other's name is Veja'Hast."

Martin interrupted him.

"Yeah, he told me that right before he threw me into the wall."

"I am sorry about that," said Çig'Allagosh. "He should not have done that."

"Why did he want to kill me?"

"You don't waste any time," said Çig'Allagosh, laughing quietly.

"Well?"

A nurse came in and began to check Martin's vitals. She told him a doctor would be in to see him soon and smiled at Çig'Allagosh as she left. Çig'Allagosh waited for her to close the door before he continued.

"You are meddling in very dangerous affairs, Dr. Lee," said Çig'Allagosh. "Veja'Hast had no right to hurt you, but you should take him at his word that this does not concern you."

"What do you mean, it doesn't concern me?" asked Martin. He tried to sit up and turn to get a better look at Çig'Allagosh but was forced to lie back down in the bed.

"You're hurt very badly, Dr. Lee. You shouldn't get too excited."

Martin closed his eyes and let out a breath. He thought for a moment about everything that had led him to here – the plane crashes, the inscription, and his interactions with Haoyu. Then he thought of Zoe, and he smiled before the pain jerked him back to the moment.

"A woman confronted me when I was back in Chicago," said Martin. "Do you know her? Is she like you? Is she dangerous?"

"Yes," he answered. "I know her well. That is Ygg'Vilerov, and she is not to be toyed with."

Martin watched Çig'Allagosh out of the corner of his eye, but he was impossible to read. For all Martin knew, Çig'Allagosh could have been a corpse but for his tan complexion.

"She told me her name was Cathaerine," said Martin, doing his best to speak quietly in order to avoid straining anything else. "You obviously know a lot more than you're telling me. People died in that plane crash, and more are going to die if we don't figure out what is causing them. You say you don't kill people, but you'll be just as responsible for their deaths if you don't do anything to help me stop whatever is happening from happening again."

"That is not her true name." Çig'Allagosh paused for a moment, before continuing. "Dr. Lee, I understand what you are saying, and I am working on that. I have been working for a very long time to prevent that from happening."

Martin exhaled again and winced. He paused until the pain subsided before saying, "What can you tell me about all of this?"

"Just know that there are beings all around you now, who are like Ygg'Vilerov, Veja'Hast, and me," said Çig'Allagosh. "Most just want to be left alone. We are not supposed to interfere in your lives, but some don't care about the rules. And, to be totally honest, Dr. Lee, most just aren't that nice. But we value human life and don't just take it. That is a hard rule that everyone follows."

Martin saw Çig'Allagosh open his mouth again to speak but quickly close it when there was a knock, and then the door opened. A young man walked into the room, wearing a white coat with a stethoscope around his neck.

"Looks like you took quite a beating, Dr. Lee," said the younger man as he picked up a chart from the foot of the bed and started reading. Martin could smell cigarette smoke on him.

"I'm Dr. Baso. You're safe now. Bruised rib and sprained elbow. Other than that, it looks like you're doing pretty well."

He put the chart down, walked to Martin's side and listened to him breathe.

After he was done, he said, "We're going to keep you here overnight. The police will be by soon now that you're awake to take your statement. Let the nurse know if you start to feel poorly."

The doctor turned to Çig'Allagosh.

"Someone will be by soon with paperwork for you to fill out," he said before turning and walking out the door, closing it behind him.

After the doctor left, Çig'Allagosh stood up and said, "Good talk, Dr. Lee, but I need to be going. I'll let Dr. Sullivan know you're in the hospital."

Martin tried to sit up but thought better of it.

"What will I tell the police?"

"Tell them that you were attacked by a Westerner, and a good samaritan saved you. The police are quite thorough here, but they won't pursue it much. It's a big city."

Çig'Allagosh turned and started to open the door.

"If you stop poking around where you don't belong, you won't be in any more danger. Go home as soon as you can, Dr. Lee. Until then, I hope you and Dr. Sullivan enjoy Indonesia. It really is a beautiful island. I owe this place a great debt."

He then walked out, and the door shut behind him with a loud thump.

*   *   *   *   *

"You should have just let me kill him."

Çig'Allagosh had just left the hospital when he heard a familiar voice. He turned to see Veja'Hast and Ygg'Vilerov waiting for him. He smiled and bowed ever so slightly to both of his friends.

"He will be fine," he told them. "Thanks for asking."

"Veja'Hast is right," said the tall woman, her reddish-blonde hair moving in the wind. She brushed it out of her face with a sweep of her hand. "We should finish him quickly. It would be more merciful."

Çig'Allagosh turned toward, anger in his eyes.

"We don't do that!" he roared before pausing to regain his composure. He closed his eyes and took a breath, lowering his voice. "We don't kill them. That has always been the rule."

"But you're okay with killing one of our own?" she asked him.

Çig'Allagosh saw her jaw tense. She was looking particularly angry today, he thought. That's not a good sign at all. He thought better of provoking her, so he tempered his voice.

"We all agreed it had to be done. She was out of control."

"Well it looks like we may have to do it again," interrupted

Veja'Hast. "Your trap is failing, and she's getting stronger."

He caught Veja'Hast studying his face.

"You knew," Veja'Hast said, "And you didn't tell us."

He saw Ygg'Vilerov look closely at Veja'Hast and then at him. He could see fury in her blue eyes. "Is this true?" she asked him. "How long have you known?"

Çig'Allagosh sighed and looked down before facing them.

"I've suspected it for a while now," he said quietly. "And, when I visited her last month, it was obvious."

"Does she know?" asked Veja'Hast.

"She's far more powerful than I thought," admitted Çig'Allagosh. "Ever since we trapped her three and a half thousand years ago, she must have figured out how to break down the barrier holding her. I didn't really notice. It was subtle, like she's been digging out with a spoon all this time."

"You didn't notice because you're an arrogant narcissist," countered Ygg'Vilerov.

"You wound me," he shot back.

"You know I go by Catharine these days," she said.

"Apologies … Catharine," said Çig'Allagosh before adding, "In any event, I'm working on it."

Catharine laughed. "Translation: you don't know what the fuck you're doing."

"Again," he shot back, "The wounds." He put his hand over his heart and feigned being shot.

"I plan on visiting her now that I'm in this part of the world again," he said. "When I'm down there I'll take a close look at the temple to see how it's holding up."

Çig'Allagosh walked up to his two friends, stretched his arms out, and did his best to embrace them both. He kissed Veja'Hast on the cheek and tried to do the same to Catharine.

"You don't get to do that anymore," she told him.

He bowed ever so slightly again and smiled at her.

"I'll let you both know what I find out.

* * * * *

Still in his serpent form, Çig'Allagosh pushed on into the black waters. Occasionally he caught sight of a strange sea creature that flashed past him in the bleakness, all white eyes, needle teeth, and huge, gaping maw. Finally, he saw a faint light coming from an overactive thermal vent that had been pumping out small amounts of lava since the beginning of time.

After a short while, the huge stone temple came into sight. Çig'Allagosh swam to it, floating a hundred meters from the columns that framed the entrance.

"I have come to pay you a visit, Uwad'Xotl," he called out to her. "Please come out and speak to me."

After a few moments, a tall woman with dark hair stepped out of the dark entryway.

"I should keep you waiting, Çig'Allagosh," she said, "But what good would that do when we have all the time in the world?"

"It is good to see you again."

"The feeling is not mutual, betrayer," she answered.

"Can we please skip the insults this time," he said, his deep, resonant voice belying the grotesque appearance of his python form.

"Call me a traditionalist," she retorted. "It's been the same with us for so very long. And how long has that been?"

"Too long, I'm afraid."

"Would you prefer we go back to the time when we were lovers?" she asked. "That was so very long ago, long before you betrayed me and imprisoned me here? But it's not like I have any real sense of time down here in this eternal darkness. There are no sunrises or sunsets, no breaks in the clouds, no cool, rainy days – all the things that break the tedium of life."

"Well I ask again if there is anything you would like from the world above?" he said. "I am happy to bring it to you."

"I need nothing from you or your allies, betrayer. Well, I would like to witness your slow, agonizing death, to see you ripped apart, limb from limb, to watch you cry and beg for mercy, but we both know that will never happen, so I just dream of it. When I close my eyes, that is what I see, and it is the only joy I ever get."

"I do not wish to relitigate our history together," said Çig'Allagosh. He swam closer to the temple to see her better and to get a better view of the front of the temple. "I only want to spend time with you, to keep you company."

He could see that the symbols he had carved all over the edifice were wearing away. He could tell that some of them were almost completely gone in some spots. He wasn't sure if this was simply the natural result of thousands of years of erosion in such harsh conditions or if, over time, Uwad'Xotl had figured out a way to erase them.

"Aw, sweet darling," she purred, "After all these years, it's nice to know you still feel terrible guilt for what you did to me." He was close enough to see the anger etched onto her face. "Don't let me assuage you of that. I want nothing more than to see you suffer as much as you've made me suffer. You let me believe you loved me. You deceived me, you …"

Çig'Allagosh interrupted her with a quick swish of his long tail.

"I did love you. That's why I couldn't bear to see you become such a monster."

Her laugh echoed in the entryway to the temple.

"All our kind are monsters," she said, still laughing, "We're the stuff of legends."

She paused before adding, "But we're not the villains in this fairytale."

He watched her turn her back to him.

She continued: "So how is that working out for you?"

He moved closer again.

"You're not going to bait me," he said. "You know how I feel. If humans destroy themselves, that's on them, but we can't help them on their way."

"I know what's been going on," she said. "Sidn'Gaabetha visited me. She told me all about the world – all about the wars, the mass killings, the weapons, the destruction, the pollution. I knew it was going to be bad, but never in my wildest, fevered dreams did I ever expect them to be so good at bringing about their own demise. It must be sad for you to watch all this, knowing you could have prevented it. The problem, of course, is that they seem bent on taking everyone else with them."

"You're wrong," was all Çig'Allagosh could muster, but even he didn't believe it when he said it.

"I can see it in your face that you know I'm not," she said. "You should have let me finish the job all that time ago. Now, there are so many more of them, and there's so much more death … and destruction."

He watched as a smile spread across her face.

"And when I am free again," she whispered, "You won't be able to stop me. You'll have to watch as I kill each and every one of them."

* * * * *

"We were close once."

The massive python floated in the salt water, waves crashing against his long serpentine body. There wasn't a cloud in the sky, and his scales shimmered in the sun, showing purple, green, and orange. A huge body, black as night, would occasionally break the surface of the water and roll in the white caps, tentacles writhing in time with the ocean's swell.

Çig'Allagosh thought back more than 3,000 years ago to the last conversation he had with Uwad'Xotl when they were alone. At the time, he had gotten word of her killing spree. The others spoke of it in hushed tones. Four villages had been wiped out, just gone, everyone who lived there either dead or displaced. Based on what he knew of that area, he figured at least a thousand humans had been killed. They had done nothing to deserve it, but that didn't seem to bother Uwad'Xotl. She saw them simply as a parasitic species, a virus that needed to be eliminated from this beautiful world before they destroyed everything.

He still remembered their talk, the harsh words. They were trading thoughts, so their emotions were bare to each other as well. Her anger was palpable. It was real. More importantly, it was clear he was wasting his time, but he had to at least try. Maybe she would see reason. Maybe she would at least acquiesce and accept it was out of their control.

"You're not the same person I loved," he told her.

"How could I be?" she answered. "With what I've seen? The question should be, how can you view the world the same way after everything we've seen?"

"That is not up to us to decide the fate of this world."

"Only we have the power to change it, to make things right," she thought, "To restore balance to this world."

"Yes, but …"

"I can't let them destroy this world," she interrupted him, "And they will. Mark my words, if not now, they will in the future when they've had so many children that they are killing each other over the last scraps of land and food that remain."

Çig'Allagosh thought for a moment. She had killed already and was not going to stop. For millions of years, the eight Tanninim were all they had. They lived in relative peace. Yes, things lived and died, sometimes in terrible, brutal ways, but the Earth was in relative balance. Too many hungry mouths? Scarcity of food solved that problem. And then, of course, there were natural disasters like a comet strike, a drought, a flood, or a wildfire, which always would help to restore a relative equilibrium.

Then, one day, apes walked out of the forest and started manipulating the environment around them. It happened slowly, and it was fascinating to watch, but it was obvious even then the world was changing and that there would be no going back. Of course, the Tanninim had helped them along, dropping hints and teaching them language and the written word, but for the most part, humans were left alone to evolve on their own.

It was hard to argue with her. He had seen it, too: the senseless killing, the waste, and the destruction, but most humans were kind and selfless. From what he saw, it was only a few that were violent and petty.

"You know I'm right," she thought to him. "If not today, the time will come when they will have taken everything. By then, it will be too late."

"You can't just kill them. That's not the answer."

"Why not?" she responded with a shrug.

He could feel the anger growing in her. It was hard to take.

"Anything else, we wouldn't even think about it," she said. "It's not like we haven't influenced our world. When it looked like they might die off from the relentless cold, we helped them find warmth by showing them a path to the south. I remember you leaving food for some of them to help them survive. They look to us as if we are gods. To them, we are. They build temples to us. They write epics about us. They say we are vengeful, wrathful, all-powerful beings, who reward them when they are good and take vengeance on them when they misbehave. It's been a long time since we have lived up to these stories."

"No! That is not what we are. That is not what we do. You are wrong to think these things. You are wrong to assume they won't solve their own problems, that they won't evolve past their petty, shortsighted, shameless ways. They will. I have seen it. The good in them will win out ..."

Çig'Allagosh stopped mid-thought, cut off by the sound of laughter echoing in his head.

"I have to believe that," he said, shaking his serpent head in the waves. A pod of blue whales swam by them, and he watched them for a moment, listening to their high-pitched songs carry underwater. "I have to believe they can solve their own problems without interference. I have to."

"We've interfered before. What's the difference now?"

"To stop them from dying out – that is why we helped them," he said. "We saw how precious they are, and, yes, we may have helped them."

He paused for a few seconds. "But that was to help them survive, not to kill them off entirely."

Uwad'Xotl scoffed. "They've already lived longer than a lot of creatures. It's their time. Maybe what comes next will be better, but we'll never know because humans would never allow anything to evolve and threaten their dominance."

"They're afraid," he shot back. "They're not evil."

"It's not like they haven't exterminated other living things, just completely wiped them out."

"You can't do this, Uwad'Xotl," he said. "You can't just kill them off."

There was silence between them. He could feel her shutting down. The conversation was over, and he could feel he hadn't changed her mind.

"Maybe it is time we revealed ourselves and helped them understand what they do," he thought, but she was already moving away.

"Thanks for the talk, lover. Always a pleasure."

And she closed her mind and swam away.

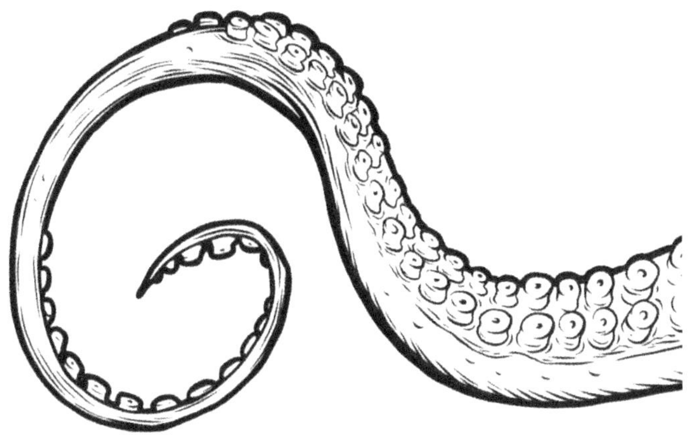

Not That Crazy

Chapter 6

For the second time that day, Martin was jolted awake, this time when Zoe came bursting into the hospital room.

"Jesus, Martin," she said. "Are you okay? What happened to you?"

He did his best to smile but he winced when he moved to get a better view of her.

"I got jumped in an alley on my way back to the hotel," said Martin. "Some guy intervened and got me here. I'm okay. Just a bit banged up. A bruised rib, and my arm is going to be in a sling for a few weeks. Other than that, I'm great."

Zoe slid one of the chairs next to the bed.

"Can I get you anything? Are you in pain?"

Martin closed his eyes. "I'm just pretty tired. They said I have to stay the night but I can leave tomorrow."

"Are you hungry? Do you need more meds?"

"I'm okay," he said sleepily. "Thanks for coming by, but you can go back to the hotel. No use in both of us being bored here."

"There's no way I'm leaving you," she said, "At least until

tomorrow when we get you back to the hotel."

Martin smiled at her, and, just before he fell asleep, he heard her say, "I'm just glad you're okay."

She took his hand in hers. She was warm and smelled of lavender.

"I'm just gonna take a nap," he said, then he fell fast asleep.

*   *   *   *   *

The next day, Martin was allowed to leave the hospital after he spoke to two police officers. Martin told them what Çig'Allagosh told him to say, that he was attacked but an anonymous good Samaritan intervened, took him to the hospital, and saved his life. It was painfully obvious that Martin was out of it from the attack and the painkillers, so the police didn't push for more information from Martin.

Martin returned to his hotel room and promptly fell asleep. He awoke the next day, still in pain. When he rolled over to try to stand up, he noticed that Zoe was asleep under a blanket, lying next to him in the bed. She stirred when he sat up and winced. She looked up at him and smiled.

"First time we sleep together, and I don't even remember it," he said. He laughed softly which turned into a cough which turned into a groan.

Zoe sat up and put her hand on his back.

"You're a funny man," she said, "But you should stay lying down. You need some more painkillers."

Martin felt dizzy. He nodded to her and then laid back against the pillow.

"I should probably just lie here for a bit," he said, closing his eyes.

Zoe had the television on. It was turned to an English channel, and there was a documentary about the Pacific Ocean. Hong Kong billionaire Li Haoyu was giving a tour of the research ship he owned. He was introducing a team of scientists he had contracted with to study the oceans. Haoyu was going over some of the new technology they used to monitor changes in, among other things, the ocean floor, including increased volcanic activity. He detailed the new deep-sea scanning equipment his team had pioneered as well as a state-of-the-art bathyscaphe they used to explore the deepest parts of the oceans.

The documentary had been done the year before, and, at the time, the ship was sailing toward the Mariana Trench, about 200 kilometers off the coast of Guam.

"That's your guy, right?" asked Zoe as she dumped pills out of bottles on the nightstand.

"Yeah," said Martin, sleepily, "That's the billionaire we met in Chicago."

Martin sat up and took the pills from Zoe. He washed each one down with water from a plastic bottle she gave to him. He then took a few bites from a granola bar that was open next to him. When he was done, he sat back and exhaled a long breath.

"There's something I need to tell you, Zoe."

Zoe sat down on the bed next to him and leaned back against a few pillows.

"I know," she said. "It's been a couple days since you showered, but you're on your own here, sport."

She smiled and let out a soft laugh.

"No," he said, looking at her, a frown spreading across his face. "I'm being serious here. I need to tell you something."

She sat up and turned to face him.

"Ok, I'm listening."

Martin watched the smile fade from her face.

"The story I told the police about getting attacked," he told her, "That was a lie."

He looked down at his hands.

"I was attacked, but I wasn't mugged."

He took a deep breath and let it out.

"I cut through an alley on my way back to the hotel when a man confronted me. He told me to stop snooping around the plane crash or else I would regret it. Then he threw me across the alley into a fucking wall."

Martin looked up at her, tears beginning to well in his eyes.

"He was getting ready to kill me when another man stopped him. They knew each other, and they knew the woman who threatened me at that event at Field."

Zoe reached out and took Martin's hand.

"I don't understand. Why would some random guy beat you up over that?"

Martin interrupted her.

"I know," he said, "but that's not all. It gets way weirder."

Martin related to her what Çig'Allagosh had told him about Ygg'Vilerov, Veja'Hast, and him.

"He knew about you, too," said Martin, "He knew your name and that we're here in Jakarta together. It was fucking creepy."

Martin studied Zoe's face, which was slowly turning from worry to anger.

"I still don't get why this Veja'Hast wanted to kill you," she said, before pausing to add, "And what kind of fucking name is Veja'Hast? How pretentious do you have to be to have a name like that?"

"That's not even the weird part, Zoe."

Martin picked up the plastic bottle and took a long drink of water.

"The guy who took me to the hospital and called you – the guy named Çig'Allagosh – said they're not human. And they're really old, like, beginning-of-time old."

He watched Zoe furrow her brow and turn her head to look away from him.

"I know," he said, sitting up abruptly. He wobbled a bit before leaning back against the headboard. "It sounds nuts, but that's what he said to me."

Zoe turned to face him. "No, it's okay. You took a pretty good hit to the head. You got a concussion. It happened to me when I used to play volleyball. Just sit back and rest for now. We can talk about this later."

"I'm telling you the truth, Zoe," Martin protested. "That's what happened. I'm not making this up."

Zoe stood up, grabbed her bag, and walked to the door.

"I'm going to get us something to eat. Try to sleep a bit while I'm gone. Call me if you need anything."

She opened the door and walked out, and the door slammed behind her.

*   *   *   *   *

"I don't know if I can stay here much longer."

Zoe stood just outside the hotel. It had just rained, and the humidity was ramping up, but she didn't care. She just needed some air. She held her cellphone up to her ear but was distracted by the passing traffic.

"What did you say?" she asked the person on the other end of the call. "Oh, yeah, he's okay, a bruised rib and sprained arm. He'll recover. It was an attempted mugging but some guy intervened."

She paused for a moment.

"Mom, I thought I really liked this guy, but I think he's losing it."

She paused to listen again.

"No, mom, I'm safe. He's not dangerous or anything. Just kind of nuts."

She stopped talking again.

"We have separate rooms. I think I'm going to see if I can change my ticket and come home early."

She saw a taxi pull up to the front of the hotel.

"My taxi is here ... okay ... Love you, too ... Bye."

Zoe ended the call and walked over to the cab. She opened the backdoor, leaned her head in, and confirmed that the driver had been called. She climbed in, shut the door behind her, and asked the driver to take her to a local cafe a few blocks from there.

The cafe was nearly empty when Zoe arrived. She ordered a coconut-infused latte and a bowl of fresh fruit and took a seat near a window. She was scrolling through social media on her phone when a tall woman with long reddish-blonde hair in an expensive suit sat in the chair across from her.

Zoe glanced up, annoyed, and said, "I'm not really interested in company right now."

Zoe watched a smile slowly spread across the woman's face. It was unnerving.

Hello, Dr. Sullivan," said the woman. "I hope you're enjoying your stay in Jakarta."

"Do I know you?"

The woman paused to sip her coffee.

"I've always loved the coffee here in Indonesia," she said. "It's so fresh and flavorful. Anything else added to it really takes away from its natural flavors."

The woman lifted the porcelain mug to her mouth and took another drink.

"Look," said Zoe, "I appreciate the review, but I'm not really in the mood for company." She looked around the cafe. "There are lots of other places you can sit and enjoy your coffee."

Zoe paused for a moment. "How do you know my name?"

"I was sorry to hear about Dr. Lee," said the woman. "I hope he's resting and healing."

Zoe put her latte down on the table and looked around the cafe again. A young woman sat behind the counter, bored and staring at her phone.

"What did you just say?" Zoe studied the woman's face. "Who are you, and how do you know us?"

"We know all about you two, Dr. Sullivan, and why you're in Jakarta. How's that working out for you so far?"

Zoe stood up quickly, causing the chair to quickly slide back from her. It made a loud screeching noise. She looked over at the young woman, but she was oblivious, still staring intently at her phone.

"Who are you?" Zoe demanded.

"Sit down, Dr. Sullivan. I'm not like my friend. I'm not going to hurt you."

Zoe's head swiveled around the cafe. A new customer had just come in and was in the process of ordering something in Indonesian, so Zoe didn't know what he was saying. Once he was done, he took a seat at the counter and waited while the young woman prepared his drink.

"Please sit down, Dr. Sullivan," said the woman. "I just want to talk."

Zoe sat down, but she held her bag tightly in her lap. The woman was between Zoe and the front door, so that wasn't an option if she needed to run. She saw a sign above the door behind the counter that said "Exit" in multiple languages.

"You might as well relax," said the woman. "If you tried to run, I could tear you in half before you made it across the room – spill your guts across the floor – and then I'd be gone before you even bled out."

Zoe tensed in her chair.

"And what a pity that would be," the woman laughed. "It looks like it was just mopped."

"So Martin wasn't making it up when he said your people attacked him," said Zoe.

"By 'my people,' you mean one of us, Veja'Hast. Again, I am sorry for that untoward incident. That isn't usually our way, but, you know, sometimes, it's just inevitable."

"Who are you?"

"My name is … well, these days, I go by Catharine."

"That was the name of the woman who threatened Martin at the museum in Chicago."

"Guilty," said Catharine, smiling. She took another slow drink of her coffee, savoring it.

"Why the fuck did you guys attack Martin?"

Catharine took another sip before placing the coffee down on the table again. Zoe wasn't sure, but there was something about this woman that was deeply unsettling. She was relaxed and confident, yet, at the same time, her movements were stiff, precise, careful – more like mindful and methodical.

"You know why, Dr. Sullivan," said the woman. "He just didn't listen."

Zoe watched the woman lean back in the chair, but her body remained rigid. Catharine casually looked around the room, her long red fingernails steadily tapping against the side of the coffee cup.

"Dr. Lee has been sniffing around in places he doesn't belong," she said. "He's a little puppy that doesn't realize it has its nose in a snake hole."

She lifted her hand, mimicking a lazy swat, before taking another drink of her coffee. Zoe forced herself to swallow, her gulping sound echoing in the empty cafe.

"And, just like you do with any puppy that misbehaves, sometimes you have to swat his little nose."

Zoe found herself recoiling when the woman smiled again.

"It's 2026," Zoe shot back. "We don't do that. Only psychos hurt animals."

"I guess I'm old school," said the woman, laughing.

"Why are you talking to me? What do you want here?"

Catharine looked around slowly then leaned forward. The cafe was again empty.

"I'm just afraid that Dr. Lee didn't get the message, so I'm telling you, too. Go home."

"But your other friend – the guy who saved Martin's life – said we could stay and enjoy the island."

Catharine sat back and looked out the window.

"He's always been too generous with your lot," she said.

"Our lot?"

You know," she said, "Humans."

"And what if we decide not to take your advice?"

Catharine turned to look squarely at Zoe, her bright blue eyes wide. "That would be very bad, Dr. Sullivan."

Catharine finished her coffee and placed the cup back on the table. "I've enjoyed our little talk, one woman to another. Please listen to what I've said. The rest of us are not as – what's the word for it? – humane as Dr. Lee's friend. Go home."

Catharine smiled, before adding, "Puppy … snake hole … Swat." She lifted her hand and slowly feigned a spanking motion. She paused as she picked up her clutch off the table and stood up. Zoe watched Catharine turn and casually stroll out the front door. The cafe was quiet except for the sound of the bells jingling as the door swung shut. She looked down to see her hands were shaking.

So Martin isn't fucking nuts, she thought to herself. She put her head in her hand and could feel sweat on her forehead. He was almost killed. *What has he gotten us into?*

* * * * *

Zoe burst into the hotel room, gasping for breath.

"You are not going to believe this," she yelled as she slammed the door shut, locked it, and threw up the chain. She ran to the bed and sat down on it, bouncing Martin slightly up into the air. She put her hands out and rested them gently on him. "Oh my god, I'm so sorry about that!"

Martin winced as he sat up and leaned against the headboard.

"I'm sorry," she repeated. "Did I hurt you?"

"Not really," he said, forcing a smile onto his face. "I'm okay."

He repositioned himself to get more comfortable. "What am I not going to believe?"

"Oh, yeah," she said, smiling all the way to her eyes. "Right. Well, first, let me say I'm sorry I thought you were crazy."

Martin eyed her suspiciously. Before he could respond, she added, "But that's not important now."

"Wait," he interrupted her. "Why the hell is that not important? You think I'm crazy?"

"Can you blame me?" she answered. "All we've talked about are monsters. And you've been saying that these things posing as humans threatened you. And, now, you're saying one tried to kill you. Doesn't that sound crazy to you?"

"It's not crazy if it's really happening," said Martin. He closed his eyes and relaxed back onto the bed. "Look, if you think I'm full of shit, you should probably just go home. I'll call you when I'm back in the United States …"

Zoe leaned forward and grabbed him by the shoulders. "That's the thing," she said to him, staring right into his eyes. "I don't think you're crazy anymore."

Martin opened his eyes wide as Zoe was leaning into him, and she kissed him, pressing her lips hard into his. She pulled back from him and added, "You got that. I don't think you're bat shit."

* * * * *

Martin watched as Zoe paced around the hotel room. She had just finished explaining to him about her meeting at the cafe with Catherine, the same woman who had confronted him at the Field Museum.

"I have to be honest with you, Martin, she's fucking terrifying."

"They're all terrifying," he told her. "Every one of them, even the guy who saved me and waited in my hospital room until I woke up."

"She wants us to go home," said Zoe, "Get on a plane immediately and go back to the U.S."

Martin thought for a minute before saying, "What if we just quietly skip town and head east. There's the Singhasari Museum in Malang. It's a 12 hour train ride from here. We could bring all our luggage like we're doing what they asked."

"If they know we're here in Jakarta," she countered. "Why don't you think they'll figure out we're just heading to the other side of the island?"

"I think if we're careful, we can at least buy us some time," he said. "They're smart, and I'm sure they have more money than they know what to do with, but from what I've gathered they don't know everything. They'll figure it out eventually, but I think we at least have a day in Malang before we'll have to move on again. We can take the ferry to Bali. After that, I need to contact Haoyu and see if we can meet him on his boat."

Martin smiled at her.

"What?" she asked him. "Why are you smiling like that?"

"You just kissed me – a really solid kiss right on the lips. Are we gonna pretend that didn't happen?"

"Yes?" she answered. "Maybe?"

Martin watched her face go red and saw her look away from him.

"You're still hurt," she muttered. "I probably shouldn't have done that. I'm sorry. Plus, we didn't even talk about any of that. Oh my god, did I go too far? Jesus, I always go too far. It's my life. I always go too …"

She stopped mid-sentence as Martin leaned forward and couldn't help but groan. His eyes followed her arm down to her hand, and he put his hand over hers.

"Don't be sorry," he said. "I've been waiting for that for a while, but I'd pretty much resigned myself to just being friends and colleagues. I didn't want to fuck up a relationship with the one person who believes in me, you know."

He watched as she turned her head, and they locked eyes.

"Thank you for believing me," he said. "We can pick up with the other stuff when we're back home safe in the U.S."

Martin saw her face flush again and watched her look down at their hands.

"Oh, yeah, one more thing," he added, laughing. "Apology accepted."

Gods Are Insecure

Chapter 7

Çig'Allagosh stood at the edge of the ancient ruins of Gobekli Tepe in southern Turkey, watching the tourists. Today, the remains of the temple are a shadow of what they once were, the stone building standing tall, a symbol of what humans were capable of even 10,000 years ago. He smiled as he thought back thousands of years to what the temple had looked like – the highly detailed reliefs of wild animals and humans of the time – when he heard a familiar voice.

"They worshiped us once upon a time."

Çig'Allagosh turned to see his old friend and the informal leader of their kind. A tall, thin man with dark skin, reddish-brown hair, and blue eyes in an expensive suit stood a few steps away. The two men walked quickly to each other and embraced, and Çig'Allagosh kissed the man on both cheeks.

"Anox'Moral," he said. "It is good to see you again. How is Paul?"

"A lot has happened since we last met," said Anox'Moral. "It's been two-and-a-half thousand years, the world has changed considerably. Paul is doing well."

Çig'Allagosh watched the man look around, admiring the ruins.

"My temple has certainly seen better days," said Anox'Moral, laughing. "I don't know what it is about humans today that they leave old places like this in such a state. Why don't they repair it or fix it up? You know, there was a time when they would have built something better right on top of these … ruins."

"Even the oldest among them live such a short time on this world," said Çig'Allagosh. "They're born, and 80 summers later, they're gone. Places like this are a reminder of just how short their lives are."

"You really have taken a liking to them, haven't you?"

"They're two sides of a coin," said Çig'Allagosh. "One day, they're creators, and, the next, the same group of people will destroy everything around them. They're like children. The only problem is, as time has gone by, they've created the most incredible things that could destroy them all in one hasty, thoughtless act."

"They are amusing little things to watch," answered Anox'Moral. "They think they're so advanced and sophisticated but they're barely out of caves."

Çig'Allagosh watched Anox'Moral quietly laugh. It was good to see his old friend again after so many years.

Anox'Moral continued, "If they're so suicidal, why did you stop Uwad'Xtol from killing them? She was probably doing the world a favor."

"Obviously, I didn't agree," said Çig'Allagosh. "Most humans seek peace. Only a small number are destructive to the world."

"Well, over time, that small number of them has become quite powerful," Anox'Moral fired back.

"So you'd kill them all because of a few bad ones?"

"A strong message might have convinced the good to rein in the bad."

"We would have to expose ourselves," said Çig'Allagosh.

"They already believed us to be gods," Anox'Moral countered, a smile across his face. "A few well-timed, obvious cataclysms would have their little heads spinning in all directions. Maybe an earthquake or even another flood that swallowed up the worst of the worst. They'd get the message soon enough."

"You know that wasn't what Uwad'Xtol had planned."

"Yes, I know," muttered Anox'Moral as he looked away toward the mountains.

"And that is why it had to be me that imprisoned her," said Çig'Allagosh. "I had to do it, because no one else could. She was too powerful and too distrustful of the others."

"Ah yes," said Anox'Moral, "They have to trust you first before you can betray them."

Çig'Allagosh watched his friend laugh, but he could see the sadness in his eyes. "It's true that I loved her, that she trusted me, and that I betrayed her," he said. "But we're not at the end. The prison I built is collapsing, and, if she ever gets free, it will be the end of us all."

Çig'Allagosh studied his old friend's face.

"Are you asking for my help?" asked Anox'Moral. "I'm not sure what I can do, and the others certainly don't want to get involved."

"Cowards," snapped Çig'Allagosh, balling up his hands and clenching his fists. "They wouldn't help me then, and now they'll sit back and watch Uwad'Xtol destroy the world in retribution for locking her up in the first place."

"Is it inevitable that she will break out of her prison?"

"Unfortunately," said Çig'Allagosh, "It's a matter of time."

Anox'Moral looked down at his hands.

"Even worse," Çig'Allagosh added, "There's a human couple, who seem to have figured all of this out and have been poking around. All it would take is for them to pay a visit to Uwad'Xtol, disturb the inscriptions or a stone or two, and she could be free."

"You really never thought humans would find her?"

The two shared a laugh.

"Honestly, no," said Çig'Allagosh. "Never in a million years."

*　*　*　*　*

Martin and Zoe slid into their two seats on the overnight train from Jakarta to Malang. The train was nearly empty except for six other passengers. Martin intentionally found seats toward the back away from the other travelers. He looked around at the shiny steel. The yellow and green seats were old and worn but had been taken care of over the years. He could smell disinfectant in the air from the cleaners, who must have just come through. Zoe took the seat by the window, while Martin was perfectly happy to stretch his legs into the aisle. Except for the din of the group at the back of the train speaking in Indonesian, the train was quiet, which was a welcome respite from the tumult of Jakarta. Martin closed his eyes and tried to relax, but Zoe's fidgeting brought him back to the moment.

By the time the train left the station, it was already getting dark. Martin watched as office buildings and apartments quickly transitioned into the jungle. Water collected on the windows, reminding Martin that it was tropical and still very hot and humid outside.

After a few minutes, a short, thin Indonesian woman in a head covering walked up to them and asked to see their tickets. Martin showed them to her, and she smiled and nodded, before quickly moving on to the people at the back of the car.

"You think they'll follow us?" asked Zoe, her head facing the jungle landscape that was going by at increasing speed. "I'm sorry. I can't sleep with the thought that they may know where we're going."

"If they do," answered Martin, "We can always say we wanted to visit the museum in Malang before we head home. Ancient cultures are what I do, and how often do you get to Indonesia anyway?"

Zoe yawned, before adding, "Yeah, but you think they'll buy it?"

"I don't see why not? What are they going to say? You can't travel in Indonesia?"

"They don't actually have to talk," she said. "They could just throw you through a wall again, and there's nothing either of us could do about it."

Martin put his head back against the seat and sighed. "I really don't see that happening. I don't think they want to hurt us. They just want us to stop looking for something."

Zoe turned her head to look at Martin.

"But you're not stopping," she said, her jaw clenched. "You're still looking for whatever it is you're looking for."

Martin shuffled in his seat to get more comfortable. The train car was air conditioned, but he suddenly felt hot. He took a drink of water from the plastic bottle on the tray in front of him and turned to face Zoe.

"This is why we're here," he said, "Why we're in Indonesia. It's to get more information before we meet with Haoyu."

Martin took another drink of water and cleared his throat.

"Somewhere not far from Malang is where the people lived who wrote the first story about the god at the bottom of the Indian Ocean," he said. "That's what started all of this for me." He wiped the sweat on his forehead. "Is it hot in here?" he asked, looking around.

Zoe smiled and leaned on his shoulder. "We're 700 kilometers south of the equator. It's hot everywhere around here."

Martin grimaced, and he watched Zoe sit up quickly.

"Did I hurt you?" she asked.

"No," he said, putting his hand on her shoulder. "I'm still pretty sore."

"Well, yeah," she said, "It's only been a few days. You're not healed yet."

*   *   *   *   *

Four hours later, the train slowed and stopped in a small village. A voice came over the loudspeaker. It was in Indonesian, but it was obvious to Martin that the speaker was announcing the stop. He watched the group at the back of the car. They were all either sleeping or reading their phones. A man entered the car, selling food and other items. He eventually walked up to Martin and Zoe but was turned away when Martin shook his head.

After 10 minutes, the same voice came over the speaker, obviously indicating the train was leaving. Martin looked at his watch. It was 2 a.m. He rested his head against the back of his seat and closed his eyes, hoping to get a little sleep before they pulled into Malang in six hours.

It didn't take long before Martin fell into a deep sleep, exhausted by events over the course of the past few days. Rather than much needed rest, Martin awoke to a feeling like he was floating above the ground. His legs and arms moved freely but he could feel the subtle resistance as if he were swimming. His head throbbed, and he felt pressure behind his eyes like he had a nasty sinus cold. He shook his head to clear it of the fog, and, when he opened his eyes, he wasn't in the train car with Zoe but was surrounded by total blackness.

Usually, no matter where you are, there is always a little bit of light from a phone, a watch, or even the moon and stars at night beaming through the clouds. Wherever Martin was now, there was not one wisp of illumination. Martin could feel his heart pounding in his chest as he floated freely, a feeling of some kind of movement pulling him in a direction that he wasn't altogether sure of. After a few moments, he began to see light below his feet, and it was getting closer. He saw reds, oranges, and yellows below him, and, even more bizarrely, bubbles floating up and around his body. He moved his arm and waved his hand, before realizing he was in water. Martin panicked and began thrashing about, before he heard a woman's voice in his head say to him, "Don't be a fool. You're not going to drown, you witless monkey."

Martin opened his mouth and tried to take a deep breath, telling himself to calm down, but nothing came of it. There was no air to take in.

"I really don't know what he sees in you" came the voice one more time. "You aren't very bright."

He felt himself sinking and looked around, panic in his eyes. After a bit, he could see, every so often, the earth was belching bouts of molten lava, causing the water around it to boil until the lava cooled and solidified into what looked like rounded stone pillows. The cooling lava cast light all around it, and Martin could see what looked like a large black granite temple rising from the barren landscape. Every so often, his peripheral vision caught a shadow moving on the edge of the light, prompting Martin to jerk his head around.

The voice came again, "Are you going to speak, little monkey, or should I send you back?"

Martin craned his neck to get a view of a temple close by. His attention was drawn back to his arms and legs, and he began to move them as if he were swimming. He felt himself moving toward the structure, and the little control he managed in his current situation calmed him somewhat. He opened his mouth, and, when it wasn't flooded with water, he tried to speak.

"What …" was all he got out at first. He looked around again at his own body before his eyes were drawn to what looked like a large open entrance at the base of the building. "Where am I?"

"Finally," the voice rang in his head. "It speaks."

"Who are you?" asked Martin. "Where am I? What am I doing here?"

"So many stupid questions," answered the voice. "We don't have much time. Is that really what you want to ask me?"

"I …" said Martin, shaking his head to try to regain his composure. "Yes, I think I'd like to know where I am first."
"Very well," the voice responded. "You're at the bottom of a sea that has had many names but what your kind calls the Indian Ocean. I brought you here. I am Uwad'Xotl. Maybe you've heard of me?"

"Nope," answered Martin. "Never heard of you. Are you like the others I've met … like those two guys named Veja'Hast and Cig'Allagosh?"

"I know you've met some of my kind," said the voice. "I can feel it in you."

"I have no idea who you are or what is going on here," answered Martin. He moved his arms and legs and tried to swim but didn't go anywhere.

"Seriously? I can't believe he's never mentioned me."

Martin floated in the current about 20 meters from the temple. He could now see a tall woman standing at the entrance. Absolute inky blackness framed her in the massive doorway. Her long black hair undulated freely in the deep. Martin wasn't cold. In fact, he didn't feel any sensations at all, which was really weird as he was clearly underwater and somewhere very deep where light could not penetrate.

"But I know all about you."

Martin blinked his eyes a few times and looked around him.

"Are you like Çig'Allagosh and Veja'Hast?" asked Martin.

"I am of their ilk, but I am nothing like them." The voice rang in Martin's head. He could have easily perceived the tone as rage, but it was deeper than that. There was sadness in it. "They are cowards who refuse to do the hard work of caring for this world. You are destroyers, and, if nothing is done to stop you, there won't be anything left for the rest of us, who call this place home."

"Are you the one that's been written about, locked away for all of time here in this temple?" asked Martin.

"So you do know of me," the voice purred. "The world remembers."

Martin tried to swim closer to the temple but an unseen force stopped him. He was close enough to see the woman but couldn't see her mouth move when she spoke. "I first learned about you after I came upon an inscription on a stone tablet that's about 3,500 years old. It was difficult to decipher, but I figured some of it out. An elder in a village near here recounted a strange visitor, who first appeared as a huge snake before turning into a man. His people cared for this stranger, and the stranger told him a story of a great battle that was fought. The stranger was victorious, and he was able to trap you in a cage at the bottom of the sea, but it came at great cost to him."

"Such flair for drama," came the voice, dripping with sarcasm. "Yes, I fought back, but we can't die. He would have been fine even without the help of you monkeys."

"Why did Çig'Allagosh imprison you?"

"They feared I was going to take away all their little pets," the voice rang in his head, "But I wasn't going to kill all of you. Just most of you." There was a pause for a moment, before the voice echoed, "Maybe a couple million."

Martin could feel his face getting hot.

"What did we do to you? It's not like we're a threat. You said you can't be killed."

"I had already lived a very long time by the time I made the decision to cull the apes. And, in that time, over the course of a hundred thousand winters, I watched armies of you slaughter each other over patches of dirt. I watched you burn down entire forests just so no one else could have them. You chose death. The leaders you picked for yourselves were the most violent among you. I watched you kill children and the old simply because you could. And it wasn't just your own kind. That was bad enough, but I also watched you kill so many animals that there was nothing left within a week's walk of you."

She paused for a moment to think.

She continued: "I would have been fine if you self-corrected. For thousands of years, this went on, until, finally, I decided I'd help you along with your own destruction. Actually, I was well on my way when Çig'Allagosh attacked me."

She seemed to relax for a moment. She ran her hands along the rough stone at the doorway where she stood.

The voice was in his head again, "I don't know how long I've been down here, but I suspect it's been at least a thousand winters."

"3,500 years," said Martin.

"What?"

"Assuming an inscription on a stone table I learned about came from the time of your fight with Çig'Allagosh, you've been down here for 3,500 years," he said. "Give or take a few hundred years."

Martin watched as the woman looked down at her feet and ran her hand through her hair. She looked up at him, and the voice was in his head again, saying, "So how's that working out for you?"

"I'll admit. It's not been great. We still kill each other for land, resources, and power. We often take things from the lowliest among us and give it to people who already have more than they need, but it's not as bad as it used to be. We have changed. A little, anyway. We're getting there."

Martin stopped for a second to look at the woman's face.

He continued: "I suppose the difference now is that we have weapons that can wipe out all life on Earth. Oh, and the trash. That's really bad. And the pollution is making storms worse, and …"

He paused before adding, "A lot of us want the death and

destruction to end. Just because a small number of us do evil things, that doesn't justify killing everyone."

Martin studied the woman's face. It was obvious she didn't care. He had seen that kind of anger before. Even at this distance, he could see her balling up her fists, and he could sense the fury in her voice.

"Why did you bring me here if you don't care what I think?"

"You all think you're so important," the voice came again, "But if your kind vanished tomorrow, life would thrive. Forests would grow back. Rivers and streams would be clean. Animals would flourish."

"That isn't true at all," he said. "A meteor killed all the dinosaurs, and it's only a matter of time before that happens again. All life is precious."

Martin watched her look up into the blackness of the vast ocean above her head before facing him again.

"You don't even understand that you are of less value to this planet than the smallest insect," she said. "Even the innocent among you takes more than he gives."

The voice suddenly was so loud in his head that it hurt. He dropped his head and tried to cover his ears, but it was useless.

The voice continued: "When I'm free again, I will make sure your kind understands their worth to this world. I will …"

Martin woke up in his seat in the train, startled, his arms flailing.

He heard Zoe's voice.

"Jesus, Martin, what the hell's wrong with you?"

He sat up in his seat and looked around. He was breathing heavily. There was ringing in his ears. His hand went to his nose, and when he pulled it away, there was blood on his finger. He shook his head, trying to clear the fog but he felt dizzy and nauseated. He looked around frantically, saw an empty plastic bag for trash, grabbed it, and proceeded to throw up his guts into it. When he was done, he wiped his mouth with his arm, drank some water, and sat back in the seat.

"That was one hell of a nightmare," she said. "Not surprising considering what you've been through.

Martin took another drink of water before gripping Zoe's arm.

"I know what they're protecting in the ocean," he said, closing his eyes to regain composure. He thought for a moment and then added, "I know what's bringing down those planes."

*   *   *   *   *

Martin stared out the window of the train. It was still dark outside, and he could barely make out the overgrown field on the edge of the track in the moonlight. Zoe sat quietly on his left. He turned his head to see that her eyes were closed, but he could tell by her breathing that she wasn't asleep. Her head was back against the seat, but she was leaning into him.

"To be totally honest," he muttered, "Up until I met these creatures, I just figured you were right, that we'd eventually find some natural phenomenon brought down those planes. I didn't actually believe there was a sea monster or some creature that had the power to crash 747s."

Zoe opened her eyes and smiled. She leaned back into her seat and looked up at the ceiling of the train car.

"I just thought you were weird," she said, "Cute and smart, but really weird. But I like weird. And who was I to talk, you know? My life is a total mess. I'm going through this ridiculous divorce where my ex and I are – what's the word people use these days? Oh yeah, 'decoupling.' We're still trying to be friends, which is a total lie. I know it, and so does everyone else, but we still say it to each other with a straight face. I really didn't think much beyond my shit life when I first met you."

Martin studied her face. Her hair was rumpled from awkwardly sleeping on the train. As exhausted as she was, she was still beautiful to him, and, somehow, despite the heat and humidity, she still managed to smell like flowers. He subtly tried to sniff himself, and he smelled of sweat. He watched her laugh at him, and he smiled back.

"We both smell pretty bad," she said, "But it's the tropics. Everyone's sweaty. And you just had that terrible nightmare. It's understandable you're even more sweaty from that."

Martin looked over his shoulder.

"I don't think it was a nightmare," he said before looking back at her. "It was real. I was there, maybe not my body but my mind was at least. My head still hurts from it all. The pressure was nearly unbearable."

"Maybe she can show you things. You know, get inside your head and talk to you and send you images."

"But I really felt like I was down there," he said. "Creatures that powerful can probably do all sorts of things we can't even begin to understand."

"Like bring down planes with their minds?" she asked him.

"Yes, exactly."

Zoe ran her hand along the side of Martin's head, tamping down his unruly hair.

"It's pretty terrifying when you think about it," he said. "What could we possibly hope to do to stop any of this? These things live forever. They say they can't be killed. One of them is trapped at the bottom of the Indian Ocean right now in a place that's incredibly inhospitable to life, and she's been there three thousand years. Does she need to eat or drink fresh water? If she does, obviously it's not much."

"Did she tell you how she's able to crash airplanes?" asked Zoe.

"I asked but she said she didn't want to fill me in on her sinister plan to commit genocide," said Martin with a sneer. "Honestly, I could barely think of anything intelligent to say. I was too terrified. Plus she kept mocking me, calling me a stupid ape."

Martin looked down at his hands and brushed some crumbs off his lap.

"I can't explain to you how absolutely frightening she was," he said.

"I met the one that calls herself Catharine," answered Zoe. "It may have just been in a coffee shop, but I got the feeling she could have crushed me in the blink of an eye if I pissed her off even a little bit."

Martin sighed. He looked at his phone; it was 4 a.m. They still had two hours to go before they would reach Malang. What was he thinking. He wasn't just endangering himself, but he was also risking Zoe's life over something he wasn't even sure he had the power to do anything about.

But now he knew what was going on. There was a nightmare trapped at the bottom of the ocean just like the inscription said, and what could he hope to do about it? The things that say they can't be killed – they haven't been able to do anything about it except delay what seemed like the inevitable. She seemed pretty confident she would be able to get out eventually, and then she was going to finish the job, whatever that meant. Does she want to kill everyone now? If she thought the world was bad in 1,500 B.C.E., wait until she gets a load of all the trash that's been piling up, the combustion engines and coal-fired power plants that are belching out toxic out fumes, the chemicals and plastics we've dumped into all the waterways, and all the animals that have gone extinct thanks to humans. She's really going to be pissed off when she sees that.

Martin slammed his head back against his seat. He could still hear ringing in his ears, and his head hurt from the pressure.

"Maybe your guy's right?" said Zoe as she closed her eyes and leaned her head on his shoulder. "Maybe we should just go home and forget all about this?"

"You're probably right."

He looked out the window at the darkness outside. "Tell you what: let's just go to the museum in Malang, maybe spend a day or two checking out the local sites. Then we can head back to the U.S."

Zoe let out a heavy sigh and pressed herself into Martin's arm. "Sounds perfect to me," she said. "Wake me up when we're at the station."

*   *   *   *   *

"The town square is just around the corner from us, and it's only a short ride to the zoo if that's what you're looking for," said the woman behind the counter.

Zoe had found them a small guesthouse that was right in the middle of Malang. It was only $24 a night, but Martin was impressed with how modern the place was. There were stained wood accents all over the lobby, and the smell of spiced meats emanated from the bar and restaurant nearby.

"Are you here for work or pleasure?" asked the young woman from behind the counter.

Zoe smiled at her and said, "We're traveling on vacation and want to really see the Singhasari Museum."

"Oh that's 20 minutes up the road," said the clerk. "Would you like me to call you a cab?"

"We just took the train all night from Jakarta," said Zoe. "I think we're going to go to sleep for a bit."

The young woman smiled at her. "Feel free to call down to us when you want to go to the museum. We can call you a cab."

"Thank you."

Zoe took Martin by the arm and turned him toward the stairs.

"We're on the second floor," she said as she began walking. "I just got us one room. It's their family room – two beds – but one room. You don't mind, do you?"

Martin looked around the place as he pulled his small suitcase behind him.

"$24 for all this?" he said to no one in particular.

"Yeah," said Zoe. "Apparently it's not even their off-season. It's just not an expensive city, I guess. I really like it."

They both walked up to the second floor and followed the hallway around a corner to their room. Zoe swiped her card and opened the door to a spacious room with two queen-sized beds, a small kitchenette, and a large bathroom with a walk-in shower. Traditional Indonesian art hung on the walls.

Martin pushed his suitcase into the closet, walked over to the bed and flopped down on it.

He watched Zoe lift her suitcase onto the gray loveseat on the other side of the room and open it.

"I desperately need a shower," she mumbled and grabbed some clothing. She smelled one of her shirts before adding, "They have a free laundry service here, which I will definitely be taking advantage of."

Martin slid further up the bed, kicked off his shoes, and closed his eyes.

"There's a heated toilet seat," he heard Zoe shout from the bathroom. He found himself laughing. It felt good.

"And there's a bidet built right in," he heard her call out again, "And it ... Ohhh ... Wait ... Now there's hot air! This place is amazing!"

Martin rolled onto his side and pulled his legs up ever so slightly to relax. The last thing he remembered was the sound of the shower coming on before he fell fast asleep.

* * * * *

Martin woke up with a start—again. The room was dark, but he could see light coming in on the edge of the curtains. He sat up and looked over at Zoe, who was sitting up, reading something on her iPad.

"How long was I asleep for?"

He reached for his phone, which was on the nightstand next to his bed.

"About three hours," said Zoe. "I figured you needed it, so I didn't bother you."

"Thanks," he answered as he sat up and swung his legs off the bed and onto the floor. His head still throbbed, and he walked over to his suitcase, took out his travel kit, and rifled through it for some Motrin. He dumped out two pills, closed up the bottle, and placed it back into the small bag. He walked over to the fridge, grabbed a bottle of water, and swallowed down the Mortin with a gulp of water. He started to strip out of his clothes before remembering that Zoe was still there.

"You can change there if you want," he heard her say. "I'm not looking."

"Sorry about that," he said, laughing quietly to himself. "I guess I'm just comfortable with you now."

"Don't be sorry," she said. "And don't let me stop you from showering. You need it after the train ride."

Martin smelled himself. "Am I really that bad?"

"Let's just say I can definitely smell you from here," she said. "I've been to some of the most remote parts of the world on research trips, so it doesn't bother me, but there's no reason not to take advantage of this place while we're here."

Martin shrugged, walked to the bathroom, and shut the door behind him. The lights came on automatically when he entered the room, and he flicked another switch to activate the fan. He took off his clothes, letting them fall to the floor. He turned on the shower and adjusted the heat. He then sat on the toilet and relieved himself. He looked around at the white-tiled room that was quickly filling up with steam.

Two days, he thought. That's how long they'll stay before heading back home. He really liked the city from what he had seen of the place on the cab ride from the train station to the guesthouse. The city was renowned for its colorful buildings that blended traditional and Dutch architecture. It was a bustling city, but Martin thought it didn't have the same frenetic feel as Jakarta.

When he stood up, he jumped forward as the toilet flushed itself. He laughed at himself before opening the door to the shower and stepping in to immerse himself in the piping hot water. He soaped up his body as best he could, wincing when he bent over. When he was done, he stepped out of the shower, dried himself, wrapped a towel around his waist, opened the bathroom door, and walked out into the coolness of the air-conditioned room.

"Feel like a new man?" Zoe asked him as he reached into his suitcase for his clothing. He had to use both hands to dig deeply to find some clean clothes, but when he did, the towel dropped off him, and he felt the cold air on his nakedness a few seconds before he realized what had happened. Across the room he heard Zoe stifling a laugh.

"You know some people would pay extra for a show like that," she said, still laughing at him.

His face flushed, Martin squatted down quickly, picked up the towel, and wrapped it around himself.

"I'm so sorry," he said as he turned to face her, his clothes in his hands. "I really didn't …"

She put up her hand to cut him off.

"It's not a big deal," she said. "Don't be embarrassed."

"I guess I should have expected something like that."

"It's not like I haven't seen a naked man before," she said. "In many parts of the world nudity isn't even an issue at all."

"I know," he said, "But it's us, and we're staying in a room together. I don't want to make you uncomfortable."

"If you made me uncomfortable, I'd already be back home by now."

"I appreciate that," he said.

Martin walked back into the bathroom and shut the door. He slipped into underwear, jeans, and a short-sleeved, button-down shirt. He checked his hair in the mirror, combing down a particularly unruly part in the back of his head. He opened the door and walked back out into the room, where Zoe was already up and putting on makeup in the mirror over the desk.

"We heading to the museum?" asked Martin as he bent over to zip up his suitcase again.

"Food, first," answered Zoe. "Museum, second. I'm starving."

Who Is the Bad Guy?
Chapter 8

Çig'Allagosh lay naked on the hot sand on a beach somewhere in the middle of the South Pacific, the cool salt water lapping at his feet. The tide was on its way out, so he didn't feel any urgency to move. He lay back and closed his eyes, thinking of an easier time before his troubles with Uwad'Xotl and the pressure he was under to fix the problem he had made for his kind. Of course there had been squabbles in the past, even violence, but it was isolated to a few of them, and it didn't threaten to spill over and force them all into picking one side or the other.

He thought back 3,000 years to the last time he was here, waiting for his lover at that time, Sidn'Gaabetha, to meet him. He considered her an ally of Uwad'Xotl, so he wanted to make sure she understood his reasons for imprisoning Uwad'Xotl. He was not concerned about the others, though. Most of them were so self-centered that he didn't worry they might try to help Uwad'Xotl, or, worse, try to break her out once she was isolated and locked away.

He did keep tabs on those who made the long trip to visit Uwad-Xotl. Over the years, as far as he could tell, it had only been himself,

Sidn'Gaabetha, and the group's quasi-leader, Anox'Moral, who made the trek. Anox-Moral would never be a problem. Çig'Allagosh knew he was, deep down, a coward unwilling to take any real risks that would threaten the group.

Çig'Allagosh remembered that day clearly, even though thousands of years had passed, and he felt a stirring between his legs. It was certainly unexpected what happened then but not unusual for his kind. After all, they had already lived for millions of years. And since there were so few of them, it was not considered strange for each of them to have been lovers after all that time. That is, except for Anox'Moral, who had been with Thexērus for so long that everyone thought they might stay together for eternity. Çig'Allagosh had his share of relationships with humans over all this time, having had both long affairs and one night trysts with everyone from queens to outcasts and everything in between.

He watched the waves crashing on the beach and thought back to when he first saw signs of Sidn'Gaabetha swimming toward the remote island he was on while still in her massive reptile form, slicing through the water, her four legs pressed against her side, her large tail driving her forward, bright scales shining in the sun. He remembered sitting up when he caught sight of another huge creature breaking the surface, an enormous squid that rolled in the waves before dropping back down. Soon enough, two tall women with dark hair and tanned skin emerged from the ocean.

"I thought it was just us today," Çig'Allagosh remembered shouting out to Sidn'Gaabetha.

He saw the smile spread across her face as she reached out to take Uwad'Xotl by her hand and lead her onto dry land.

"I assumed you wouldn't mind if I brought a friend."

He looked up as Sidn'Gaabetha walked to him, bent over, and kissed him hard on his mouth. She tasted like salt and red wine, and she smelled of flowers. Çig'Allagosh started to stand, but he was abruptly stopped when Sidn'Gaabetha put a hand on his shoulder.

"No need to get up," she said. "We can all relax on the sand unless you have somewhere to go."

Sidn'Gaabetha's other hand was still firmly in Uwad'Xotl's as she stood back up. The two then embraced and kissed passionately as Çig'Allagosh looked on, feeling his lust taking over. When they were finished, Uwad'Xotl dropped to her knees, placed her hands on Çig'Allagosh's shoulders, and kissed him deeply. Over her shoulder, Çig'Allagosh watched as Sidn'Gaabetha dropped to her knees as well, slowly moving down him. He lost sight of her, but he could tell exactly where she was by the feel of her mouth on him.

Çig'Allagosh smiled, thinking of how the three of them spent the rest of the day, lying languidly on the beach, sometimes sleeping and other times engaged in acts that even to this day make his heart race.

He knew that Sidn'Gaabetha never forgave him for what he did to Uwad'Xotl, but he felt he had no choice. Sidn'Gaabetha had sided with Uwad'Xotl, and the two had destroyed at least one village that Çig'Allagosh was aware of, but there may have been more.

He was brought back to the present moment when he saw far off in the distance the shape of something large moving toward him. He had reached out to her in his mind, asking her to meet at the one island in the South Pacific that today is referred to as the Tuamotu Islands, but she never responded. He sensed that she had received his message. It came as fuzzy emotions—mostly rage—but there was sadness in it, as well.

He gathered that their meeting would be different today than the last time they saw each other thousands of years ago. Çig'Allagosh paced in the sand as Sidn'Gaabetha swam closer. Eventually he watched her, in human form, step from the ocean, water flowing off her muscular olive-colored body. Many things had changed. The world today was completely different than it had been so long ago. Back then, early Polynesians had not even braved the oceans yet to populate this chain of islands. In those days, he and his kind had them to themselves.

Also, he noted that, unlike thousands of years ago, a considerable amount of trash had washed up on the shore and was pushed into the jungle. Birds, bugs, and coconut crabs picked among it, looking for food. Çig'Allagosh had chosen an island that was still pretty remote. Even now, few humans had ever set foot on these beaches. Nonetheless, fishing nets, bags, plastic buckets, and even shoes could be seen nestled among decomposing palm fronds.

Sidn'Gaabetha was as beautiful as ever as she walked toward Çig'Allagosh, but he could tell by the look on her face she wasn't exactly happy to see him.

"Thank you for coming to talk," he said as he walked toward the water to meet her.

"Don't thank me yet," she shot back at him. "I have half a mind to wrap my hands around your throat and watch your face turn all shades of purple."

He smiled and bowed slightly to her.

"You don't actually mean that," he said. "Do you?

"You fucking better believe I do," she roared at him, "you scheming, traitorous pig."

Çig'Allagosh put his hands up.

"I didn't bring you here to open old …"

She cut him off.

"Yes, you fucking did. You brought me here to try to convince me what you did was noble and right. You know it wasn't, otherwise you wouldn't have asked to meet me alone."

He tensed up as she began to walk faster toward him.

"You imprisoned my friend at the bottom of the sea to save your favorite pets," she said. "She was doing what the rest of us were too afraid to do. Look where we are now."

"She had no right to kill the humans," he said. "Yes, not all of them are good, but it's not up to us to save them. They have to figure it out for themselves."

He took a step back and braced himself as she rushed toward him. His eyes went to her hands she placed them flat on his chest and shoved him hard, throwing him back into the jungle, flattening several palm trees. He fell hard onto his side, rolled over onto his back, and stared up to the cloudless sky. He exhaled heavily and started to get up, but, before he could, he saw a blur of light as Sidn'Gaabetha ran up to him again. She took a step forward, drew her leg back, and kicked him in his side. He put his arm out to try to block her but it was useless. He flew even further this time, smashing through another half dozen trees before skidding to a stop on his stomach in the middle of the island. He again tried to get up, but she kicked him in his side, launching him a few meters further into the jungle.

As soon as he landed, this time, he jumped to his feet and turned to face her.

"Stop doing that," he shouted out to her, but it didn't seem to faze her. She blurred again, coming up in front of him. She reached both her arms back, ready to shove him again, but this time, he stepped aside at the last moment, and she fell forward off balance. He reached around her, grabbing her by her hair and her throat.

"I told you to stop," he screamed at her.

She craned her neck, snarled, and spit right in his face.

"You fucking traitor," she yelled at him. "You made your choice. Now live with the consequences."

She pulled her hand back ever so slightly, closed her fist, and jabbed him right in his stomach as hard as she could, forcing him to bend over and let go of her. She quickly stood up, clasped her hands together, raised them over her head, and slammed them down on the back of his head, driving him into the ground. He went down so hard that it actually dented the ground several inches.

Çig'Allagosh pushed up with his hands, lifting his whole body up and away from her. He landed several meters back, but before he could even get his bearings, she was on him, again slamming both of her arms into his chest, sending him flying back toward the beach. He rolled out onto the sand, coming quickly to his feet as Sidn'Gaabetha raced out of the treeline toward him.

"Will you please ..."

But before he could finish, she hit him across his face with her balled-up fist, hurling him dozens of meters into the ocean. By the time he landed in the water, he had already changed into his snake form, sending a tsunami that was four stories high straight at the island. Undeterred, Sidn'Gaabetha changed her form into a massive monitor-lizard-like creature hundreds of meters long. As the huge wave swallowed the island, Sidn'Gaabetha pushed up and through it, powering her way in the direction of Çig'Allagosh.

He watched it all from the edge of a dropoff about 20 meters from what used to be the shore. He floated in the current, coiled up and ready to spring when she came into view. As the water settled, he saw her slowly swimming over him, her tail splashing about. Çig'Allagosh launched himself at her, driving his long serpentine body up and over her. When he was upon her, he opened his mouth, bit down, and wrapped himself all around her over and over again, squeezing her legs tight against her. She thrashed and rolled over in the water, her massive jaws opening and clamping shut. He slowly tightened his grip on her, and the two sank beneath the waves even as she struggled.

He reached out to her in his thoughts.

"You need to stop this," he thought. "I just wanted to talk, not fight."

He felt her struggle even harder after that.

"You know I can hold you forever," he thought again. "Please, just talk to me."

Çig'Allagosh felt his grip go limp as the large lizard he had caught simply vanished. His head swiveled around until he caught sight of Sidn'Gaabetha in her human form, swimming toward the surface. He quickly dropped his snake shape and followed her up to daylight.

When he surfaced a few moments later, he swam to her and began treading water next to her. He quickly looked back in the direction of the island only to see it flattened. The trees lay smashed and broken and the beach was awash in trash and other detritus.

"That was a pretty good beatdown," he said to her, a smile on his face, "But did you really have to destroy my favorite island?"

"You fucker, that was all you," she shot back at him. "You're the one who changed …"

He interrupted her. "After you punched me so hard I flew into the water."

He paused for a second to gauge her mood.

"Can we talk?" he asked. "Or are you going to start hitting me again?"

"Day's still young."

Çig'Allagosh turned from her and began to swim toward the shore. He looked back over his shoulder and saw her following right behind him. After he made it to the beach, he bent over to clear some trash from his leg. As he brushed at it, he saw Sidn'Gaabetha quickly raise her leg and kick him, knocking him to the ground. It was clear she wasn't using anywhere near the strength she had right before the island was flooded.

He got up on his hands and knees and spit sand out of his mouth.

"Was that really necessary?"

"You're the one who stuck your ass in the air," she said, laughing. "I can't help it if you make an easy target."

He sat down on the beach and began to brush the sand off himself. She sat down next to him and began to pick pieces of palm fronds and other garbage out of her hair.

"Can we at least talk now?" asked Çig'Allagosh. "Are you done hitting me?"

"Day's still young," she repeated.

"Right, well …" stammered Çig'Allagosh. "Will you at least hear me out?"

"I'm still here."

"Okay," he said, pausing to read her face. She was looking off over the water into the distance away from him, and, even though she was sitting next to him, her body was tense and turned away from him. He could see the muscles in her arm flexing as he looked at her.

"I can see you're angry with me about Uwad'Xotl," he said, "But I had no choice…"

"You're a liar," she blurted out, cutting him off. She was staring right at him now, and he could see the anger in her eyes. "Of course you had a choice."

"Will you let me finish, please?" he asked her. "At least hear me out."

"Fine," she said. "Say your peace."

"I tried to talk to her," he said. "I tried to convince her what she was doing was wrong, that she was no better than the worst of the humans if she were to continue murdering all those innocent people, but she would not hear me. She felt so strongly. It was clear to me that she was going to wipe out all of them if I did not put a stop to her, so I did what all the others were too cowardly to do. I stopped her."

Çig'Allagosh studied her. She still refused to look at him, but he could see the tension dissipating in her. Her shoulders had relaxed, and she wasn't clenching her teeth anymore. He tried again to reason with her.

"It's been a few thousand years since I stopped her," he said, "And you know I'm right. You know I did the right thing. She was wrong to kill all of those innocent people."

Sidn'Gaabetha turned and their eyes met. He saw tears welling up as she tried to blink them away. She looked down at her hands.

"I still fucking despise you," she said, wiping her eyes. Çig'Allagosh laughed.

"You can hate me and still know I did the right thing," he said.

"I'm not sure that's true," she muttered, looking back toward the water again.

"What? That you hate me?" he asked, "Or that I did the right thing."

"I think we could have convinced her to stop without having to lock her away by herself for all those years," she said. "Do you know what that does to someone, locking them up like that for thousands of years with no one to talk to? She's not the same as she was before you did that. She's consumed with anger and vengeance now more than ever."

Çig'Allagosh put his hand on hers.

"I know," he said. "I visit her often." He turned his head toward a squall that was passing to the south of them. "And I know you do, too."

"I've visited her many times," she said. "To be honest, I've even tried to figure out how I could help to free her, but nothing came of it."

He turned his head to look at her again. The growing wind had pushed her dark hair in her face, and she reached up and brushed it aside.

"Well," he said, "There is a problem. I think she's figured out how to free herself. It's taken millennia, but she's been working away at it, and, somehow, her power is growing."

"And why would you think I'd consider that bad news?"

"Because, if she gets free, she will try to destroy this world," he said, doing his best to keep his voice cool and calm. "And she could do it."

*   *   *   *   *

Çig'Allagosh stood at the entrance to one of the ancient limestone temples on the island of Gozo, just north of Malta in the middle of the Mediterranean Sea. He glanced at the sign posted at the entrance as he waited for some of the others to show up for an impromptu gathering he had called.

He laughed as he read the temple's history.

"Believed to have been built by a giantess and her child," read the sign.

It continued: "Built over 5,000 years ago during the Stone Age, the temple predates the pyramids of Egypt. Legend has it that her child was the product of a love affair with a human man. After he was born, the child built the temple and then used it as a place of worship."

Çig'Allagosh smiled when he thought back to those heady days when early man accepted that supernatural forces controlled their fate. Humans have come a long way from that time, but not all of it could be considered good. Perhaps the world was ready again for his kind to reintroduce themselves rather than continue to hide in the shadows. Coming clean about their existence and their power would make it a lot easier to deal with Uwad'Xotl. If humans only knew the truth behind this ancient temple and most of the others scattered around the globe. Çig'Allagosh was lost in thought when he heard a familiar woman's voice behind him.

"They built this for her," said the woman, "Gigante, indeed."

He turned around quickly to see Sidn'Gaabetha in a light, sleeveless white gown that reached her feet. Her gold bracelets and necklace sparkled in the sun.

"Nice to see you again."

The two embraced before Çig'Allagosh took a step back and eyed her from head to toe.

"Still pining over your little pets, I see," Sidn'Gaabetha told him.

Çig'Allagosh frowned.

"Did I hit a nerve?" she asked.

He tightened his jaw and pursed his lips.

"Our last get-together didn't go to your plan, I assume," she added, smiling.

"Careful," answered Çig'Allagosh. "The others might hear you. Honestly, I'd rather forget it, and they certainly don't need to know about it."

Çig'Allagosh watched as it was now Sidn'Gaabetha's turn to frown. She glowered at him, adding, "We still don't agree on any of this, Çig'Allagosh. You'll never change my mind."

"The others might not see …" Çig'Allagosh cut himself short as he watched Anox'Moral walking along the long concrete pathway to the entrance of the temple. Another of their kind by the name of Olivion – a tall dark-skinned man with black hair and dark brown eyes – walked beside him. Çig'Allagosh caught a moment of recognition on Sidn'Gaabetha's face, as she turned to see who else was coming.

"Anox," she called out. "It's so good to see you again! You, too, Olivion!"

"It feels like old times," Anox'Moral said, as he stopped abruptly at the entrance where the other two were standing. "Who else are we waiting for?"

"I reached out to Thexērus, but he said he's stuck in Chicago and can't make it without throwing his current situation into considerable disarray," said Çig'Allagosh. "I'm sure you know more about that than I. Veja'Hast and Ygg'Vilerov should be here soon. That makes six of us."

Çig'Allagosh craned his neck, looking back toward the pale limestone villas that make up the neighboring town of Xagħra. He watched as Sidn'Gaabetha and Anox'Moral traded a brief kiss. He then bowed slightly to greet Anox'Moral and Olivion.

"Hello again, my old friend," said Anox'Moral. "I've seen more of you in the past month than I have in 1,000 years."

Çig'Allagosh looked down at his feet before meeting Anox'Moral's eyes.

"It is good to see you again, too," said Çig'Allagosh. "I wish we were meeting under better circumstances. I have concerns."

He looked at Sidn'Gaabetha, who averted her eyes.

"Not all of us agree that imprisoning her was the right decision," said Anox'Moral. "Some say you acted too presumptuously, and now we could all suffer."

"I acted because she was murdering humans," roared Çig'Allagosh. "She was killing innocent people. I couldn't sit back and just let that happen."

"You should have talked to us," interjected Sidn'Gaabetha. "I could have convinced her to stop, but you took it upon yourself with the help of …" She paused while two others walked up to them. "Oh look, here they are now."

A tall woman with long reddish-blonde hair, pale skin, and blue eyes was walking slowly next to a tall, thin man with olive-colored skin, green eyes, and dark hair. Çig'Allagosh watched a smile spread across the woman's face as she clearly recognized the group.

"The gigantes are home again," said Veja'Hast as he drew near to the group, his arms extended. The six of them exchanged laughs, kisses, and hugs before turning to face the temple. Ygg'Vilerov paused to look around the ancient site. She walked up to the ropes as close to the temple grounds as she could before turning to a security guard who was breezing by, staring at her with a watchful eye. She smiled and waved at him.

"If that guard only knew who this was really for," she muttered under her breath before turning to face the group.

"Fitting place to meet," she said. "Such a pity how it looks. It's seen better days."

"She would be sad to see her temple in such disrepair," added Sidn'Gaabetha, shaking her head. She turned and looked at Çig'Allagosh, saying, "So why exactly are we here again?"

Çig'Allagosh frowned and looked down at his feet. "It is Uwad'Xotl. She is breaking free of her prison. It is only a matter of time before she is free."

"I guess, now that we've gotten the formalities out of the way, we get right to it," said Veja'Hast. "How long do we have?"

"Could be years," answered Çig'Allagosh. "Could be days. I really don't know."

"How do you know?" asked Anox'Moral.

"Every day, she's growing more powerful," he said. "Surely you can sense it, too."

"I have been able to hear her thoughts more clearly in the past few years," said Ygg'Vilerov, "But I still have to listen very hard for them."

"And you thought to tell no one of this, Ygg'Vilerov?" replied Anox'Moral.

Çig'Allagosh could see the anger etched on his face.

She dismissed him with a wave of her hand. "I thought little of it. I figured, after all this time alone, she had just learned to project them better."

"Maybe that's your problem," Anox'Moral shot back. "You don't think enough."

Çig'Allagosh watched her turn toward him. Her face flushed red.

"I go by Catharine these days," she blurted out. "You know that."

Çig'Allagosh saw her ball up her fists and take a step forward. He quickly stepped between them. "I didn't ask you to come here to fight," he said, his head going back and forth between the two. "We're here because we have a problem."

Sidn'Gaabetha coughed and cleared her throat. "Correction," she said. "You have a problem."

"It is a problem for all of us," he fired back at her.

She turned away and faced the old village of clay and stone buildings. The sun, shining in a cloudless sky, beat down on them.

"We would not be here if you three had not acted on your own," said Anox'Moral.

Çig'Allagosh could tell Anox'Moral was trying to temper the anger in his voice. "Someone needed to act," Çig'Allagosh answered. "Something had to be done, and none of you had the will to do it except for us three."

Sidn'Gaabetha turned and faced the group again. She waved her hand in a wild gesture. "Look around you," she said. "She was right. Humans are destroying everything. Their trash is everywhere. They're poisoning this world, pouring toxins into the air and the water. Let's face reality. Uwad'Xotl was prescient. She was an oracle, and you treated her like the villain."

She paused to let her words sink in, before adding, "Maybe it is you, Çig'Allagosh, who should have been locked away, not her."

Çig'Allagosh felt his face get hot, but he did his best to relax his shoulders and arms. He took a deep breath and exhaled. "What is done is done," he said. "We can't turn back the clock, so we're here now. She is a threat to this world."

He met Sidn'Gaabetha's eyes.

"We have to deal with it together," he said. "Otherwise, the prison will fail. She will escape, and she will wage war not just on humans but on us as well."

"You forget," interrupted Sidn'Gaabetha. "I visit her often. She only seeks revenge against the three of you. The rest of us have nothing to worry about."

"Is that what you're hearing, Catharine?" asked Çig'Allagosh.

Ygg'Vilerov shook her head. "Her thoughts aren't coherent," she said. "What she allows me to hear, anyway."

She looked down at her feet and then back up at the group.

"She is consumed by rage," she added. "And, while most of it is directed at Çig'Allagosh, she sees all of us as betrayers."

Silence fell on the group as a half dozen tourists wandered onto the temple grounds. One of the tourists, an older Japanese man, walked up to Veja'Hast and held up his phone to him. Çig'Allagosh watched the man point to the screen before barking at the others to gather in front of the temple for a group photo. Veja'Hast rolled his eyes and sighed heavily before telling the nice, old man in fluent Japanese that he can take the picture if the old man moves his ass and gets in the shot. In a moment, it was over, and the group walked back in the direction of the village, thanking Veja'Hast profusely as they left.

Anox'Moral was the first to speak up: "Have you figured out how she's breaking down her prison?"

"I'm not sure," said Çig'Allagosh. "I have noticed some of the etchings on the temple are degrading. I suspect she has figured out somehow a way to exploit naturally unstable fault lines in the deep to physically and quite literally shake apart her prison."

"Can you repair them and stabilize it?"

Çig'Allagosh shook his head. "I don't know," he said. "It took me a century to build the temple. I can start to fix the etchings, but I just do not know if I will be able to catch them in time before she breaks out."

"So, if I understand you correctly," said Anox'Moral. "You're telling us it was a mistake to build her prison at the bottom of the ocean?"

"What he means to say," interjected Ygg'Vilerov, "Is that, not only did you fuck us by acting so rashly, you fucked us by putting her in a place she'd eventually bust out of."

Çig'Allagosh threw his hands up in the air and walked to the ropes blocking the temple's entrance.

"I had to put her in a place where no one would ever just stumble upon her," he said, staring at the ancient site. "I didn't think she'd ever figure out how to free herself."

"And that's not all," said Veja'Hast. "There are two humans, who have been poking around. I think they're close to figuring this all out."

Anox'Moral shot a glance at Çig'Allagosh. "Is this true?"

"Don't act like you don't know any of this, Anox'Moral," said Çig'Allagosh. "You know Dr. Lee better than any of us. You even tried to bribe him to make him go away."

Çig'Allagosh watched Anox'Moral look down at his feet. "That is correct, Çig'Allagosh," he said. "Thexērus and I did make him an offer we thought he couldn't refuse, but he rejected it."

"Just kill them and be done with it," quipped Veja'Hast. "You all worry too much about this stuff."

"You cannot kill him," said Anox'Moral. "Thexērus and I have grown fond of him. He is a good man. He is just misguided right now. That is all."

A strong gust of wind picked up sand and stone, blowing it all around the six Tanninim standing before the ancient temple, before it passed. The air smelled of soil and saltwater.

"So you didn't think, Çig'Allagosh," mumbled Ygg'Vilerov loud enough for all of them to hear. "Why did we ever trust you knew what you were doing?"

Çig'Allagosh turned on them and shouted, "I brought you here to ask for your help, but I can see clearly that I am wasting precious time. I will fix this myself just like I've always fixed our problems."

"Seems to me," said Anox'Moral, "You've made even more of a mess here, and now you have dragged us all into it."

"I'll take care of it," said Çig'Allagosh before turning back to face the interior of the site. "You all can just go about your lives oblivious to the world changing, like nothing is happening, like you always do. I'll let you know when it's done."

He turned and walked off, leaving them in silence.

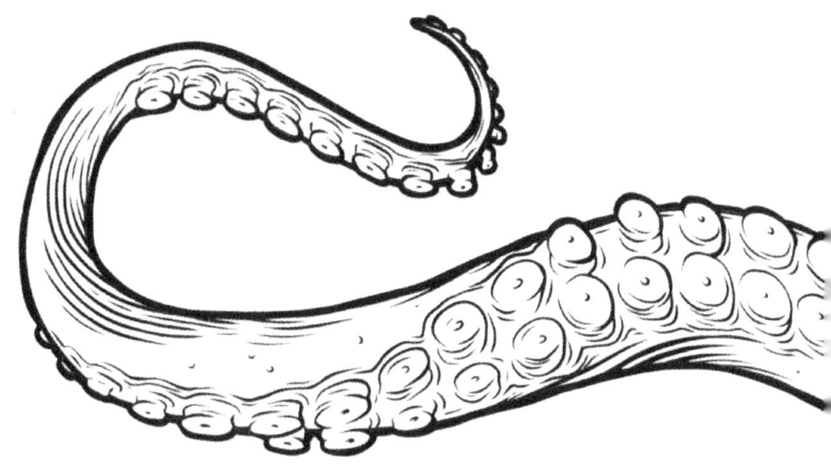

Bury the Secret

Chapter 9

A cool wind blew off the sea as Manuk sat on the beach, mending his fishing net. He watched the seagulls soaring above, diving into the water to catch fish. He made a mental note of the spot where the seagulls landed to throw the net there when he was finished. As a young boy, his father had told him to watch the birds to see where the fish were schooling. His father said he learned that from his father, who was taught the trick by his father, and so on and so on, up the line.

The sun had barely peaked in the sky, and, already, Manuk had caught enough fish to feed his family as well as the older couple who lived next door. The boys had been out earlier that day but had moved on, frustrated that they couldn't catch anything. Manuk knew better. He had quietly watched the seagulls, waiting for them to head out over the water before he started casting his own net. He quickly pulled in a dozen fish, most of which were too small to keep. Three, however, were near perfect size, so he quickly dispatched them, bled them out, cleaned them, and placed them on a wooden plank under a palm frond. He repeated this process several more times, catching another six keepers for meals later this evening and tomorrow morning, until he snagged the reef and cut two large holes in his net. Manuk cursed at himself for not taking more care when he pulled in his net, but there was no use whining about it now, so he sat down to repair it.

As his village's elder, Manuk really shouldn't have been out fishing. There were so many other more pressing issues he should have been dealing with, such as several ongoing disputes and plans that needed to be made to build more homes for his growing village. Fishing relaxed him, though. The problems would still be there tomorrow, so, for now, he figured he might as well take a day to himself to ease his mind a little. And who knows? In the past, some of his best ideas had come to him while he was off by himself fishing, so he figured he could get his family and his neighbors dinner and problem-solve all at the same time.

He was busy winding the hemp rope through the net and tying it off when the sea began to bubble a hundred meters in front of him. He dropped the hemp cord and net, sheathed his stone knife, and stood up quickly to get a better view of the commotion, prepared to run into the jungle if whatever was surfacing showed itself to be a threat. Considering the recent visitor to his village, Manuk was rightfully concerned that others of the strange man's kind may one day show themselves, and, from what he had gathered, not all of them were friendly.

The seawater boiled and bubbled before it went completely still except for the waves breaking on the beach. The seagulls had all flown back to the jungle, and, for a few moments, Manuk was thinking they probably had the right idea – that is, until the odd man, who his village healer had helped nurse back to health, broke the surface and started swimming to shore.

Still concerned, Manuk slowly walked to the water's edge, stopping just at the edge of the incoming tide. Despite the wet, the sand was hot on his feet, but he didn't care. He knew this man showing up could not be good news for his village, so he decided it would be better for him to meet him at the water rather than have him follow him back home.

"It is good to see you again, Manuk," said Çig'Allagosh.

Manuk watched the man stand up in the waves and start toward him. He looked up and away when an incoming wave pulled water back toward him, revealing the man was completely nude. It was obvious the man didn't care, so Manuk just smiled.

"It is good to see you again, Çig'Allagosh," he said. "And I can only hope your arrival means better news this time."

Manuk felt tension leave his neck and shoulders when Çig'Allagosh nodded his head and smiled back at him.

"I do not come with bad news," he said. "I hope that is good enough."

Manuk scanned the horizon but didn't see anything else that looked out of place. The seagulls were all slowly coming back, and, except for the sound of the wind and waves, an uneasy quiet fell over the area.

"When you left last time," started Manuk, "you said I'd never see you again."

He watched as Çig'Allagosh stepped out of the water and ran his hands through his wet hair, pushing it back and off his face.

"Yes, well, I clearly had other thoughts," said Çig'Allagosh," And I figured I should come share them with you."

Manuk watched Çig'Allagosh sit in the sand. The tide lapped at his feet. The man was very strange, Manuk thought to himself, but it was still clear something was bothering him, which was absolutely terrifying considering who this man was. What exactly could a god be worried about?

Manuk looked back toward his net and then down at the man. He looked like any other young man staring off into the ocean, worry etched on his face. Manuk smiled. Maybe he really isn't a god after all? Maybe he's just like the rest of us?

Manuk sat down next to Çig'Allagosh and said, "I can see on your face that something is troubling you." He paused for a moment before asking, "Do I really want to know what it is?"

Çig'Allagosh laughed. "That's a very astute question," he said, still laughing. "Should the gods trouble lowly humans with their affairs?"

"You don't look much like a god sitting here beside me in the sand," answered Manuk.

"I suppose you're right," said Çig'Allagosh. "Fear, doubt, and worry aren't very godly."

"Well you already told me the last time we met that you're not a god," answered Manuk, "I didn't believe it then, but I think I do now."

Manuk felt Çig'Allagosh's hand on his shoulder. It surprised him that it was no heavier than anyone else's. "I need you to know something, my friend. In case something happens to me."

Manuk waited for Çig'Allagosh to continue, but he spoke up when he didn't. "I thought you said you can't die. Now you're telling me you can?"

"The truth is," muttered Çig'Allagosh. "I don't know if I can."

The sound of the waves, followed by the rustling of the palm trees in the wind, seemed excessively loud to Manuk as he sat there staring into the ocean.

"In all the years," said Çig'Allagosh, "none of us have ever died, so we just figured we can't. We've survived fiery volcanoes, poisoned air, and catastrophic earthquakes. We've lived through freezing ice, and we've outlasted fires that fell from the sky and darkened the world for many seasons. Of course, none of that means we can't die. All it means is that we're pretty hale."

Manuk ran his hand through his hair and scratched at an itch.

"At some point, a father has to explain to his son all of the troubles of their world for his own good," said Manuk. "I guess that's where you and I are now."

"Yes, my friend. That is where we're at."

"So what is it you want to tell me today?" asked Manuk.

Çig'Allagosh turned to face Manuk, and their eyes met.

"I want to teach you my language," answered Çig'Allagosh. "And I want you to teach it to others."

Manuk watched as Çig'Allagosh looked back toward the ocean. He followed his gaze toward a small squall that raged far off the coast.

"At some point you're probably going to need it," said

Çig'Allagosh. "And, by you, I mean your kind – humans. And, like knowing all of the secrets about someone, once you know it, you'll have power over us. Then you'll really understand that we're not gods after all."

"Isn't it dangerous to know these secrets?" asked Manuk.

"It is, my friend, but, by the time my kind learn of it, you'll already have power, and there will be nothing any of them can do about it."

*   *   *   *   *

For the next three years, Çig'Allagosh met Manuk several times a month on the beach near his village when the weather was clear and taught him how to speak, read, and write the ancient language of his people – words that had never been seen by and had never been on the tongues of humans. It was similar to cuneiform and other forms of proto-writing but with some odd symbols and script mixed in. It was actually more of a proto-language than a detailed form of communication. Çig'Allagosh explained to Manuk that most of his kind had already adopted the language of the humans they lived among, but the words had power for his kind, and it was critical that someone besides the Tanninim knew about them.

Soon enough, Manuk could write simple messages in the sand and speak with Çig'Allagosh. That was when Çig'Allagosh finally decided to teach Manuk the words he used to trap Uwad-Xotl at the bottom of the sea, several hundred kilometers from where they sat.

"It's important you know this," said Çig'Allagosh, "Because, in all honesty, I don't trust the others. I don't think they'll do what is right."

He first drew the words in the sand before explaining to Manuk the full meaning of them.

"I'm pretty sure that it only works on my kind," said Çig'Allagosh. "Don't ask me why, but it just does."

Once Manuk had memorized all the words – much like an epic poem – the two worked together to etch them onto a flat andesite stone that Çig'Allagosh had brought from the bottom of the Sunda Trench. Its provenance was not important, Çig'Allagosh explained to Manuk; it was the script that mattered.

It took several tries, but the strange symbols were all etched in order to Çig'Allagosh's satisfaction. Manuk was also tasked with building a temple nearby for the Tanninim's language. Manuk knew he would never live to see the temple firsthand, he assured Çig'Allagosh that it would be built and that the same writing would appear all over it – the same words that were on the temple Çig'Allagosh created to hold Uwad-Xotl over 10,000 meters down in a hole at the bottom of the sea.

"So that's it?" asked Manuk after he carved the last line of the final symbol. "Are we done?"

"Yes," he answered, "Those are the symbols that I used to imprison Uwad'Xotl."

"If your friends ever find out I have this," Manuk questioned, "Will this put us in danger?"

Çig'Allagosh stopped to think. It is unlikely that Manuk and his people will be able to keep this inscription a secret forever, but Manuk had to know. More importantly, Manuk had to pass this information on down through the years to make sure that, if Uwad'Xotl ever broke free or the others decided she was right, that they could put up a fight and, hopefully, save themselves.

"Yes, it is possible you will be in danger from at least one of my kind," he said. "But I don't think so, because my kind are arrogant and mostly self-centered, though not everyone agreed that imprisoning Uwad-Xotl was the right thing to do."

"They may also fear we could abuse this power," said Manuk, "And lock every last one of you away forever."

Çig'Allagosh laughed. "Yes," he said, "There's always the possibility of that, but I trust you, Manuk. You could have run from me and left me on the beach that day. But you didn't. You didn't let your fear get the better of you, and I respect that."

He leaned back in the sand and looked up at the huge white clouds that floated high above them. A Java sparrow called out and flew over their heads into the jungle. Çig'Allagosh watched it and smiled. He picked up the stone inscription and studied it.

"Do you have a safe place to keep this?" he asked Manuk.

"I do," said Manuk. "I can bury it in my joglo."

"You'll need to teach others my language."

"I know just the person," said Manuk, smiling. "Aji, the boy who rescued you."

Çig'Allagosh turned to Manuk and put his hand on his shoulder.

"I'm trusting you with this," he said. "There are many others just like you."

Cig'Allagosh could tell Manuk's head was swimming as Manuk struggled with all the information he had given him.

After a few moments, Manuk asked him, "Are there many other people out there like the people in the villages around me?"

Çig'Allagosh smiled again. "This world is huge, Manuk. There are many, many, many other people on it just like you and the people of your village."

Manuk's eyes went wide as Cig'Allagosh continued, "One day, people will figure out ways to travel all around it. I hope, then, that people will come together and not treat each other as enemies."

Manuk laughed. "I doubt that very much," he said. "We don't even get along with villages that are only a day's walk away."

Çig'Allagosh handed the stone tablet back to Manuk. "It is time for me to go, my friend. I can't say that I will be back, but who knows? Perhaps we will see each other again some time."

Çig'Allagosh patted his friend on the shoulder once. He stood up, shook the sand from his body, and walked into the sea, disappearing beneath the waves.

ABOUT THAT IMMORTALITY

CHAPTER 10

Martin and Zoe headed down the stairs from their hotel room to the lobby. They asked for and received a recommendation from the young woman behind the check-in counter for a small cafe that served traditional food close by the hotel. After a brief lunch, they hailed a cab and made their way to the Singhasari Museum.

Once settled in the car, Zoe asked Martin, "What exactly are we looking for in this museum?"

"This is the museum that has the stone tablet that tells the story of the god imprisoned at the bottom of the sea," said Martin, "You know, the creature those scary people don't want us to know about."

Martin watched Zoe sit up and turn to face him.

"Hold on," she said. "Hold on."

He could see anger in her eyes.

"I thought you said we weren't going to mess with these guys anymore?" she shot back at him. "You said we might as well check out the other side of Java since we're here. I didn't know we're still poking around."

Martin put his hands up. "Hang on. We're in Indonesia. We

might as well check out this stone tablet while we still can."

"These things nearly killed you. They followed us here. Don't you think they're smart enough to know we might come to the very museum that has evidence that they actually exist and that they did this to one of their own?"

"I mean …" Martin stammered. He looked out the window at the buildings they were passing. "I … uh … hadn't really thought about it that way."

"What do you mean, you hadn't thought about it that way?" she said. "Please tell me what other way there is to think about it than these things threatened us to stop messing around in their world?"

"We're just going to take a quick look and then get out of town," he said after letting out a deep breath. "What harm could it do?"

Zoe pressed her fist into Martin's side that had been hurt in the fight in Jakarta. He pulled back and winced, crying out, "Ow! What the hell?"

"What harm could it do?" she blurted out. "How about they kill you? And, to be fair, you're so dumb, I can't say I'd blame them."

Still holding his side, Martin's eyes went wide, and he felt his face get hot. "Hey now," he said. "That's not very nice."

"We're way past nice," she said, looking away from him. "We're well into 'you're going to get me killed, too' territory here."

Martin tried to put his hand on her arm but she pulled away from him.

"Don't touch me," she said. "I can't believe I'm that much of an idiot that I keep getting dragged into this."

Martin felt the car slow down. He looked out the window to see they were pulling into a turnaround in front of a large building. It stood out among the other buildings due to its traditional design.

"That'll be 80,000 rupiah," said the driver.

"Pay the man," said Zoe before opening the door and stepping outside.

Martin pulled his wallet from his pocket, grabbed a few bills out of it, handed it to the driver, and slipped out of the vehicle. He looked around and saw Zoe was already at the front doors to the museum. It looked like she was reading something on a window nearby. Martin walked quickly to her just as the cab pulled away. As he got close to her, she opened the heavy glass door and walked inside. Martin abruptly had to stop to catch the door as it closed on his face. He took a deep breath, shook his head, and followed Zoe into the entrance hall.

Once through the doors, Martin and Zoe were greeted by a young Indonesian woman behind the check-in counter. There were no tours being offered at the present moment, but the woman told them they were welcome to wander the museum and could come back and ask her questions if they had any.

"We're actually looking for something specific you have here," said Martin. Out of the corner of his eye, he caught Zoe glaring at him. "It's a stone tablet that dates to around 1,500 B.C.E. It has some early Javanese writing on it. Do you know what I'm talking about?"

"I certainly do," she answered. "Through those doors, you'll find it in a glass display case in the middle of the room."

Martin started to turn in that direction before pausing and looking back at the woman.

"I'm actually a paleoanthropologist from the United States," he said. "I don't suppose there's a curator, exhibit director, or similar staffer I could talk to?"

"I'd be happy to call Dr. Hidayat to see if she's available," said the woman.

"Thanks," he said. "We'll be in the exhibit hall."

Martin turned to see that Zoe was already well on her way into the neighboring room. He stepped up his pace and caught up with her quickly.

"One quick peek, and then we can be on our way," he said. "I promise."

"I swear to god," said Zoe without turning to face him, "If you get me killed, I will haunt you for eternity. Not one moment's peace for you."

Martin let out a quiet laugh, but it didn't look like Zoe was amused.

They entered a large room with tile floors. Rows of display cases made pathways throughout the place. Martin looked around quickly before settling on one case toward the middle. He stopped right in front of it and bent over to look closely at the 18-inch by 18-inch beige stone tablet. It was clearly very old and had faded script that had been meticulously etched into it. He began to pore over it when he heard a woman's voice behind him.

"Abi said you're from the United States, and you came here to visit us," the voice said.

Martin stood up and looked over several displays to see a middle-aged Indonesian woman walking toward them.

"My name is Naimah Hidayat, and you are?"

"I'm Dr. Martin Lee, and this is Dr. Zoe Sullivan," said Martin. "I'm an anthropologist and Zoe is an environmental scientist. We're just visiting. My specialty happens to be Southeast Asia, but I'm sad to say I've never been to this part of Indonesia before. Your museum is amazing."

"Thank you, Dr. Lee," said Naimah.

"Please call me Martin, Dr. Hidayat"

She smiled before adding, "And I insist you call me Naimah."

Martin watched as Naimah studied both of them before looking down at the ancient stone tablet. "Ah," she said. "I see you've found this remarkable piece. It's unique as it is the earliest stone inscription we've ever unearthed here."

When Naimah looked back up at him, Martin met her eyes.

"I've been studying this find for a few years now," he said. "It tells quite the story. It's obviously a metaphor. Do you have any thoughts on it?"

"Why yes," she answered. "Based on where we found it in the Alas Purwo, the so-called primordial forest, we feel it more speaks to an event like some natural disaster. We know there were volcanic eruptions at that time, 3,500 years ago, so perhaps it related to tsunamis or some other event that the people saw as an act of the gods."

She paused for a moment to let that sink in before adding, "But we're not 100% sure of that."

"That makes sense," said Zoe. "That's what I thought when Martin told me about this tablet before we came here."

Naimah turned to Martin.

"So this part of the world is your focus?" she asked him.

"It is," he said, "Lately I've been using my expertise to research items for museums and collectors."

"That's very interesting," she said. "We have another stone tablet that we've been unable to date from that same time period. We store it in the back of the museum. If you think this tablet is interesting, wait until you see this one."

She turned and started to walk the way she came in.

"If you'd follow me, it's right this way," she said without looking back.

Martin glanced at Zoe before following the museum curator through a set of doors and into a large warehouse area. A half dozen tables and desks framed the room, while around 50 crates—some open with their contents exposed while others remained closed—had been set randomly about the place.

Naimah walked them to the back of the large room, where a glass display case was, and she took out a set of keys and unlocked it. Martin caught up with her and immediately saw that a dark stone tablet with strange etchings on it had been carefully placed in the center of the case under soft fabric.

"Our experts say this stone tablet dates to around the same timeframe as the other one that we have on display for the public," she said, looking up at Martin and Zoe, "However, it remains a real mystery to us."

"Why do you say that?" asked Martin as he bent over the tablet to get a better look at it.

"Well," she answered, "For one thing, this doesn't even look like any language that has ever been documented before. It is loosely based on cuneiform, which would be crazy. I'm sure you understand, Martin."

Zoe looked at the two of them.

"How so?" she asked.

Martin didn't look up but continued to pore over the tablet.

"At that time, cuneiform was found in the Middle East, Zoe," said Naimah. "If this is real – and we don't know if it is – it would provide evidence that distant peoples were already interacting with early Javanese culture 1,000 years before we thought."

Martin looked up and smiled.

"It would upend what we know about early Java civilization," he said. "And it further demonstrates what many people already believe: that a vibrant civilization existed on Java before migrants from India showed up."

"That is correct, Martin," said Naimah, adding, "Ancient peoples on Java believed that the world was created out of the Alas Purwo, the primordial forest. That is where we found these two tablets in what our researchers believed to be an ancient village. The story goes that the first kingdom of Java, called the Medang Kamulan, was lorded over by a cruel, cannibalistic king – that is until a man by the name of Aji Saka came to depose him. In a great battle, the king didn't die, though. He became a giant crocodile while Aji Saka became the ruler. Aji Saka had a son who was a snake, and he was tasked with hunting down the great crocodile. The story goes, detailing epic battles between all sorts of monsters, but it really was just a metaphor for Hindu rulers coming to Java."

Naimah looked down at the tablet.

"We really don't know what to say about this find, however," she said. "No one recognizes this language. It appears to be just gibberish."

Martin removed his cellphone from his pocket.

"Would you mind if I took some photos of the tablet?" he asked her.

"Be my guest," she said. "I'll be honest, most researchers believe it's just nonsense, like if people from the future were to try to decipher songs like 'Zip-a-Dee-Doo-Dah' or 'Supercalifragilisticexpialidocious,' believing they had some serious significance to our time."

"But those songs are very popular," said Zoe, "They do have cultural significance. We can't just dismiss them."

"Yes," countered Naimah, "But those words still don't mean anything, so it's pointless to try to translate them."

Martin took multiple photos of the front of the tablet. He also had

Naimah lift it up and take some shots of the back.

"We're leaving tomorrow for the U.S.," he said. "When I get back I'll see what I can do about this. In the meantime, can you email me any scans or MRIs you've done of it?"

"Certainly," said Naimah.

She looked at her watch and then turned toward the two of them.

"I have a conference call in a few minutes," she said. "I do have to run. It's been very nice meeting you two. I hope you enjoy your stay in Malang."

She gestured toward the double doors, and Martin and Zoe saw themselves out.

*   *   *   *   *

Martin and Zoe sat in silence as the cab wended its way back to the guesthouse on the other side of Malang. Martin stared out the window, watching locals on the sidewalks making their way around the city. He was lost in thought about the strange tablet held by the museum when he heard Zoe shuffling in her seat.

"I'm sorry I blew up at you earlier," she said. "I was just really freaked out when you said we were going to see that inscription."

Martin turned and smiled at her. "It's okay," he said. "I get it. I invited you on this trip, and you really didn't sign up for any of this, especially the thought that we could be killed."

He put his hand on her arm and gently squeezed. "We're heading home tomorrow, so let's just try to ha …."

Martin stopped abruptly mid-sentence. He caught a flash out of the corner of his eye, before something hit the cab they were in, crushing its side and flipping it onto its roof. Martin hit his head on the door as the car rolled over. He looked over to see Zoe, her face covered in blood, lying limply on the ceiling of the overturned car. Martin tried to crawl toward her, but his head was cloudy, and he found his arms and legs wouldn't work. He called out to her, but she didn't respond. The car moved again, this time lurching violently before the door nearest to him was wrenched open with a squeal of metal. He turned his head to get a better view when he saw the same man with olive skin, green eyes, and dark hair, who had attacked him in Jakarta, looking in at him.

"Hello stranger," said the man.

The last thing Martin remembered was watching helplessly as the man reached into the car through the door frame, grabbed him by the leg, and started to drag him out. His world went black after that.

*　*　*　*　*

"I know you're awake," said Veja'Hast. "I can hear your breathing's changed."

Martin opened his eyes and blinked. It hurt to breathe. He still hadn't healed from his previous encounter with Veja'Hast, and now, after the car accident, he could feel that all-too familiar sharp pain in his side again. He tasted metal in his mouth, and, when he rubbed his hand along his face and pulled it away, there was blood on his hand. He rolled onto his back and groaned.

"Didn't I tell you to go home?" roared Veja'Hast. "Didn't I say to keep your fucking nose out of our business?"

Martin tried to get up, but he didn't have the strength. He made it to his knees before collapsing back onto the ground and rolling onto his back. He took a deep breath and let it out. He managed to look around. They were in a small clearing in the jungle, no more than a dozen yards in diameter. Something incredibly strong obviously had cleared it quickly. He could see six hardwood trees that had been torn from the ground and tossed into a pile. Bushes and other plants had been ripped up, revealing sand along with decomposed leaves beneath him. A few dozen yards away, through the jungle, Martin caught sight of an old stone temple – the ancient site he had seen in photos that had odd script etched onto it, writing that, to this day, no one had been able to decipher.

"Recognize this place?" he heard Veja'Hast ask him. "This is where it started, more or less, where Çig'Allagosh hatched his plan to save your kind from a goddess's wrath. I got to say, in hindsight, I should have let her kill you all, but what's done is done. Can't go back now."

Martin could see Veja'Hast pacing at the edge of the circle like a predator toying with its prey. "And I'm certainly not going to let you fuck it all up and let her out by …"

Veja'Hast stopped mid-sentence. He craned his neck, trying hard to hear something. He shook his head, before adding, "Çig'Allagosh seems to have a soft spot for you, but he isn't here to save you now. I'm going to tear you in half and leave you in the jungle for the bugs and animals to feed on you. At least you'll be able to do someone some good."

Martin closed his eyes and tried to calm his breathing. The realization that this would be his end was sinking in, and he felt like crying, but instead, he found himself chucking softly.

"What are you laughing at?" yelled Veja'Hast. "You're an insect, and I am a god to you, and there's nothing anyone can do about it. How's that for funny?"

Martin saw Veja'Hast stalk toward him with a slow swagger, swatting a large mosquito that flew at his face, killing it. Veja'Hast squatted down next to him, put his hand on Martin's side with the injured rib, and squeezed. Martin let out a yelp and tried to flinch away but Veja'Hast's grip was too tight.

"I like it when they struggle," said Veja'Hast. "It makes it better."

Veja'Hast paused for a moment and lifted his head, listening again. Martin could see him looking around before he dropped his head toward him, and the two of them made eye contact. A wide smile spread across Veja'Hast's face.

"I'm going to enjoy this."

And that was when all hell broke loose.

Someone or something that was very fast rushed out of the jungle and slammed into Veja'Hast, knocking him to the ground. Martin caught sight of it out of the corner of his eye. He looked over to see Veja'Hast roll backward into a crouch as he frantically scanned the thick foliage and trees, trying to find what hit him.

Martin carefully slid onto his side so he could get a better view of Veja'Hast, and he saw that wicked grin spread across the man's face.

"Don't be a tease," sneered Veja'Hast. "Come out and show yourself if you want to play that badly."

A tall, muscular woman with olive-colored, tanned skin and black hair stepped out of the jungle and into the clearing. Veja'Hast saw her, and his eyes went wide. He stood up slowly and brushed the dirt and leaves from his body.

"What are you doing here?" he asked the woman.

Martin could see Veja'Hast was noticeably unnerved by the sight of this individual. He pushed himself into a seated position, his arms behind him for support and his legs spread out in front of him.

"He's brought me here to kill me," said Martin. "He was just about to ..."

Veja'Hast cut him off. "Shut up, worm. You talk when we ask you to."

"Now that's not very polite," said the woman. "Apologies for my rude friend, but we haven't been formally introduced. My name is Sidn'Gaabetha, and I know who you are, Martin Lee."

Martin watched as the two began to move around the circle, like two feral cats sizing each other up.

"If you have any sense of self-preservation," she said to Martin, "you may want to get out of the way."

Martin crawled towards the jungle and hid himself partially behind a huge teak tree. He could see Veja'Hast was smiling as he stalked around the clearing.

"First we fight, then we fuck, and then I get to end this annoying little worm's life," said Veja'Hast. "This is going to be fun."

He looked directly at Martin and smiled, saying, "Now is the time of monsters."

But things didn't go according to Veja'Hast's plans.

In a flash, Veja'Hast moved across the circle, but Sidn'Gaabetha was either quicker or a more experienced fighter, and she slid low, taking his arms in hers. She used his momentum to throw him hard into the jungle. He smashed into several trees, splitting them in half before skidding to a halt in the dirt. Veja'Hast stood up, looked down and brushed the leaves off of him.

"You little bitch," he said. "I was only playing. I'm going to make this hurt now."

He stupidly rushed at her again, and, again, she used the force of his own body in motion to throw him into the jungle on the opposite side of the clearing. Veja'Hast stood up and threw his hands down in a fit, before screaming, "Fuck!"

He ran at her again, but this time, rather than try to slam into her, he abruptly stopped, pulled his arm back, and tried to throw a punch at her face. Even Martin could see his projection, so it wasn't a surprise when Sidn'Gaabetha ducked under the haymaker and shoved him back the way he came. He fell hard onto his front and kept going until a particularly large hardwood tree stopped him by way of his confused face.

He stood up, shook his head, and called out, "This isn't funny anymore. I'm going to rip your he …"

All Martin saw was a blur of light before Sidn'Gaabetha was on Veja'Hast. Her arms were outstretched, and she placed one hand on the roof of his mouth and the other on his tongue, pushing her arms apart. Veja'Hast's eyes went wide in surprise as he struggled to push her off him. Martin could see Sidn'Gaabetha straining, but, after a few seconds, there was a loud crunching sound followed by a snap – kind of like the sound plastic makes when it breaks – and she ripped the upper part of his head clean off, leaving only his bottom row of teeth and tongue attached to his body. She let go of his lower half, spun around, and hurled the upper part of his head up and over the jungle where it quickly disappeared from sight in the direction of the sea. Veja'Hast's headless body stood on its own for a few seconds, its tongue, arms, and legs still twitching, before collapsing into a heap in the sand and mud.

"What an insufferable twat," said Sidn'Gaabetha as she turned away from Veja'Hast's corpse, wiping her hands on her pants.

Martin watched her walk into the middle of the circle and pick up the gold necklace that had fallen off her in the middle of the fight. "You can come out now if you can walk," she said, as she turned to face the corpse. "Well I guess we know now. We really can die.

Hmmm."

Martin struggled to get to his feet. He did his best to walk into the middle of the clearing, but he stumbled several times and nearly fell. He walked to Veja'Hast's headless body and looked down at it.

"You may be a monster, but you forgot the important part," he stammered. "The old world's dying, you dumb fuck. Welcome to the new world."

He kicked Veja'Hast's body as hard as he could and then turned to see the woman smiling at him.

"I know who you are," said Sidn'Gaabetha, "And I know what you've been doing."

Martin blinked at her, doing his best to keep from falling over. "What have I been doing?"

"You're looking into my friend, Uwad'Xotl," said Sidn'Gaabetha. "Çig'Allagosh locked her away for thousands of years at the bottom of the ocean just over there, because she wouldn't listen to him."

Martin paused to think for a few seconds. He had just watched this woman tear the head off of an immortal godlike being that can change into an actual monster – and he figured it'd be best if he chose his words carefully. No, he thought. Fuck it. He had already been beaten close to death twice. If she were going to kill him, he couldn't stop her, so why not tell her exactly what he thought.

"Hold on a second," answered Martin. "Uwad'Xotl killed a lot of innocent people. It wasn't just because she wouldn't listen."

Sidn'Gaabetha turned on Martin, rage in her eyes.

"He didn't even try to talk to her," she said. "He attacked her with the help of this garbage and another by the name of Ygg'Vilerov. She goes by the name Catharine these days."

Martin caught her studying him.

"You know her."

"Yeah," he mumbled, "We've met." He paused for a moment before asking, "Are you going to kill her, too, because I wouldn't object to that. She's an asshole."

"Not sure yet," said Sidn'Gaabetha as she brushed the remaining dirt and leaves off of her. "If she gets in my way, I have no problem taking another life."

Martin felt dizzy, and he took a step back. He waited for a moment for his head to clear. "I thought you guys were immortal?"

"We live forever," she said, "But, evidently, we're not invincible – a subtle, but important, distinction."

"Right." Martin slowly walked back to the edge of the jungle and leaned against one of the hardwoods. "Why did you save me?"

"I want you to tell me everything you know about my friend," she said. "I want to know if she can be freed."

Martin thought for a moment. "I honestly think she's already doing that," he said. "At least that's what I've come to understand."

"Do you know how she's doing it?"

"Not really," said Martin. "Çig'Allagosh seems to know about it, but he hasn't told me much."

"And what can you tell me about her cage, the temple?"

"I've seen it," said Martin. "There's this strange writing on it, like that temple over there." Martin pointed in the direction of the ruins, adding, "I just saw a tablet that has similar script on it, but I couldn't translate it."

"That's our language," said Sidn'Gaabetha, "But it is just an artifact. No humans today know it."

"This tablet was 3,500 years old," said Martin. "It's from the same time as another tablet that documented the great battle between Uwad'Xotl and Çig'Allagosh."

Martin paused to catch his breath. He felt very tired and out of breath.

"Do you mind if I sit down?" he asked. "If you're going to interrogate me much more, I think I'm gonna pass out."

"I will get you back to your friend in Malang once we finish speaking."

"Right," said Martin as he slid down onto the ground. He leaned back against the tree and tried to take a deep breath, but it hurt too much. He winced.

"Back then," he continued, "People only wrote important things on tablets because it took a long time to do it. I mean, this isn't always the case, but it's mostly true. If someone went to the trouble of etching something on a stone tablet it usually meant it was a big deal to them."

"Why have I never heard of this tablet before?"

"The one with your language on it?"

"Yes."

"The museum doesn't know what to do with it," he said. "They think it's nonsense, so it sat in a warehouse ever since it was found right near where we are."

"Where is this tablet?"

"I have pictures right here …" Martin fumbled around for his phone. "My phone's gone, probably lost in the crash. If you take me back to Malang, I can show you the images, but you have to help me translate them?"

"I make no promises," she said, "And I owe you nothing. But I will look at them."

"Great," he muttered. He closed his eyes and leaned his head back. "I'm … just … uh … gonna out now. Can you please get me back to Zoe?"

Martin didn't hear her answer before he slumped over and lost consciousness.

*   *   *   *   *

Martin blinked several times. He raised his hand to wipe the crust from his eyes, but when he tried to move sharp needles of stabbing pain shot up his side. He tried to sit up, but his head swam. As he relaxed back into the cot, the pungent chemical smell of rubbing alcohol and cleaning detergents assaulted his nose. He slowly looked around the room. He was alone in what looked to be a medical clinic. The walls were a pale chalky white. There were no windows in his room, so the only light came from the fluorescents overhead, casting an unnaturally white light that hurt his eyes. He was dressed in some medical gown, and he could see bandages on his arms. He heard a steady beeping sound and people talking outside the room. He tried to sit up again, but a sharp pain in his mid-section stopped him, so he settled back down. The talking outside the door grew louder, and he could tell it wasn't English.

After a few minutes, the door to his room opened, and Zoe and Sidn'Gaabetha walked in. Startled, Martin sat up quickly and winced from the pain.

"Oh my god, Martin," shouted Zoe at him. "Just be still. You're lucky even to be alive."

She ran to the bed and helped him slide back down. He smiled up at her. He figured the doctors must have dosed him up with something good, because he really didn't feel that poorly.

"I'll be okay," he said. "I just need a few days."

He closed his eyes and felt the smile broaden across his face, almost like he had no control over it.

"You have bruised ribs, and you're covered in cuts," said Zoe. "You're not going anywhere for a while."

Martin put his hand onto Zoe's arm and patted it. "I feel pretty good," he beamed.

"Yeah, they hit you up with morphine," she said. "You should be feeling no pain, but you're very far from good."

Martin scratched his forehead and dropped his arm down by his side.

"I see you met my new friend," he said, smiling.

He watched Zoe turn toward Sidn'Gaabetha, who was still standing by the door, and then back to face him. "Yeah, she saved your ass. For now, anyway."

Martin chuckled. "What do you mean?"

"Jesus, Martin," she shot back at him.

He watched Zoe look at Sidn'Gaabetha again.

"She killed one of her own," Zoe said in a hushed tone. "That's not easily forgiven. What about …"

Sidn'Gaabetha cut her off. "That's my problem," she said, "Not yours."

Zoe stood up and turned to face the tall woman.

"I've met a few of your people," she said. "They don't seem like the live-and-let-live type.

Zoe paused to look back toward the door. She turned back to Sidn'Gaabetha. "For fuck's sake," she hissed, "You ripped that guy's head off."

"Like I said," said Sidn'Gaabetha, casually looking down at her nails, "I killed him, not you or Martin. You don't have anything to worry about, it."

"Catharine's psycho," said Zoe. "I think we got a lot to worry about."

Martin watched Sidn'Gaabetha's body move as she laughed softly. "I can handle Ygg'Vilerov."

Sidn'Gaabetha walked to a chair and sat down. Martin thought she walked like a predator, turning her back on Zoe, confident that she was the top of the food chain and there was nothing anyone could do to her.

"How are you so sure?" asked Zoe.

"When they find out about Veja'Hast, all of us will know at once," she said, a wide smile spreading across her face. She flipped her hand over and held it up to her face. "Damn it," she said, sitting up. "That little fucker broke one of my nails. I just had them done."

Martin watched as she shook her head several times and then looked up at Zoe. "You wouldn't happen to have a nail file on you?"

"Really?" Zoe shot back, waving one of her hands over the other to show off her closely cropped nails. "Do I look like I have one?"

Sidn'Gaabetha looked her up and down, before turning to look out the window. "Right," she said. "Sorry for asking."

Zoe sat down in the chair next to the bed where Martin was. She reached out and pulled the covers over him. She picked up a plastic mug and held a straw to his mouth. Martin took a long pull off it. When he was done, Zoe put the mug back onto the side table. She turned to Sidn'Gaabetha and asked, "Why are you even still here?"

"That's a good question," she answered. "Martin has something on his phone I need to look at."

"I don't have your phone, Martin," said Zoe. "The police took it when I told them he had been kidnapped. Try your iCloud?"

Martin shook his head. "I turned that off."

He looked around the room at the two women. Zoe rolled her

eyes.

"What?" he said. "I have an old phone."

"What were you going to show her?" asked Zoe.

"That old tablet with the odd script," he said.

"Wait a second," answered Zoe. She fumbled in her bag for her own phone. "I took a few photos of the tablet, too. I have it right … yup … here it is."

She held up her phone to Sidn'Gaabetha, who took it from her and peered down at it. Sidn'Gaabetha dragged her fingers across the image to blow it up.

"Huh," she said, staring at the photo. "Incredible."

Martin tried to sit up to get a better look at Sidn'Gaabetha.

"This is it," she said. "This is exactly how Çig'Allagosh was able to trap Uwad'Xotl. It has the script he had to carve into the stone temple as well as the chant to … I'm not sure how to translate this word … I guess, it's activate or, maybe, empower it. I'm not sure what it is in English."

"Does it tell you how to free her?" asked Martin.

"No, but I think I know how to free her anyway."

"Look," said Martin. "Are you sure it's a good idea to free her? She's pretty pissed – and I'm not saying she doesn't have a right to be pissed – but don't you think she's gonna want to get revenge?"

"I can reason with her," said Sidn'Gaabetha.

"You seem pretty sure of yourself," said Zoe, "But I've seen what happens when we get caught in the middle."

"I think I spoke to her a few nights ago," Martin slurred. "She brought me to her at the temple, so we could … I guess … chat. She seemed pretty pissed."

Martin paused to watch Sidn'Gaabetha's reaction, but she seemed distant and cold to him, like she was deep in her own thoughts. "She's mad at the world," he continued. "She's ready to burn everything down."

The silence between the three of them filled the room. Martin looked back and forth between Zoe, who was staring at her feet, and Sidn'Gaabetha, who was back to looking out the window.

Without turning back to face the room, Sidn'Gaabetha said, "She's my friend."

Zoe looked up and smiled.

"What if we help her get justice?" she asked.

Martin's eyes went wide, and he shot a look at her. "I don't think that's a good ..."

"Hear me out," she said. "She's mad at the guy named, Çig'Allagosh, and that fucking headcase, Catharine. You already killed Veja'Hast. What if we help her get her justice on the last two? Would that keep her from going bathshit crazy on the world?"

"That's my friend you're talking about," interrupted Sidn'Gaabetha.

"I think there's a better way to handle this," said Zoe. "Besides, you'd be nowhere without us had we not figured out the other tablet."

Martin did his best to read Sidn'Gaabetha's reaction. He sighed heavily and winced. "I don't think we should be making any promises right now," said Martin. "We don't even know how she'll react, if she'd even agree to this."

Zoe turned to Sidn'Gaabetha. "Can you talk to her without the others knowing about it?"

"I can," answered Sidn'Gaabetha, nodding her head as she got up from her chair. "Go back to the your own country as soon as you can. Do not delay. I will get in touch after I speak with her."

She paused and studied Martin's face. "You will listen, yes? You will leave now and never return to this place?"

Martin did not speak. He just nodded his head, looking down at his feet.

Sidn'Gaabetha frowned and turned away. She opened the door and walked out, leaving Zoe and Martin alone in the hospital room.

Zoe brushed Martin's hair off his face, smoothing his cowlick, and smiled at him. "I can't tell you how glad I am to see you. I really thought I'd never see you again."

"How much did she tell you about what happened?" he asked her.

"Pretty sure it was most of it. Well, the important parts anyway."

"I guess they can die after all," said Martin, leaning back and closing his eyes.

He was just about to fall asleep when he felt Zoe lurch up out of the chair and run for the door. "You okay?"

"Yeah," she said, as she grabbed the door and threw it open. "Be right back. That bitch stole my phone!"

You Are Not That Special
Chapter 11

The wind whipped sand and dried leaves around Çig'Allagosh and Anox'Moral as they stood naked in a clearing in the Alas Purwo forest, staring down at the headless corpse of Veja'Hast. It was a grim sight. The putrid smell of feces and death hung in the air. Veja'Hast's clothes were dirty and torn, and the flesh on his pale arms and neck was nearly gone, eaten by the insects and crabs that were crawling all over the body.

Anox'Moral was the first to break the silence. "I guess that answers the question."

Çig'Allagosh looked up at Anox'Moral for a second before directing his gaze back at the body. "For millions of years, he survived fire, ice, famine, disease, only to be killed by in such a truly sad way," said Çig'Allagosh as he stared down at Veja'Hast's corpse.

Çig'Allagosh could feel Anox'Moral looking at him. He lifted his head, and their eyes met.

"Any idea who did this?" asked Anox'Moral.

"I have my suspicions, but I'm not sure."

"Who could do this unspeakable evil to one of us?" blurted out

Anox'Moral. "We are so few. I can't even understand who could do such a thing."

Çig'Allagosh nodded his head in agreement. "It is beyond my comprehension. I didn't even think it was possible."

All around him, hardwood trees were broken into pieces, and large divots of earth had been dug up.

"It looks as though a battle took place here," he said. "You can see where his body was tossed around here and here. When I got here, his head wasn't anywhere to be seen. I found what was left of it a hundred meters that way near the sea."

"Do you know what he was doing out here?" asked Anox'Moral.

"I'm afraid I do not. There was no reason for him to be here."

He looked at Anox'Moral, doing his best to try to read him. There was anger in his eyes but also sadness.

Çig'Allagosh continued, "I felt something wasn't right, and it was drawing me to this forest that means so much to me. I never, ever thought I'd find this, though."

"Well, we can't just leave him here," mumbled Anox'Moral. "What should we do?"

"I can bury him deep in the ground here, I guess," said Çig'Allagosh, "We don't really have a custom for this."

He paused for a moment, then he added, "It's never been needed."

Anox'Moral turned and began to walk toward the sea.

"Let me know when you find out who did this. Something has to be done to punish them. I will think on it."

Çig'Allagosh didn't bother to respond. He picked up one of the smaller broken trees and began to dig at the edge of the forest. It didn't take long for him to create a deep pit. When it was done, he picked up Veja'Hast's remains and carefully placed what was left of him into it. He then used the tree to push the dirt back over the top of Veja'Hast and rolled a large stone over the top of it, leaving his friend buried four meters under the soft ground in the ancient forest.

When he was done, he threw the tree as far as he could into the jungle and screamed. His cry was so loud, it silenced the noisy jungle.

He looked down at Veja'Hast's grave and muttered, "What did

you do to deserve this terrible fate, my friend?"

He paused for a moment as the din of the jungle picked back up.

"I think I know who you pissed off."

Then he turned and started to walk to the sea.

"And, if I am right, there can be only one response for this: death."

* * * * *

"I called Haoyu last night."

Martin put his coffee down on the table and watched Zoe, who was staring out the window and watching people walk by the small cafe.

"Why did you do that?" she asked him as she turned to face him. She picked up her tea and took a sip.

"I wanted to see if he could meet us before we head back to Chicago."

Zoe put her tea down on the table and stared at Martin. He watched the smile disappear from her face. "Why would we want to do that?"

Martin looked down at his feet before meeting Zoe's eyes.

"Don't you want to see for yourself what's at the bottom of that trench? We can do that if we want to."

Zoe's chair screeched on the tile floor as she sat up straight. "You're fucking kidding me, right? This is a joke."

Martin laughed, trying to lighten the mood, but it was obvious even to him that Zoe was not in the mood this morning for anything other than getting on the plane to make the long trip home. She had said as much the night before as they walked back to the hotel room. It had been two weeks since the car accident, and they had not heard from any of the Tanninim. Martin's side still hurt him, but that didn't stop them from seeing more of the city and even traveling all the way to the sea.

The quiet moments together in Malang had also given Martin time to think about what they could do. He could always head home and take over the research firm from his boss, Paul, but that didn't make any sense. He got into this because he discovered something in the ocean was taking down airplanes and killing people, and, now, he saw an opportunity to stop it from ever happening again. To be fair, he didn't trust any of them. While Sidn'Gaabetha had saved his life, she scared the crap out of him. It wasn't that long ago that he watched her rip the head off of what was about as close to a god as you could get. While she was never violent to him, he certainly didn't trust her.

As for Çig'Allagosh, Martin didn't really know what to make of him. Yes, he saved Martin from getting killed once, but Martin didn't know if he could trust him either. And when it came to Çig'Allagosh's allies – well, he had one less to worry about there – but the one that calls herself Catharine is about as terrifying as you can get.

He didn't start all of this, he thought. Had Çig'Allagosh just killed Uwad'Xotl, there would be no problem today. She was killing innocent people, so you could easily say he had the right to do it, but they clearly didn't live by humans' rules, despite the fact that everyone suffers now because of them.

Martin took a deep breath and let it out.

"I think we have to see this through," he said. He watched Zoe's reaction, before adding, "Please don't hit me."

"I've never hit you," she scoffed. Looking down, she added softly, "I have thought about it a few times, though."

"Seriously?"

"No, not seriously," she laughed. "Besides you've taken enough of a beating lately. And I don't want to pile it on."

Zoe took another sip from her tea. "So what did he say?"

"He told me he could send his plane to us here to pick us up and take us to Singapore where his ship is."

Zoe nearly choked on her drink. After a moment of coughing, she shot back, "Are you crazy? I don't want to die when some sea monster sinks us."

Martin laughed again. It hurt.

"Oh, so now you believe me that sea monsters are real?" he said, mocking her.

He watched her laugh.

"Yeah," she answered, "I guess I do now. Who would have thought most of what you believed turned out to be true?"

Martin reached out his hand and placed it on hers resting on the table.

"Most of what I believed?" he said. "Everything I believed turned out to be true. In fact, I can't think of one thing I was wrong about."

"You thought Javanese tribes worshipped what's in that temple."

"Okay," he said. "You got me there."

"And you didn't know these things walk among us."

"Right," he said, looking down, "Okay, that's two."

"And there's eight of them," she said. "And you actually admitted to me that it was most likely some natural phenomenon causing the planes to crash. And –"

"Okay," he blurted out. "Okay, I get it. I really didn't know much about anything."

Martin met her eyes and watched a smile spread across her face. They both started laughing.

"So what do we do now?" she asked.

"I guess I will call Haoyu, and we will head to Singapore," he said.

He paused for a moment to think but then continued: "And, from there, we get on his boat, sail to the Sunda Trench, get in his bathyscaphe, and go see an ancient, magical temple where a world-destroying monster's been trapped for three millennia – all the while evading a bunch of monsters that are about as close to gods as you can get."

"Oh boy," muttered Zoe, shaking her head.

*　*　*　*　*

Çig'Allagosh sat in the salon of his hotel room in Jakarta. The double doors were open, and he looked around the place and sighed. He could see the outline of a woman in the large double bed, the white sheets clinging to her curved body.

"It is time for you to get up," he called out to the bedroom. "I have to get some work done, and I need to be alone."

A woman's voice called out from the other room.

"What time is it?"

"It is morning, and it is time for you to leave," he said.

He watched as a tan arm appeared from under the white sheet and pulled the cover back. The woman sat up, rubbed her eyes, yawned, and stretched her arms. Çig'Allagosh watched her look around before her eyes met his. She smiled at him.

"You sure you don't want another round before I go?"

"I am sure," he said. "You must go."

Her smile sank into a frown.

"Can I at least shower?" she asked. She smelled one of her armpits. "I definitely need it."

"I left cash on the nightstand for you to take an Uber home," he said. "You can take as long a bath as you need there."

The woman huffed, threw off the covers, and stood up. She walked to a chair by the window and began to dress. Çig'Allagosh watched her as she bent over to grab her bra and panties off the floor. She took a moment to put on the small black strapless bra but grabbed her small clutch and shoved the tiny thong into it before picking up her dress.

She was beautiful – tanned skin, long, muscular legs, curved hips, and pert breasts – Çig'Allagosh thought. When this was all over, he would have to spend a few days with her at the very least.

"I promise I will make it up to you the next time I'm in town," said Çig'Allagosh. The woman didn't respond. He watched her walk in front of him and grab a bottled water before unlocking the door and slamming it behind her. He smiled for a moment before the anger inside him began to well up. He sat back on the sofa and stared out the window to the bustling city outside.

"Sidn'Gaabetha."

He thought her name as clearly and as strongly as he possibly could. If she were listening, he knew there was no way she couldn't hear his thoughts.

"I need to speak with you immediately. You must know already that something terrible has happened, and we need to talk."

He waited for a moment, but there was no response.

"I am in Jakarta, but I can come to you if you are far away. Please, Sidn'Gaabetha. We must speak right away. I need you to hear me and respond."

He closed his eyes and listened, tuning out the sirens and other noise of the city.

After a few moments, a voice came to him. It was Sidn'Gaabetha, and he could sense the anger in it.

"I know what has happened," came the voice in his head. "Everyone knows what has happened."

After a brief pause, the voice continued, "I certainly don't need to talk to you. As far as I'm concerned, the world is better off without him …"

He cut her off. "You can't mean that. We are so few. The loss of one of us is a great tragedy, and we must know who is responsible for this."

The voice came back quickly, but it was much louder this time. "We're not that special, you arrogant prick. None of us."

"We were made in the …"

It was her turn to interrupt him.

"Yes, yes, I know," she said. " 'Conceived in the stars.' Blah blah blah."

Çig'Allagosh sat up quickly. Her mocking tone was palpable. "What did you say?"

"Everyone comes from stardust, you ass," came the voice. "Everything on this planet was conceived in the stars and born here on Earth – just like you and me and the rest of us."

Çig'Allagosh could feel anger welling up inside him. He did his best to calm himself and relax.

"Veja'Hast was a dear friend," he said. "His loss matters."

"Now you know how it feels to lose someone close to you," came the voice. "The only difference is, Veja'Hast hadn't been tortured for thousands of years. His end came quickly."

Çig'Allagosh stood up abruptly. He was so angry he actually said out loud, "Uwad'Xotl isn't dead."

"What you did to her," the voice came back, "She would have been better off."

"Did you do this, Sidn'Gaabetha?" he shouted. "Did you kill him?"

He waited for her to answer, but there was no response.

"Answer me," his thoughts screamed in his head. "Did you do this?"

Nothing came to him.

"Sidn'Gaabetha," he shouted out to her in his head. "I will find you, and you will pay for the life you took. I swear it."

There was only silence.

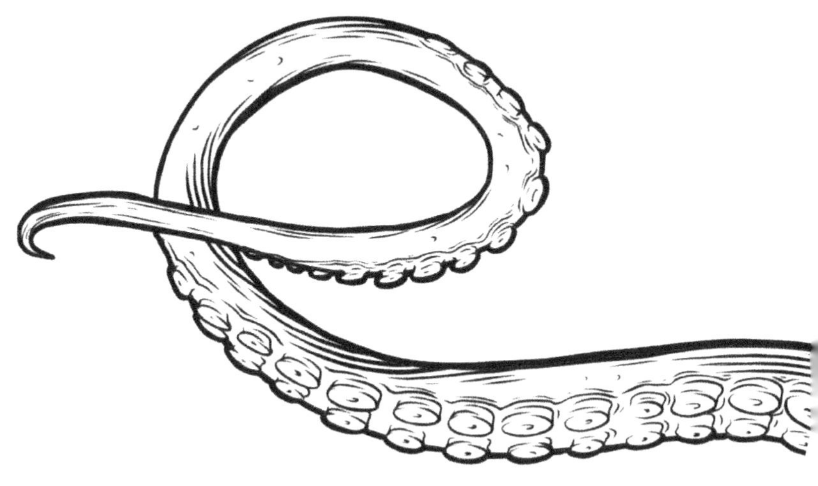

Before the Plunge

Chapter 12

Martin had had a few hours to sleep on Haoyu's plane during the eight-hour flight. It wasn't exactly restful, though. It was one of those moments you steal, but the weight of the choices he had made hung over him and plagued even his dreams so much that his brain never really shut off and reset.

He had to admit to himself that this had to be, by far and away, the most exhausted he had ever been. Traveling across the island of Java from Jakarta to Malang and then onto Singapore had taken a toll on him.

At one point, Martin woke up abruptly. He rubbed his forehead, and he was drenched in sweat. He looked around to see Zoe fast asleep in one of the reclining tan leather seats. Her chest was slowly moving up and down, and he could hear her making little breathy noises, indicating she was fast asleep. He exhaled heavily and closed his eyes again.

Truth be told, it had only been a few weeks since he learned of an entire world that changed the course of history. Everything he had studied his entire life was wrong. It turned out that nearly all of the early myths about monsters, giants, and gods weren't metaphors for situations and circumstances that can be easily explained in the modern world. Maybe the stories were embellished as they were passed down by word of mouth for centuries, but, most likely, they happened.

When this mess was settled, Martin figured, at the least, one of the Tanninim owed him an explanation. He wanted to hear first-hand from one of these creatures what really happened. They owed him that at least. Was the flood myth real? Was the epic of Gilgamesh really a story about early man's interactions with these monsters? When the Greeks talked of giants battling gods, were they really documenting these creatures fighting amongst themselves? It was crazy to think – and, honestly, no one would ever believe him – but all of these early epic stories could have really happened.

Martin closed his eyes again and nodded off, only to be abruptly awakened by the flight attendant, who told him that they were starting their descent.

A few minutes later, Martin stepped off the jet at the Singapore airport. Even though the departure tunnel was air conditioned, he could still feel the oppressive heat and humidity outside. Welcome to Singapore, he thought. Next trip will be to Iceland.

After clearing customs, Martin saw a young Chinese man, standing by the baggage claim, holding a sign that read, "Drs. Martin Lee and Zoe Sullivan."

"That's us," Martin mumbled to Zoe, pointing to the man.

They picked up their luggage and followed the man to a black sedan that was waiting outside the airport for them. After loading their suitcases, they climbed into the back of the car with the man, who told them, "Mr. Li is not at the ship yet. He will be there tomorrow. The weather window looks good, so the captain expects it will take about a week to sail to the eastern portion of the Sunda Trench."

After a short drive, the car eventually pulled up to the Singapore docks, where a massive white ship sat, moored to the pier. Martin caught sight of the boat's name, Nansen, as the car drove up to it. Martin turned his head and met Zoe's eyes.

"Fridtjof Nansen," she said.

"Huh?"

"The famous 19th century Norwegian explorer," she said. "That's probably who the boat's named after."

"Ah, that makes sense."

"Dr. Sullivan is correct," said the young man. "Mr. Li liked Nansen's courage and tenacity so much he named the ship after him, particularly Nansen's work in oceanography."

The young man went on to explain that the RV Nansen is a 138-foot Scandinavian-built deep-water research ship owned by Haoyu. It had just finished ferrying environmental scientists to study the effects of warming oceans on fish populations in the South Pacific before docking at the Port of Singapore.

He added that Haoyu was extremely excited to test out his new bathyscaphe, *Tiě lóng* —Iron Dragon in English—in the mysterious hole that his researchers had first thought to be only a software glitch when they were studying the warming water temperatures in the Sunda Trench last year and their effect on the strange and unique sea creatures that call that particularly inhospitable place home.

"It's possible that this part of the trench is even deeper than Challenger Deep in the Mariana Trench," said the man. "If true, that means the three of you will go down in history as the first people to go to the deepest point on any seabed floor on Earth."

When the car stopped, the driver stepped outside, walked to the rear of the car, and opened the door for Martin, Zoe, and Haoyu's aide. The young man gestured toward the door and said, "I recommend you not tell any of your colleagues about what you will be doing on this trip. For security purposes, Mr. Li has always ordered his crew to be tight-lipped about this all. Believe it or not, this type of research is quite cut-throat."

The man stepped out of the car, bent over, and offered his hand to Zoe.

"I will not be leaving Singapore," he said as he helped her out of the car, "But the crew is expecting you, so, please, head up the gangway and check in with the captain."

Martin and Zoe grabbed their bags and began to walk up the long aluminum walkway to the ship.

"Bon voyage," said the man. "Have a safe trip." And he disappeared back into the car.

*   *   *   *   *

Martin and Zoe sat on a metal bench, both of them staring at the largest ultra-deep submergence vehicle ever built. In a couple of days, this thing would take them almost 11,000 meters to the bottom of a pit at the southeast end of the Sunda Trench.

Martin stared out at the vast ocean. The hum of the boat's engines mostly drowned out the sound of the waves, but he could see them crashing against the side of the ship. He thought about how far they had come and the terrible realizations they had faced over the past month.

He sighed heavily before saying, "Can I tell you how absolutely unsure I am of all of this."

Zoe looked at him and blinked rapidly a few times.

"It's a little late now," she blurted out before breaking down in laughter.

Martin just stared at her, and he could see realization dawning on her face. She put her hand on his forearm.

"I know. I know," he answered, shaking his head, his eyes going to the deck of the ship. "I think we need to tell them what we're going to see down there."

"You really think they'll believe us? They're gonna think we're nuts."

For the past week, they had traveled over 4,000 kilometers on the Nansen just south of the Indonesian island of Java.

Martin had spent the first two days in his cabin, seasick, doing his best to keep whatever he ate and drank from coming back up. During the initial orientation meeting with the captain, he had been told he was going to get seasick, but, if he couldn't manage it, the captain would have him flown back to Singapore on a helicopter. He was told that it's extremely rare, but seasickness could be extremely dangerous if left untreated. It was nothing to be ashamed of, the captain told him. In all his years sailing on ships, he had seen some pretty tough crew members break down due to the unrelenting dehydration, and sickness.

True to form, both Martin and Zoe had gotten quite sick in the first few days. The weather hadn't actually been that bad, but the never-ending rolling of the ship had left them both hugging toilets.

Zoe bounced back quicker than Martin, and she checked on him periodically when she wasn't roaming the ship, talking with the crew and all of the scientists on-board.

The only time before this that Martin had been on the ocean was when he took a cruise in the Caribbean with a past girlfriend's family 15 years ago. He had never been in such a remote location, though, and it unnerved him how far from anything they were. Once they had sailed past Java, the commercial vessel traffic dwindled to practically nothing except for a few cargo ships that travelled that far south and east.

After the first few days, Martin and Zoe settled into a routine, eating with the crew and researchers three times a day. The other time was spent sleeping or reading. It would have been incredibly restful and peaceful on the ship were it not for the deep sea dive they'd be making in a matter of days. The thought of climbing into the bathyscaphe that was mounted on the rear of the ship terrified Martin. He had never so much as scuba dived, let alone climbed into a submersible that would take him 11,000 meters below the ocean's surface. At times he felt like he was stuck in some terrible nightmare and he would be waking up any minute now. Usually, the nearly constant low-level nausea he had would jolt him back to reality, but sometimes it took a quick look or a nudge from Zoe to bring him back to the moment.

In that time, Martin and Zoe never saw much of Haoyu, who made himself pretty scarce. When they did see him, he was almost always surrounded by assistants and researchers, just like the first time they met him at the Field in Chicago.

On the one occasion that Haoyu ate with the crew, he chose to sit at the same table as Martin and Zoe. The three of them discussed what they might see at the bottom of the Sunda Trench—not that much, considering the total darkness at those levels.

Martin started to bring up the dream he had in the bathtub in Malang, where he believed he had seen the temple down there, but Zoe's quick kick to his shin silenced him.

Haoyu explained that the deep-submergence vessel's complement would hold Martin, Zoe, Haoyu and the French pilot, Jean Auclair, whom Martin and Zoe had met wandering the ship's passageways. Martin was told that the whole trip would take about five hours, which left them some time to sit at the bottom and collect data.

"It's going to be amazing," said Haoyu, "And if these scans we did already are accurate, we will go down in history as having dived to the deepest point on Earth. This will be a historic trip."

Martin stared at him and then met Zoe's eyes.

Haoyu continued, "I haven't alerted any reporters yet, but I'm thinking we should probably get in contact with a few we trust sooner rather than later. I don't want it to look like we're hiding anything from the world."

Zoe swallowed a bite of her sandwich, cleared her throat, and said, "We've mapped the entire world. Why do you think no one has found this deep chasm before us?"

Haoyu took a sip of the thick, green liquid in his glass and placed it on the table again.

"Every day, researchers make new discoveries, like that massive cave in China that can house an entire city," he said. "We found that a decade ago. We accidentally found Challenger Deep, because it's a few hundred kilometers from Guam."

Haoyu paused to think for a few moments.

"Right now," he continued, "We're in the most remote part of the world. Even cargo ships don't really go this far south. When we stumbled on this during our own surveys, even my own researchers dismissed this chasm as a software glitch."

He reached into this pocket, pulled out his cellphone, and flicked it open.

"I was just reading this morning about a new sea creature that was just found last year in the Atacama Trench off the coast of Chile," he said. "Look at this thing. It's not just a new crustacean they found. It's an entirely new genus. We have no idea what else is down in these really deep areas of the oceans. We're only beginning to realize these regions have quite a bit of life in them."

Haoyu turned his phone so Martin and Zoe could see the screen. "I've actually been down to the bottom of that trench," he said. "It's not hard to think that there's a lot of life down there that we haven't discovered."

He took another sip of his drink and swallowed, before continuing his thought. "People say what we know about these parts of our world is like if you travelled to California, spent five minutes there, and then just left. It's pretty humbling to admit we just don't know a lot about this. We probably know more about space than we do about the hadal zone in our oceans."

Martin looked back and forth between Haoyu and Zoe. He could see the joy on her face. While he felt apprehension about this whole endeavor, she was clearly excited about the prospect of climbing into a tin can and riding it 11,000 meters down in the ocean to look around. He did his best to smile, but she knew as well as he did what was out there now and what this trip could mean not just for them but for the entire world should it go badly.

It had been two weeks since he had heard from Sidn'Gaabetha or Çig'Allagosh or any of the others. When this was all over – assuming he survived – he figured he was going to need a lot of time to process what had happened to him. As for what happened to Veja'Hast, he was conflicted. He couldn't help but feel relief that this violent monster would never bother him again, but he was also saddened by the loss of such an interesting, unique creature.

He also found himself sympathizing with the dilemma Çig'Allagosh had obviously struggled with when he chose to imprison Uwad'Xotl. He realized that locking her away would have been a death sentence, but he did it anyway to save a bunch of lowly humans.

Martin was brought back to reality by a tap on his arm.

"Hello, Martin?"

He turned to see Zoe staring at him.

"You with us?"

"Uh …" he stammered. "Yeah, sorry, I was lost in my thoughts."

He looked back and forth at Zoe and Haoyu.

"Was there a question?"

"Yes," shot back Zoe. "Haoyu asked you if you're ready for tomorrow."

He forced a smile onto his face. "Oh," he said, "Yeah. Definitely."

He watched concern spread across Zoe's face.

"It's gonna be great," she said, turning back to Haoyu. "We're both just a bit nervous."

"I've personally dove to these depths a dozen times," said Haoyu. "Iron Dragon is the safest DSV out there. There's nothing to be nervous about. You're going to be perfectly safe."

Martin caught Zoe's eyes. He felt his jaw clench, and he pursed his lips. Haoyu wouldn't be so confident if he really knew what was out there.

"Yeah," Martin said, nodding his head. "It's gonna be great."

*　*　*　*　*

Martin couldn't sleep, so he slipped out of bed, walked down the passageway, and climbed the stairs to a hatch that would take him outside and onto the deck of the ship.

There wasn't a cloud in the sky, and the moon hung low and reflected off the ocean, highlighting white caps on the waves that broke against the side of the boat. His eyes had adjusted to the darkness, and he could see a fair distance out past the ship. The smell of salt water was in the air, as the ship's motor hummed along. He had gotten used to the constant rolling as well as the vibration from the engines, so, other than the hum, it was a brief moment of peace out there in the warm night.

Martin rubbed his eyes. His new-found knowledge of what was out there in the world came rushing back to him, and he shivered. It was both amazing and terrifying.

He was lost in his thoughts when he noticed something break the water a few dozen meters from the ship. Whatever it was, it didn't look like any whale or dolphin he had seen in the past few days, riding the ship's wake.

For a brief moment, it happened again. At any other time in his life, he would have thought he was losing his mind when he swore he saw human legs kicking in the water, but now he knew what was out there, and his body immediately tensed.

He frantically looked around for whatever it was that seemed to be following them when, suddenly, a naked woman launched herself from the water and landed on the deck right next to him. Martin flinched as the woman began to straighten up, brushing water from her body, but he relaxed a little, as a familiar figure stood up and took an extra moment to wring the ocean water out of her long black hair.

"Hey," said Sidn'Gaabetha, nodding subtly.

"You scared the shit out of me," he said, looking around.

He watched her smile brightly before walking toward him. She stepped close to him, turned, and then leaned over the gunwale. Martin felt his face flush, and he did his best not to stare at the beautiful naked woman, who was casually standing next to him.

"Don't worry," she said. "No one saw me. I never changed from my human form, and I made sure I was quiet."

The sound of a large wave breaking on the side of the ship forced Martin back to reality.

"What …" he stammered. "What are you even doing here?"

"I know where you're going," she said to him, "And I know what you're gonna do."

She took a moment to stretch her arms out, adding, "I'm here to help you."

"What exactly do you think I'm doing, because I don't even think I know for sure."

She looked over at the bathyscaphe hanging in the gantry at the back of the ship, then back at him, and laughed.

"It's obvious you're gonna see her for yourself," she said, "And I want to help you bust her out."

"That's not what I'm doing," he said. "Should we even be talking like this? Won't the others hear us?"

Sidn'Gaabetha stared at him. She didn't blink, and it freaked him out. "They can't hear us right now," she said. "We can block them out if we want. We can speak freely. No one's listening."

"Fine," he said, "I mean, yes, I'm going down to the temple, but I'm not breaking her out of there."

He watched her turn and lean back against the railing, stretching her arms out on either side of her. Her rounded breasts bounced slightly as she moved. Martin looked up to see her looking at him. Their eyes met, and he quickly looked away. He heard her laugh again.

"That was a long swim in my human form," she said. "Your people are such prudes. It's just a body. There's nothing to be ashamed of."

"It's just," he stuttered again. "We just don't really do that."

"Do what?"

"You know," he said, still looking up at the sky. "Walk around naked everywhere."

"I get why human women don't want to walk around naked, because human men are gross and violent," she mused, "But you couldn't be a threat to me, so what do I care what you think about my body?"

"You wear clothes normally around us."

"That's only because my kind don't want to draw attention to ourselves," she said. "It wasn't always like this. For thousands of years, humans didn't wear clothes much of the time."

Martin shot a glance up at the ship's wheelhouse and said without taking his eyes off of it, "Look, I'm interested in learning about you and your … uh … people … but I don't think this is the time or the place."

Sidn'Gaabetha turned away from him and went back to leaning over the rail. Martin unconsciously followed her lead and did the same. They stood for what felt like minutes, just staring out across the waves. He was the first to break the silence. "I'm telling you. We're not going to bust her out. It would be incredibly dangerous. I couldn't do that to the world."

"It doesn't matter," she said. "That tablet told me how to do it, so I'm going to, whether you help me or not."

Martin turned on her quickly, but she didn't budge.

"You can't do that," he said. "You can't let her out."

Sidn'Gaabetha faced him, and their eyes met again. He could see her demeanor had changed, and she had a serious look on her face. "Darling, maybe I didn't make myself clear. I'm going down there alongside you, and there's nothing you or anyone else can do about it."

She reached out and cupped Martin's cheek, patting it three times. Martin clenched his jaw. "I could let the others know."

He watched her face change again. Her eyes partially closed, and her flat look turned into anger. He gulped hard.

"You wouldn't fucking dare." She enunciated each word.

"You're not giving me much choice."

She turned her head back toward the ocean and looked down. "I could sink this ship and kill everyone on it before you could call out to Çig'Allagosh."

Martin stared at her. He could see she was watching him out of the corner of her eye. "If you haven't figured it out," he told her, "I'm so far beyond caring about my life there isn't a threat you could make toward me that would make me change my mind if I really wanted to do something. You'd have to kill me."

Sidn'Gaabetha turned to face him. "How about your friend? You know, the pretty one. What's her name? Zoe?"

He watched her as she studied him.

"I could grab her in a heartbeat," she continued, "Drag her from her warm bed, and take her to the bottom of the sea. It's probably a few thousand meters down from here."

She leaned toward Martin to emphasize her point.

"I've been alive for millions of years, and I've seen a lot of death, but I've never seen what happens to a person as they're dragged thousands of meters under the water. I wonder if she'll drown before the pressure crushes her? Maybe her eyes will pop before she dies? I bet there'll be a lot of blood."

She looked back at the ship, focusing her eyes on the nearest hatch. "You wanna find out?" she said, smiling.

"I thought you weren't supposed to kill people?"

She threw her head back, laughed, and began to spin slowly on the deck.

"If you haven't figured it out," she said, "I am so far beyond caring about all of those old rules. It's a new world, Martin. Either get on board, or get left behind. Makes no difference to me."

Martin sighed and dropped his shoulders. He thought better of it, but he still reached out and tried to grab her. She was too strong for him and broke free of his grip without much effort.

"Can you just give us more time?" he said. "Please? I promise I will help you free Uwad'Xotl, but we have to talk to her first. We have to get assurances from her that she won't go homicidal on the world."

He watched her take a deep breath and let it out. She walked back to the gunwale and leaned over it, watching the waves below.

"We humans didn't do this to her," said Martin. "Your kind did it. But we'll be the ones who suffer if you release her now. You have to see that."

"There has to be some justice for what's been done to her," said Sidn'Gaabetha. "Something has to be done and soon. I can't let her rot in that temple. It's already been too long."

"That's on you then," said Martin, "But leave us out of it. We don't want anything to do with your drama. Having met a few of you already, I've seen it first-hand that humans caught in the middle of you guys don't fare so well."

She dropped her arms, resting them on the railing.

"So we're good?" asked Martin after a moment. "We're not going to free her – today anyway?"

"Fine," she said, throwing up her hands, "But, when the time comes, I want you to promise me you'll help me free her."

"I ... uh"

"Promise me," Martin.

"Okay," he said. "Okay, I promise I will help you free her."

"Great!" she yelled.

She grabbed him by both arms, pulled him toward her, and kissed him on both cheeks. He looked up at the wheelhouse, but no lights came on and no one stepped out onto the deck above him.

"Keep it down," he said. "They don't need to know about any of this."

"Fine," she huffed, "But I'll be keeping an eye on you for the next few days. You know, just to make sure nothing happens to you. We take oaths seriously, Martin, so don't try to fuck me over."

Martin watched her grab the rail with both hands and start to climb over it.

"Wait," he said, grabbing her arm.

She looked down at his hand and then up to his face.

"You're just gonna swim away?" he asked her, his eyes going wide.

"Why not?" she said, as she deftly slipped out of his grip, climbed up and over the rail, and quietly dropped into the water, feet first.

Of all the dumb things he'd ever done in his life, riding inside a metal ball to the deepest point on Earth to visit an ancient temple where an angry, vengeful monster once revered as a god had been imprisoned for thousands of years had to be the stupidest move by far. Martin shook his head, turned, and walked to the hatch on the side of the ship. He turned the handle, stepped inside, and took the stairs down to his room where Zoe was still fast asleep. She mumbled incoherently as he climbed into the bunk next to hers.

As he laid back on the pillow, staring up at the ceiling, he muttered, "We're so fucked."

He rolled on his side to watch her sleep. He could see her eyes flutter, and she snored quietly. He closed his eyes and tried to think of something soothing, like waves crashing on a quiet, sandy beach, but it only reminded him of the ocean and the horrifying secrets that lay beneath its surface.

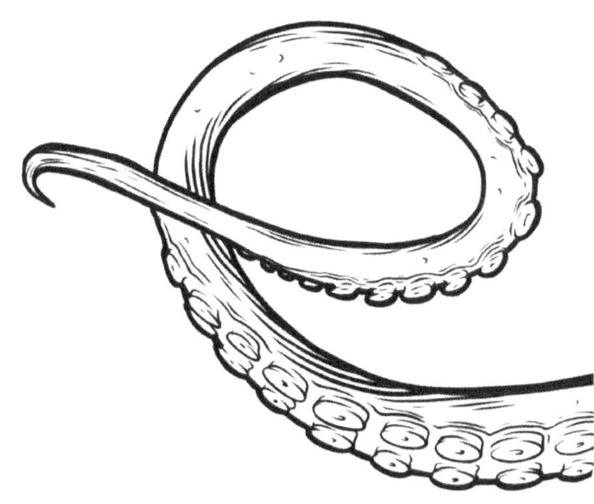

That Didn't Go as Planned

Chapter 13

Martin watched on one of the computer monitors as the blue-green of the ocean's surface slowly faded away, leaving behind only darkness and terrifying silence. He sat in a jumpseat next to Zoe, who was looking at another monitor on the opposite side of the bathyscaphe that showed nothing but blackness beneath them. Haoyu and Jean were in the front of the vessel, closely watching two monitors positioned just over them. Every so often, Jean would reach forward with his left hand to make some adjustments on the instrument panel, which was loaded with buttons, switches, and LED displays, while his right hand remained gripped around a joystick that controlled their slow descent into the dark depths of the Indian Ocean.

Martin had already seen the interior of the Iron Dragon on videos on the Internet, including a YouTube documentary on its construction, but it was nothing like being in it. From the inside, he could see the rounded walls that formed the perfect ball that was intended to spread out the incredible pressure at the depth to which they would be going. In an effort to assuage his growing feeling that he was locked in a death trap, Martin stared at the small observation window in the front of the vehicle, but it really didn't do much. It didn't seem to show much other than an occasional bubble passing by.

He caught Zoe's eye as he looked around the interior, and she flashed him a nervous smile. He did his best to smile back, but the truth was, he was terrified. The vessel kept making random popping noises, and, the deeper they went, the more it felt like the walls were closing in on him. It was bad enough that if he stretched he could palm each side, but it felt like the interior was getting smaller and smaller and smaller as the seconds ticked away.

He shook his head to clear his thoughts. He was having trouble dispelling the idea that there was only about 10 centimeters of steel and titanium separating them from a watery death. If there was any good news here – from what he understood – should the vessel's structure fail, it would happen so quickly it was unlikely his brain would even have time to react before pressure that was 1,000 times what it was on the surface turned them all into pancakes.

All of these thoughts were spinning in his head, and he sat there, quietly, doing his best not to freak out – as Haoyu and Jean laughed and joked right in front of him.

At one point, after a particularly loud banging sound, Haoyu craned his neck back and said, "Perfectly normal, guys. No need to sweat it."

Nearly two-and-a-half hours into the dive, Jean spoke up for the first time in his strong French accent.

"Passing 10,935 meters. That's it. We have officially been to the deepest point on Earth, and we still have a few hundred meters to go."

Haoyu tapped the intercom, bent a small microphone on a flexible gooseneck arm toward his face, and said, "Uh … Nansen … Are you registering our depth?"

A crackling voice came back, "Yes, we do Iron Dragon. Congratulations are in order, but we'll wait until you're back on the ship to pop the champagne."

Haoyu turned toward Martin and Zoe and smiled. "We'll go

down in the history books for this dive. It's a huge deal, and we have you two to thank for it."

Martin looked at Zoe and smiled. For the past few hours, his anxiety over being locked inside this metal vehicle had been a rollercoaster. One minute, he'd feel the need to close his eyes and take deep breaths, and, the next minute, the feeling would be gone as the team discussed a fish that swam by one of the monitors, then it would come crashing back as a pop sounded, signaling the vehicle was adjusting to the changing pressure.

About 30 minutes after that, Haoyu looked up at one of the monitors.

"Huh," he said. "I think I'm seeing light below us."

Martin watched Haoyu type something into a keyboard, and he watched as a camera beneath the vessel began to scan below them. He reached up and pointed at one of the monitors.

"I see it, too, Mr. Li," said Jean. "This is incredible. It must be a volcanic vent, and you know what that means: where there's heat, there's life."

He punched more keys on the keyboard, before bending the microphone to his face.

"Redirecting our course to head toward what we suspect is a volcanic vent," said Haoyu into the mic.

A muted voice crackled on a speaker over their heads: "Roger that, Mr. Li. We can see you adjusting course on the radar."

Martin saw Haoyu move in his seat and turn to face them. "This is really incredible. We're going to get a ton of data down here."

He paused before adding, "It's new findings like this that make all the work worthwhile."

After a moment's pause, Jean chimed in. "Sir, I'm seeing something on the monitor here. It doesn't look like natural rock formations."

Haoyu quickly turned to look at the flat screen, picked up the keyboard, and began to type on it. Martin looked up at the monitor and saw one of the cameras repositioning itself to face down and in front of them. After a few moments, what looked like a giant temple began to take shape in the darkness. Martin could clearly make out the columns supporting some stone overhang, which framed an opening in the temple. The camera focused on the building as the vehicle continued its descent. As they got closer, Martin could make out etchings all over the edifice, similar to the stone tablet in the museum in Malang. He shot a glance at Zoe, who was fixated on one of the monitors near her.

"What the hell is that?" blurted out Haoyu, who was leaning forward to see out of the observation window. "That looks like some kind of temple, but how the hell did it get down here? Water levels have never been this low in the past 10,000 years, and there's no way it sank and landed fully intact like it is."

He turned around and faced Martin. "This is really weird, right? Like finding-a-stone-temple-on-the-Moon weird."

Haoyu began frantically punching keys on his keyboard. "I gotta make sure we're filming all this," he added. "No one is gonna believe this."

Martin felt the vehicle stop. When he leaned forward, he could see dirt and debris clouding the observation window.

"We've hit bottom, folks," said Jean, looking around the inside of the vehicle. "We're officially at 11,157 meters – the deepest dive ever recorded, beating Challenger Deep by over 200 meters."

Haoyu was too busy staring at one of the monitors to pay attention. Jean pointed to the screen displaying their depth.

"Yes, Jean," he said. "I got that. I'm more focused on this building. For the life of me, I can't figure out how it got here. No human could have built this thing."

Haoyu was focused on one of the displays when Jean tapped him on the shoulder and pointed toward the radar. "So what could that be?"

Martin looked up at the radar screen to see six large blobs rapidly making their way toward them.

"They can't be whales," said Haoyu. "They don't go this deep."

He tapped the computer monitor a couple times, before leaning into the microphone again. "Uh, Nansen," he said. "Are you seeing what we're seeing on radar?"

The voice came back again, "Yes, sir. We have no idea what those are."

Haoyu tapped on his keyboard. "I'm repositioning camera number six to face above us so it'll hopefully catch whatever swims over us," he said.

"Well whatever those things are," said Jean, "They're massive, even bigger than the Nansen."

Martin saw Zoe lean toward him. "We need to tell them," she whispered. "Like, everything. And right now."

"They won't believe us," said Martin. "No one would."

"Just tell them," she hissed. "We can worry about that if we all make it out of here alive."

Haoyu awkwardly turned his body so he could see the two of them. "Tell us what?" he said, studying the both of them.

Martin saw Zoe look at him angrily.

"What are you talking about?" asked Haoyu. "Do you know what these things are?"

"If you don't tell them," said Zoe, "I will."

Martin looked up at the radar screen. He could see the blobs getting closer. "Aright," he said. He took a deep breath, exhaled, and added, "Remember what I told you back in Chicago? The monsters? They're real."

As quickly as he could, Martin brought Haoyu and Jean up to speed with what they knew about the Tanninim, the temple, and what was imprisoned inside it. "That's not all," said Martin. "One of them – a woman who goes by the name of Sidn'Gaabetha – visited me on the ship late last night while I was out on the deck getting some fresh air."

He looked over at Zoe, whose eyes were wide. He watched her jaw drop. "She wanted me to help her free what's inside the temple, but I talked her out of it," he said.

Zoe sat back hard in her chair.

"You're telling me this now?" yelled Zoe. "What the hell were you thinking, Martin?"

"I thought I took care of it," he said. "She said she was just gonna follow us to the bottom of the trench, but she said she'd do it quietly. She said we wouldn't see her."

Zoe ground her teeth, squinted her eyes, and waved her hand in front of the radar. "And there she is."

Martin looked at Haoyu. Both he and Jean stared at him. It was obvious they were trying to process what he was telling them, but for the moment, they were speechless.

"You have to believe me, I had no idea they'd all be coming here now," said Martin, looking around at the others in the vehicle. "Honestly. Had I known I would have called this off."

"We can't just sit here," said Zoe.

Haoyu's head swiveled between Martin and Zoe. His face was flushed, and he tightened his jaw. "You guys are serious?" he said. "These things are real?"

"Does it look like we're joking?" quipped Zoe. "We've met them a couple times, and they nearly killed Martin." She looked at Martin and then back at Haoyu. "Twice."

"To be fair, they saved me, too," said Martin, as he looked down at his shoes. "One of them even killed another of their kind. Apparently, that's bad, and I think they may be coming here to sort it all out."

"They're moving really fast for their size," said Jean. "They're gonna be on us in just a couple minutes."

Martin met Zoe's eyes.

"We can't be down here if they're gonna fight," she said. "We've got to get out of here."

*   *   *   *   *

Çig'Allagosh knew he was close to the temple. He looked back to see Anox'Moral as a whale and Ygg'Vilerov as a huge bipedal lizard right behind him. He could sense others were near. He figured it had to be Sidn'Gaabetha, but the two others were shielded from him. He reached out to Anox'Moral and Ygg'Vilerov with his thoughts.

"I can sense six of us are near," he said, "But there are two – I can't read their thoughts."

"I sense the same," said Anox'Moral. "I have tried to reach out to Sidn'Gaabetha, but she won't respond. It has to be Paul and Olivion, but they won't respond."

"What difference does it make?" said Ygg'Vilerov. "They'll die, too, if they try anything."

"We came here to talk," said Çig'Allagosh, "So don't do anything rash, okay?"

"Whatever you say."

"I'm serious. Don't do anything to provoke her."

"She killed Veja'Hast," said Ygg'Vilerov. "She deserves the same fate."

"I said, wai …"

Çig'Allagosh stopped mid-sentence as the last two Tanninim came into view behind Sidn'Gaabetha. The first was a huge bipedal monstrosity with a long neck that ended in a massive sharp beak. It had thick arms that ended in three-fingered claws. Shiny brown, green, and purple feathers covered its entire body. Right behind it was a massive spider-like crab powering through the dark waters by the use of its eight long, spiked legs.

Anox'Moral's voice pierced the quiet, so loud Çig'Allagosh had to wince.

"Paul?" he screamed out. "What are you doing here?"

A man's voice rang back.

"We were wrong to imprison her for so many years," said Paul. "She needs to be free."

The six monstrosities stopped just short of each other, floating effortlessly in the water. Light spilling out from volcanic vents on the ocean floor illuminated them from below, casting dark shadows across their huge forms.

Çig'Allagosh swam toward the huge birdlike creature. He reached out to it with his thoughts.

"Olivion," said Çig'Allagosh. "It is good to see you again."

The head of the monster stared at Çig'Allagosh before lowering its head to the temple below them. Its legs pumped slowly in the current.

"I wish we were meeting under better circumstances," added Çig'Allagosh.

The monster looked back up at Çig'Allagosh, and a deep voice rang in his head.

"You've had plenty of time to make this right," Olivion said. "It is time to free Uwad'Xotl."

"Well," answered Çig'Allagosh, "I guess I see whose side you picked."

"There are no sides here. There is only right and wrong," said Olivion, "And you, Çig'Allagosh, are wrong."

Çig'Allagosh flexed his tail and pushed himself back from Olivion.

"We didn't come here to fight," he thought, "But we will if you try to free Uwad'Xotl …"

A woman's voice rang in their heads, interrupting Çig'Allagosh. It was Uwad'Xotl. "I'm right here," she said. "There's no need to speak of me as if I'm not."

Çig'Allagosh ignored her.

"Uwad'Xotl was wrong when she started murdering humans," he thought. "She has never expressed remorse or admitted she was wrong. She has already said, if she is freed, she will continue what she started. We cannot allow her to do that."

He studied Olivion and Paul as they traded looks. Even in their monstrous forms he could read the doubt and worry on their faces.

Another voice echoed in their heads. It was Sidn'Gaabetha. "Uwad'Xotl has suffered long enough. We can make sure she does not murder any more humans. The time has …"

Çig'Allagosh swam toward Sidn'Gaabetha, shouting out in his mind, "You cannot stop her. It took three of us to trap her the first time, and it nearly killed me. We won't allow you to do this."

An eerie silence took hold as Çig'Allagosh watched the other five monsters eyeing each other. As he looked around, a small light below him caught his attention. That was when he noticed the white metal ball sitting on the ocean floor right below them. Quickly, he shielded his thoughts to the others and reached out to his friend, Martin Lee.

"Please tell me you are not in that thing," he thought.

A familiar voice came back to him in his head.

"As much as I'd like that to be the case," said Martin, "I'm afraid

Zoe and I are in this thing underneath you."

"You are a fool, Martin. If the Tanninim go to war, you will be crushed."

"It's not like we knew you'd be here."

"Well, you should have listened, gone back to your home, and left this business to us."

"That doesn't help us now," asked Martin.

"I will let the others know that you are here with a group of humans," answered Çig'Allagosh, "And that we should let you leave."

"Will the others allow that?"

"I do not know," said Çig'Allagosh. "You have seen too much of us. I'm not sure the others will allow you to go, knowing what you know."

Çig'Allagosh felt something shove him. He turned to see Anox'Moral's tail swinging back to hit him again. He opened his thoughts to the others.

"Are you listening?" he heard Anox'Moral asking him. "There is a question before us. We need to answer."

Çig'Allagosh apologized. "I am sorry, but there are humans here, right below us."

His tail stretched out to point at the steel ball that sat on the ocean floor right beneath them all.

"Martin and Zoe are inside it," he said, "Along with two other humans. They have asked us for safe passage …"

"They cannot leave," interrupted Anox'Moral. "They know too much."

"They mean no harm," said Çig'Allagosh. "I do not believe they will tell anyone about us."

Angry thoughts flooded their minds. It was fast becoming clear to Çig'Allagosh this meeting was not going to end without violence.

"Anox'Moral, we're talking about Martin," Paul thought to the others. "This has gone too far already. We have to allow them to leave, and then Uwad'Xotl needs to be freed."

After a brief moment of quiet, Sidn'Gaabetha chimed in. "Debate's over, kids. We gonna fight."

* * * * *

"Martin?"

Martin shook his head to clear it, but he had trouble focusing after Çig'Allagosh had been in his mind.

"Martin? Are you with us?"

"Is he catatonic? This is really stressful, but it's a bad time to check out."

It had been a few moments, but the voices were starting to make sense again. He shook his head and blinked rapidly several times. "I'm okay. I'm okay."

He looked around the submersible. Zoe and Haoyu were staring at him, concern etched on their faces. Jean was focused on the monitor that showed what was happening above them. Martin looked up at it. It was mostly dark, but, every so often, something moved through the light. It was hard to tell exactly what it was, but it looked like a massive spotted snake's tail undulating in the current.

Zoe pushed his shoulder with enough force that he fell sideways. "Wake the fuck up, Martin," she yelled. "What's going on?"

"Uh," Martin stuttered. "I was just communicating with Çig'Allagosh. It was a lot to take in. I could hear the others, too. I think it hurt my brain to have so many voices in my head."

He wiped his nose and saw there was a bit of blood on it. He looked up at Haoyu.

"Is that the leader?" Haoyu asked.

"No," answered Martin. His head hurt, and he felt tired. He wanted nothing more than to rest his head back against the seat and go to sleep. He shook his head for a third time. "He … uh … He's the one who started all this by locking up Uwad'Xotl. He knows we're here. He said he's going to tell the others to let us leave, but, honestly, I didn't get from him that he was confident they'd listen. I don't think this is going to end well for anyone."

Haoyu turned back to the monitor at the front of the submersible.

He punched a few keys on the keyboard in front of him, and Martin saw one of the monitors zoom in on the temple. "This is incredible," said Haoyu. "I can't believe we're witnessing this."

Out of the corner of his eye, Martin saw Zoe grab the seat in front of her and sit forward. "I don't think you guys realize just how much danger we're in," she said. She turned to face Martin. "Reach out to Çig'Allagosh again. We have to leave now."

Martin shook his head. "If we start our ascent, we'll be right in the middle of them if something happens. We should stay here until we get the 'all clear' about leaving."

Zoe sat back hard in her seat and crossed her arms. Martin tried to meet her eyes, but she looked at the wall. He put his hand on her arm; she ripped it away. "There's nothing we can do right now," said Martin. "I tried to talk to him. It's out of our ha …"

Before Martin could finish his sentence, the deep submergence vehicle was jolted hard and was sent spinning away from the temple. The four crew members were thrown about the submersible.

After a few moments, Martin slowly pulled himself back to his seat and looked up at the monitors to try to see what was going on, but all he could see were clouds of dark debris around them.

Martin watched Jean frantically punching buttons on the submersible. "We're okay," said Jean, his French accent coming through strongly as he spoke rapidly. "All systems appear nominal, but it's going to take a few minutes to bring up the cameras again. We should stay put."

Martin heard Zoe exhale hard. He wasn't sure what happened, but he suspected Çig'Allagosh was trying to be helpful by knocking them out of the way of the fight.

Jean rebooted all the cameras, and they were slowly coming back online. After what seemed like an eternity, Martin saw the two forward cameras being repositioned so they were focused on the area in front of the temple, which was illuminated by three volcanic vents near it. He watched in horror as six monsters came into view on the two monitors: a giant snake, a monstrous whale, and a huge bipedal lizard were facing down a grotesque crablike creature, a huge, weird bird monster, and an actual, honest-to-god dragon.

He looked around. He could see fear etched on everyone's faces. They should be afraid. It's the old saying about elephants: whether they fuck or fight, the grass still gets crushed.

*   *   *   *   *

Paul, in his monstrous crab form, was the first to move, springing quickly at Anox'Moral, grabbing the two short flippers in each claw, and pushing him back 100 meters away from the others. Anox'Moral swung out with his tail, but Paul held him steady. The two of them wrestled against each other, stirring up thick detritus, Anox'Moral twisting and squirming. Paul managed to hold him fast, though.

Çig'Allagosh could hear them cursing each other, but it was obvious they were being careful. Dark blood still began to seep out of the wounds on Anox'Moral's flippers as Paul pushed and squeezed him.

Before Çig'Allagosh could react, he felt something big hit him in his side. Out of one of his eyes, he caught a glimpse of enormous multicolored feathers moving in the water right before he felt pain just below his neck where something had bit into him. He was being held fast, and all he could do was coil his long serpentine body around Olivion and start to constrict.

"We know we can all die thanks to your new ally," thought Çig'Allagosh. "I don't want to kill you, but I will if you don't let me go and back off."

The only response he received was a grunt and more pain as Olivion doubled down on the bite just behind Çig'Allagosh's head. As the two of them rolled in the current, he caught sight of Sidn'Gaabetha in her sleek dragon form, her claws extended, rushing toward Ygg'Vilerov. She hit her hard, grabbing the tall bipedal lizard's short arms and pushing them back as she sunk her massive, sharp fangs into Ygg'Vilerov's exposed neck. Blood began to pour out of Ygg'Vilerov, and, in seconds, Çig'Allagosh noticed a metallic taste in the salt water from all of the blood.

Ygg'Vilerov's screams filled his head, as she threw her body back and forth, fighting for her life, but Sidn'Gaabetha refused to let go.

"You're killing her!" yelled Çig'Allagosh in his head, but his voice was drowned out by desperate screams. He uncoiled himself from around Olivion and tried to break free, but the massive bird held onto him by his neck. With everything he had, he lashed out his long tail and caught Sidn'Gaabetha in the ribs. He heard her grunt, but she never let go of Ygg'Vilerov's neck. He watched as she readjusted and bit down even harder. Ygg'Vilerov continued to fight Sidn'Gaabetha, but it was clear she was losing strength. With one final push, Ygg'Vilerov tried to throw off Sidn'Gaabetha, but the dragon held fast. In a last ditch effort, Çig'Allagosh managed to wrap his tail around Sidn'Gaabetha, but he could only pull her toward him. He couldn't break her grip.

Sidn'Gaabetha started to thrash her head, like a dog with a chew toy, ripping and tearing at Ygg'Vilerov's neck, then Ygg'Vilerov's head just popped off – jagged cuts marking the spot in her neck where Sidn'Gaabetha had simply decapitated her.

"No!" screamed Çig'Allagosh, but it was too late. Sidn'Gaabetha let Ygg'Vilerov's giant lizard form float away in the current, and it sank limply to the bottom of the ocean.

Laughter filled his head, then he watched as Sidn'Gaabetha turned toward him.

"Hold them," came Sidn'Gaabetha's voice in his head. "This won't take long."

*   *   *   *   *

All eyes were on the two monitors at the front of the submersible. The pressure in Martin's head had subsided some, but he still thought he could feel the surge of emotions – anger, sadness, fear – emanating from Çig'Allagosh.

He heard Zoe audibly gasp when the long dragon's snout closed on the neck of the two-legged dinosaur, biting its way entirely through its neck. Haoyu blurted out, "Oh my god. How is this even happening?"

Martin could just barely see the whale and crab wrestling off in the distance, and it was obvious Çig'Allagosh was being held firm by the giant bird.

"We have to leave now!" he shouted out to no one in particular.

"You don't have to tell me," responded Jean as he began to type on the keyboard next to him. "Ascent commencing in 3 … 2 … 1. …"

Martin could feel the submersible lifting off the surface and beginning to rise. Haoyu slowly adjusted the two front-facing cameras to keep an eye on the monsters still thrashing about just above the ocean floor. The giant dragon was not engaging, though. It was just floating there in the current, staring at the huge serpent.

Haoyu quickly looked back at Martin, saying "Do you know what's going on?"

Martin shook his head. "I … uh," he stammered. "I'm not sure, but something's not right. I can't hear what they're saying exactly, but I think I can still feel emotions, and, to be honest, I'm getting what I think are waves of panic. And fear."

Haoyu turned to Jean. "Fuck the bends. We need to push our ascent as quickly as possible. Just get us to the surface as fast as you can."

Jean tapped the keyboard and leaned into the microphone near him. "Uh, Nansen," he said in his French accent. "Please have medical ready. We'll be coming up fast."

*   *   *   *   *

Çig'Allagosh could hear the chanting in his head. It was the language of the Tanninim. He recognized it immediately as the incantation he had used to trap Uwad'Xotl, but it had been changed ever so slightly. Some of the words were clearly different.

"Lag'vachem erg anum mai," chanted Sidn'Gaabetha. *"Una mas, una mal. Una mas, una mai. Una mas, una sol. Eena som. Eena so."*

He reached out in his thoughts: "What are you doing? What is this?"

More laughter filled his head; this time it was Uwad'Xotl. "You'll see soon enough, lover," was her response that echoed in all their heads.

The chant repeated several more times, and Çig'Allagosh could feel electrical pulses coursing through the water.

"Anox'Moral, you have to break free and help me stop this!" Çig'Allagosh screamed. "She's going to free Uwad'Xotl!"

Anox'Moral's voice came to Çig'Allagosh: "Paul has me pinned to the floor. There is nothing I can do."

The chanting continued as Çig'Allagosh struggled to break free from Olivion's hold, but he knew it was futile. Neither Anox'Moral nor he were going anywhere, so he relaxed, hoping Olivion might loosen his grip, and then he might be able to slip out.

Ten minutes later, Sidn'Gaabetha's voice crescendoed. Çig'Allagosh could feel electricity pulsing through the water. The last time this happened was 3,500 years ago, but he still remembered that feeling – the tingling in his body, the involuntary muscle twinges. Çig'Allagosh recognized the rhythmic phrases were peaking when, all of a sudden, Sidn'Gaabetha paused. He saw her turn, and their eyes met. She called out to him in the language of the Tanninim: "I speak for all! The time has come to trade one for another! Free Uwad'Xotl, and let Çig'Allagosh take her place for the rest of time! "Una mas, una mal. Una mas, una mai. Una mas, una sol. Eena som. Eena so."

There was a flash of light, then all Çig'Allagosh saw was complete darkness except for a tiny distant frame of illumination. He called out in his head. He waited. He tried again, but he heard nothing in return. No response.

He instantly knew what had happened. He was trapped, and cut off, and there was nothing he could do except walk slowly to the light.

*   *   *   *   *

Martin felt a wave of electricity hit him, causing the hair on his arms to stand up. He looked over and saw Zoe's brown hair lifting ever so slightly. He met her eyes. The anger on her face abruptly changed to confusion as the submersible was hit by something from below, causing it to buck and roll. The four of them – along with clipboards, pens, articles of clothing, empty water bottles, and other items – were all thrown across the vehicle.

A few seconds later, Martin looked up and saw Jean crawl back to his seat, blood smeared across his face and his arm pressed against his side.

He heard Haoyo call out, "Is everyone okay?" and looked around frantically for Zoe. She was on her hands and knees in the back of the submersible, shaking her head.

"I'm okay," she said as she slowly worked her way back to the seat.

Jean called out, "One hour until we hit the surface. Nansen, can you hear us? We're still making our ascent but were hit by something, maybe an internal wave. Not sure. Do you copy?"

There was only silence. No voice came back. The four crew members traded concerned looks. "Do you think something happened to the ship?" asked Zoe.

Jean tapped a few keys into his computer and tried to ring the ship again. "Nansen, do you read? We're making our ascent still? ETA is one hour. Do you copy?"

There was no response for a few long seconds, but, eventually, a broken voice crackled over the intercom: "Uh, we copy Iron Dragon. We were hit by something that knocked out the electric. Took a second to reboot, but we're good now. We're standing by with a medical crew."

Haoyu looked back at Martin and Zoe. "Any idea what that was? Right before we were hit, the air here felt like a lightning storm."

"No idea," groaned Martin as he wiped blood from his face.

"Can you still hear or, you know, feel your friend?" asked Haoyu.

"No," answered Martin. "I got nothing. No words in my head, no feelings anymore."

The remainder of the ascent was uneventful. The crew sat in silence for the rest of the hour that it took. They didn't even speak when the bathyscaphe was lifted onto the ship, the door was opened, and they were allowed to deboard.

The four crew members were immediately shepherded to sick bay, where the ship's medic examined them. Except for some minor cuts and bruises, they were all fine.

None of them spoke much except for some cursory explanations about what happened on the dive. Martin left it up to Haoyu to do most of the talking as no one else was interested in relating the truth about what they had all witnessed at the bottom of the Indian Ocean.

*   *   *   *   *

Three hours after the dive, Martin was trying to sleep in his private berth when he heard a timid knock at his door. "Come in. It's open."

The door slowly opened and Zoe stepped into the room. She smiled at him before his eyes went to the floor.

"Can't sleep either?" she asked.

Martin smiled back and nodded his head. Zoe stood at the door, before Martin sat up and slid the chair out from his desk, motioning for her to sit on it. He lowered his head and put it in his hands, looking down at the floor.

"I'm sorry I snapped at you down there," said Zoe. "That wasn't helpful. I know."

Martin looked up at her, his jaw tight. "You have nothing to apologize for. I should have told you about Sidn'Gaabetha visiting me the night before. I should have asked Haoyu to cancel the dive. I should have …"

Zoe cut him off. "No, she lied to you. You had no idea any of this was going to happen, and I know if you thought our lives would be at risk you would've said something."

They sat there in silence for a few moments, before she added, "I just shouldn't have shouted at you. That's all I wanted to say."

Martin put his hand on her arm. Their eyes met. He smiled at her, and the two of them sat there for a minute enjoying the moment.

Martin was the first to speak up. "So what do we do now?"

"I saw Haoyu an hour ago in one of the ship's hallways," she said. "I could tell he didn't really want to talk, but I asked him what he was going to do. He told me he talked to Jean, and they decided to keep this all quiet, at least for a bit. He mumbled something about equipment failures or issues or something."

She paused before adding, "I mean, we don't even know what happened. For all we know, they're all dead down there, and that's the last we'll ever hear of them."

"That's probably the right thing to do," said Martin. "I'm sure Haoyu is just as afraid of being labeled a nutcase as he is knowing these things actually exist out there. I can say that from my own experience."

"If they're all gone," said Zoe, "That's not a bad thing, right? They seemed like they were a lot more trouble than they're worth."

"I can't say I feel the same way. It was pretty incredible that these amazing things lived for so long. It'll be a tragedy if they're just, you know, gone."

He thought for a moment. "Uwad'Xotl thought it'd be good to wipe us all out," he said. "She was wrong. We'd be just as wrong to wish the same for them."

Martin laid back down in the bed and rolled onto his side. He slid up against the wall, looked up at Zoe, and patted the mattress next to him. She smiled and stood up. She took a step toward him and laid down on the bed, facing away from him. She pushed herself as close to him as she could. He put his arm over her side and let out a breath he had been holding.

"I think I'm gonna sleep the whole way to Singapore," he said to her.

And he closed his eyes and fell fast asleep.

*   *   *   *   *

Çig'Allagosh, in his human form, stepped through the frame of light out onto the front stone stairs of the temple. The columns loomed up over him. He could feel pressure holding him back, and it took physical effort to keep himself from being sucked back through the doorway behind him. He looked around but saw no one – except for the lifeless corpse of Ygg'Vilerov and a massive bloodied and bruised whale floating in the current about a few hundred meters in front of him.

"Am I to understand that Uwad'Xotl is free, and I am in her place?" he thought.

Anox'Moral's familiar voice came back. "That is correct."

"All I remember is a blinding light," he said. He paused and then added, "What happened next?"

"You were just gone, and Uwad'Xotl in her human form was in your place. She quickly turned into her squid form, and she and Olivion and Sidn'Gaabetha swam away. When Paul saw what happened, he let me go and swam away, too. I didn't try to stop him. He never even looked back at me."

Çig'Allagosh didn't say anything. He just watched the giant whale. Its huge blue eyes blinked rapidly, and he could feel anguish emanating from its thoughts.

"You know what she's going to do," said Çig'Allagosh. "She wants to finish what she started. She wants to burn everything."

"I know," came Anox'Moral's thoughts back to him. He could feel the sorrow heavy on him.

Çig'Allagosh watched the whale's body pivot toward the limp, headless body of what was once Ygg'Vilerov.

"With you trapped, and Ygg'Vilerov and Veja'Hast dead, there isn't much I can do to stop them."

"You must try," said Çig'Allagosh. "Find Paul. Find Olivion. Convince them Uwad'Xotl is wrong. Make them see what is right."

Anox'Moral's voice rang in his head. "I will stop her, then I will free you, my friend. This has to end."

"Thank you," said Cig'Allagosh. "I look forward to your return."

Çig'Allagosh watched as the whale circled around, swung its tail, and swam off into the dark waters above him. He looked at the barren landscape in front of him, and he turned and walked back into the total blackness of the temple.

EPILOGUE

The short, stocky man dropped his hard hat and ran from behind a stack of cargo containers that had fallen off the cargo ship down onto the concrete pier. At least a dozen of his fellow dock workers were most likely dead, buried underneath the twisted and broken steel that had come crashing down when a colossal squid had attacked Fremantle Harbor just west of the Australian city of Perth.

The man watched as the creature picked up steel boats in its tentacles and threw them at warehouse buildings up and down the docks. A brave security guard had drawn his pistol and unloaded a clip at the beast – that is, until she dropped an entire 30-ton metal shipping container right on top of him, crushing him into the pavement.

Screams were everywhere, and he could smell caustic smoke from the fires breaking out all around.

He ran as fast as he could in an effort to flee the chaos, but then what appeared to be a huge dragon launched itself out of the water and into the air. He stopped short and looked up, just in time to see one huge clawed foot coming down right on top of him. He put his hands up and shouted, "Motherfu …," but it was too late. The huge scaled foot slammed down onto him and the concrete pier with a loud crunch. The creature roared and smashed its other foot down on top of one of the warehouses, ripping through the metal roof as if it were paper.

Martin watched the footage of the destruction on television. A local news crew, on location for an interview at the harbor, had caught most of it, just barely escaping with their lives.

When it was over, all of the harbor had been destroyed, and at least 500 people had been killed. Martin could see from the newscasts that no one knew what to make of any of this.

His cellphone rang, and he looked down to see a familiar name pop up. "Li Haoyu." He picked it up and swiped on the screen.

"Hello?"

He waited a moment before answering, "Yeah, I just saw it."

Another moment passed.

"Yup, that's Uwad'Xotl and Sidn'Gaabetha."

A few seconds went by.

"No, I haven't heard from Zoe yet. She's still at work."

Martin stood up and walked over to a desk.

"Sure, I can meet you tomorrow. Sure."

He slid out a drawer on a filing cabinet, grabbed a manilla folder, opened it, and flicked through some papers until he came to a page with detailed drawings of the Tanninim on it. He pulled that aside and saw what he had been looking for: An image of the ancient tablet from the museum in Malang, Indonesia.

"Yup. Looks like they're not dead. Absolutely. We can all meet tomorrow. See you then."

- End -

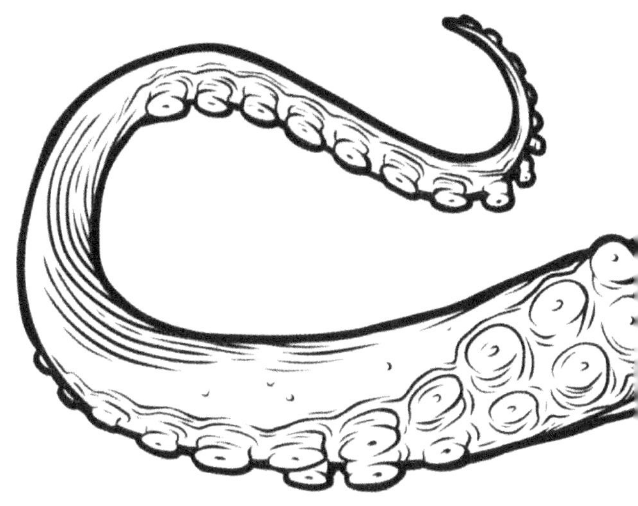

ACKNOWLEDGEMENT

I would like to take a moment here at the end of this story to acknowledge all of my great friends and family who, over the years, have cheered me on, listened to me work through my thoughts, and gave me great feedback – especially when it was difficult to hear.

I want to specifically thank my wife, Allison, for not just her unwavering support but her uncanny ability to rein in what can best be described as some pretty terrible ideas for stories and characters that I spitball at all hours of the day and night.

I also want to thank my friends, Tharen, Jason, Mara, Josh, and Brian, for lending an ear and offering helpful comments and criticisms. I have asked you to tear apart my stories, and you guys always come through. I will concede it doesn't always feel good, but it's important, and I always take what you say to heart.

Finally, I want to thank my mother, Nancy, who as I grew up never stopped supporting me. Even though she's no longer with us, her voice still resonates, always encouraging me not just to do more but to try to do better.

ABOUT THE AUTHOR

Chris Petherick is a fiction writer, who lives in Maryland with his wife and two children. Born in Sydney, Australia, he moved to the United States when he was two years old, but his heart has always been with New Zealand. He is a graduate of George Washington University and worked in music, media, and politics for the past three decades. While *They Once Were Gods* is technically not his first book, the inaugural novel he wrote in 2016 will likely never be released just like a new chef buries his early culinary disasters.

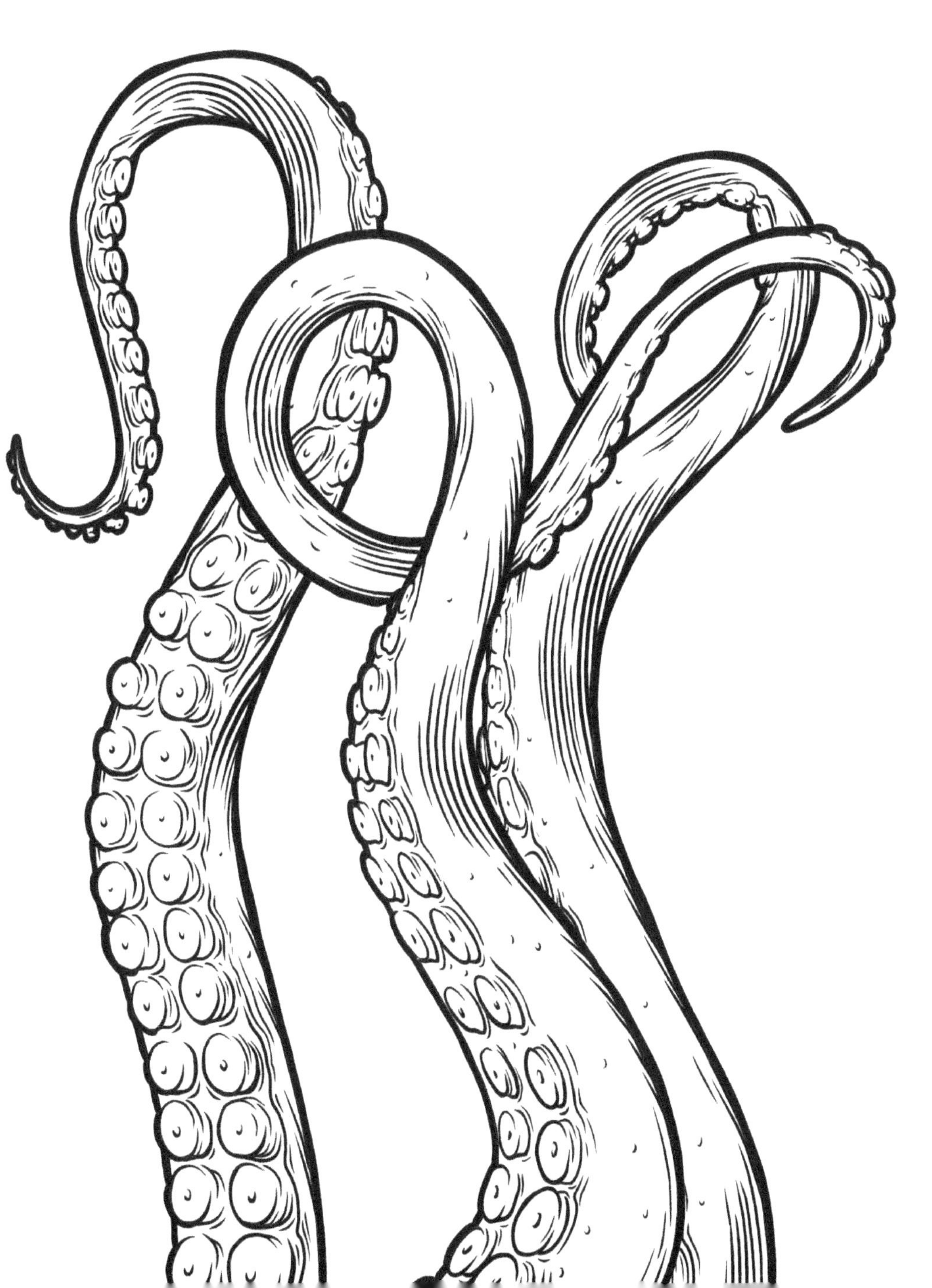

The Night Mare

The following short story is a teaser from Chris's upcoming anthology of horror and dark fantasy short stories, Things That Shouldn't Be.

It was late on a moonless night. It could have been a Tuesday, or maybe it was Wednesday. And it was dark – the kind of dark where you stumble into small holes in the street. It was dead quiet on Celestial Lane in the Teaberry Farm housing complex. Beto Kirby walked slowly, his hoodie pulled up over his head, hiding his face.

Beto could see the lights were out in the modest single-family homes that lined the street. He frowned and shook his head, but, deep down, he was jealous of the outdoor swings, the front porches, and the mulched gardens which were lined by the meticulously trimmed suburban lawns. Maybe one day he'd have something like that, he thought, but for now he was going through a bit of a rough spot. He told himself it was just temporary, and, hopefully, his luck would turn around soon. Until then, though, he was going to take life moment by moment, just like the latest opportunity of which he had taken advantage.

Beto had spent the day walking around the little town of Burning Well in Pennsylvania, about 50 miles from Pittsburgh. He had had a nice nap in the grass in a park until a cop hassled him for no reason. The nice lady at the diner had even given him some dinner out the backdoor. It was some kind of meat in some kind of stew – he wasn't sure what it was – but it was hot, and he could taste the vegetables in it.

The warmth from the pills he had taken 30 minutes ago were just kicking in when he saw the white house at the end of the cul-de-sac. His hands had begun to tingle, a welcome feeling that helped to numb the cold of the night.

For the past week, Beto had been "phrogging" in the attic of a house, and the 30-something single woman, who lived there, had no idea. That's the term used by his friend, who had introduced him to squatting in basements, crawlspaces, and attics unbeknownst to the individuals or families who lived there.

The build of this woman's home, with its low, overhanging eaves, made it easy for him to slip in and out, undetected. He just had to wait until dark and sneak into her backyard where he could jump up onto the railing of the back porch and climb up onto the roof. From there, he would simply shimmy open a window on one of the dormers and climb inside the unfinished attic.

Most of the time, so far, he'd spent sleeping under some old blankets the church in town had given him. A few nights this week, though, he had been able to watch her through a crack under the light fixture in her bedroom. He watched her sleep, all snuggled up in her bed. One morning, he couldn't sleep. The pills had worn off, and he was able to catch the woman as she got dressed for work. He didn't get to see that much, mostly just her walking around in her underwear, but he smiled as he thought about it.

In the past few days, he had learned her routine, which was pretty consistent, so it was simple to predict where she would be, and he could avoid getting caught. During the day, when she was at work, he would slip down from the attic and eat some of her cookies or make himself a sandwich. She had a black cat, but it's not like that thing cared. It would eyeball him, but he would scratch its head and give it some cheese, and the cat would purr and rub against his leg.

The other morning, he figured out her name was Laura Samuels after she had left some mail on the kitchen counter. He didn't know much about her, other than that. And, yes, he realized that what he was doing was wrong and super illegal, and that it was also pretty violating. A couple nights, when he was nearly asleep and the pills had just kicked in, he was hit by guilt, but in his head he justified it, figuring, if he never was caught and she never found out, she wouldn't know any better, and there would be no harm – so she would be okay. He was not going to hurt her, he told himself. He was not that kind of guy. He just needed a place to crash for a while until he got back on his feet.

On this night, as he lay under the blankets, trying to get warm, a thought hit him: what if some stranger was doing this to his sister? Sure, they hadn't spoken in three years, but the idea stirred up some emotions. He shook it from his head. It was just temporary, and he'd be on his way to another town soon. Don't dwell on it too much, he thought, and he swallowed another pill to try to forget about everything.

Beto couldn't sleep. He had warmed up nicely, and his stomach growled, so he sat up, pulled a muffin from his backpack, and started to eat it. After he was done, he crawled over to an electrical junction box. He had already slid the insulation to the side, so he could get a view of her bedroom through the crack under the main light in the ceiling.

The woman – Laura – was sleeping on her right side tonight. Her arms were under the bedding, and her legs were stretched out. Beto stifled a laugh when she suddenly snored and rolled over onto her back. As she lay there, Beto felt his eyes getting heavy, and his head dropped. He closed his eyes and shook his head to wake up.

"Guess it's time to sleep," he mumbled to himself.

When he looked down at Laura, he could see she was still sleeping on her back, but, to his horror, a small black creature was crawling along the edge of her bed, its dark, unblinking eyes focused on her. It was difficult to make out well, but from what he could see, it was built like a cherub, short and plump. Unlike an angel, though, this creature looked to be a deep, dark blue, and its short, stubby fingers ended in long black talons.

Beto pulled his head back as the creature looked around. He caught himself breathing hard, and his heart was racing.

"What the hell?" he muttered quietly.

When he peeked again through the crack, he could see that the creature was sitting on Laura's chest, its pudgy little legs pulled up tight against itself. It was staring at the woman as her head tossed back and forth. She writhed in the bed, and Beto could hear her calling out, "No! Please! No!" in her sleep.

He watched the creature on top of the woman for what felt like an hour, and, in all that time, it never moved. It just sat there, unblinking, looking right down at her face. If he had not watched it crawl across her bed a short time ago, Beto would have thought it was a weird teddy bear, but this thing – whatever it could be – was definitely real.

Laura lay on her back, but she rocked side to side, occasionally letting out soft whimpers or cries. Beto just about jumped out of his skin when he heard her yell out, "Help me! Please!" When he looked back again, however, the creature was gone – just vanished off her like it was never even there.

He continued to watch Laura to see if the thing came back, but it never did. After another ten minutes or so, her eyes opened, and she slowly sat up, her feet going to the floor. She rubbed her head before lifting the covers off of herself. He watched as she stood up and carefully walked across the floor until she was out of sight. He saw light spread across the room and, a short time later, heard the toilet flush before she walked back to the bed and laid down, pulling the sheets and comforter back over herself. He noticed, however, she didn't go back to sleep this time. She turned on the small lamp on the nightstand next to her bed, picked up her phone, and began flicking her finger across its screen. Another minute later, he could see her smiling and chuckling to whatever it was she was watching. As he continued to watch her, though, he felt his eyes growing heavy again, and he decided to sleep himself.

He carefully crawled back to his makeshift bed and got under the blankets, but he could not bring himself to sleep. Every time he closed his eyes, he could see the small creature.

Did it know he was in the attic, watching Laura? Was it doing the same thing to him when he slept, but he didn't know it?

He sat up with a start and rubbed his forehead.

The questions kept coming, and he did not have any answers.

What was this thing doing to her? Was it dangerous? Was it going to kill her and then come after him? If he left here and found someone else's attic across town to hide in, would it come after him? Damn it, he thought. What had he gotten himself into?

It took about another hour, but he eventually fell asleep. When he awoke, he crawled over to the dormer and looked out the window.

Laura's car was already gone, so she must have left to go to work. His stomach rumbled, and he felt like he could use the bathroom, so he decided to climb down from the attic and help himself to her house. He used the toilet and then took a shower. Just like always, he was careful to clean up after himself and use a dirty towel out of the laundry hamper so he did not raise any suspicions.

His head was in the refrigerator, grabbing some lunch meat and bread, when he thought he heard the front door to the house open. He closed the door, careful not to make any sounds when the magnet pulled it tight. Just as he lifted his head to listen intently, Laura walked around the corner of the hallway right into the kitchen, freezing at the sight of Beto.

"What the fuck are you doing in my house?"

Beto looked around quickly. He was not far from the backdoor, but he knew both the doorknob and deadbolt were locked. He thought about running for the front door, but Laura was in the way.

"I … uh … uh …"

Before he could continue, she turned and ran back down the hallway toward the door. Beto bolted after her. "Wait!" he yelled. "Please! I don't want to hurt you. You need to know something …"

She reached the front door and started struggling with the locks. Beto stopped halfway down the hallway and put up his hands.

"Okay, I've been in your house," he said. "I know it's wrong, but you gotta know something else's been here, too, something … I don't know how to explain it … something evil."

"Leave me alone!" she screamed just as she finished with the deadbolt and threw open the front door.

Beto watched her run into the street in front of her house, screaming, "Someone, please, help me! There's someone in my house!"

She soon ran out of the frame of the front door, but he could still hear her crying. He knew it was over for him, so he didn't bother running. He just sat down against her wall, his feet stretched out across the hallway.

He figured it took all but about five minutes for the police to show up. He could see the four cops running up the walkway to him. They had their guns out, so he put his hands in the air and mumbled, "I swear I wasn't gonna hurt her."

It wasn't his first time getting arrested. In fact, it was all pretty normal for him. He rolled onto his stomach just like the one cop in the front told him to do, and he put his hands behind his back. He was cuffed and then frogmarched out of Laura's house before being placed in the back of a cruiser. As he was sitting there, he could see Laura talking to one of the police officers, another woman standing next to her, comforting her, then he turned his head to the floor of the car and tuned out the world.

The next day, Beto went before a judge, who tore into him for terrorizing Laura and told him he was being charged with trespassing, burglary, breaking and entering, and about a half dozen other crimes. He was told he would be getting a public defender, but until then, because of his prior convictions, he would have to remain in the town jail. It all sounded pretty fair to him.

"So do you have anything to say for yourself, young man?" the judge asked him.

"I know what I did was wrong, but can you please tell her there's something really bad in her …"

The prosecutor cut him off. "This guy clearly needs a mental health evaluation, as well, your honor."

"I'll note that," answered the judge.

Beto was ushered back to his seat. He waited through another half dozen other criminals before he was led out of the courtroom and back to jail.

Three days went by before Beto met with a psychologist, who asked him questions about his life, his childhood, and, of course, phrogging. When the topic came up about what he claimed he saw in the woman's house at night, he thought better than to disclose everything and, instead, chalked it all up to his heavy drug use. The psychologist smiled at him when it was done.

"Did I pass, doc?" he asked him.

"You seem to be coherent, son," said the psychologist. "And you can tell hallucinations from reality. That's positive."

An hour later, Beto was back in his cell, reading a magazine when he received a letter. It simply read "Laura" on the envelope, and the return address was a post office box. He sat up quickly and ripped it open, revealing a hand-written note that said, "Please call me when you get this note at 878 555-1343."

He dropped the letter onto his bed, walked to the bank of phones on the wall in the common area, and dialed the number. A few seconds went by and a woman's voice came on the line.

"Hello?"

"Um … hi … this Beto. I … uh … I got your letter."

"Hi, Beto, this is Laura."

"Yeah, I figured."

Beto heard the woman on the other end take a deep breath.

"I'm sorry," he said. "I never woulda hurt you."

He heard her take a sharp breath.

"What you did to me …" Her voice quavered. "I don't feel safe in the home I loved."

"All I can say is I'm sorry. I never …"

She cut him off. "Look, I don't care about an apology. I didn't ask for it. I don't want it. I just want to know what you meant when you said something evil's inside my house."

"Yeah, I … uh … I think I saw something the night before we met …"

"We never met, you …"

Beto heard her take a deep breath and let it out.

"We never met. I found you. You broke into my house. You violated my home."

Beto didn't answer. He could hear her short, rapid breaths.

"How did you see it? Were you watching me?"

He started to answer, but she interrupted him: "Never mind. I don't wanna know." She paused for a moment before continuing. "Tell me what you saw that night."

Beto looked around. "I'm not sure that's a good idea, Laura. These phones are monitored."

"Tell me!" she roared.

"Okay … Okay … Right … I saw a small … thing, I guess. It wasn't a person, but it was about the size of a child. It had arms and legs, and it was dark, like jet black, and it was pretty fat. It had long black nails, and its black eyes, they never blinked."

He could hear her breathing get faster as he spoke.

"I watched it. It crawled along the edge of your bed while you were sleeping. Then it sat on your chest. But it didn't do anything. It just got real close to you, right up to your face, and then it just watched you."

There was silence on the other end of the call.

"You looked like you were having a real bad nightmare. You yelled a couple times. I don't really remember what you said, just that you screamed out stuff."

"How long did it sit on me?"

"I don't really know. I looked away when you screamed, and then it was gone. It just, like, disappeared."

Beto stopped to give Laura time to speak.

"And then what happened?"

"I don't know. You just woke up. I think you had to use the bathroom or something. You got back into bed and looked at your phone for a bit, then I tried to sleep, but I was too freaked out. Every time I closed my eyes I saw it. I couldn't get it out of my head."

He heard her take another deep breath and exhale.

"I think I've seen this thing in my dreams," she said quietly. "It was just like you described it. I saw it on my bed at night when I woke up once. It was just sitting there, staring at the ceiling."

He didn't have an answer.

"Did you bring this thing into my house, Beto? Tell me."

He felt his face get hot. "I don't know what it is, Laura. I swear. I had nothing to do with it."

Again, there was quiet on the other end of the line.

"Is that the first time you ever saw it? When you were watching me?"

"First and only time, Laura. Honest."

"Okay," she muttered. "Thanks for calling me."

The line went dead.

Beto let out a breath. He placed the phone back into its cradle, walked back to his cell, and slumped onto his bed, his head in his hands.

A few days went by before he was taken back to court. This time, he had been assigned a public defender, who got the judge to release him so long as he agreed to show up for his trial and stay away from the woman whom he had victimized.

He walked out of the courthouse that morning, a free man for the time being anyway, and he sat down on a park bench to enjoy the sun and breathe some fresh air.

"I was just at the hearing, and I wanted to talk to you again before you disappear."

Beto immediately recognized the woman's voice.

"I can't be seen anywhere near you, Laura," he said as he stood up without even looking at her and started to walk away.

"Please, just talk to me for a minute," she said. "I really need your help."

"I can't …"

"No one believes me."

He stopped short but didn't turn around.

"I can't help you. They said I'll be back in jail if I'm caught harassing you."

"I tried to talk to my family and my friends, but they all think I'm suffering from some kind of PTSD or something. They don't believe me that it's real."

"I'm sorry, but I can't do anything to help with that."

"I think it's still coming into my bedroom at night."

Beto walked farther from her. "So set up a camera or something. Or sell your house and move. I just can't do …"

She interrupted him.

"I know it's real, and you're the only one who's seen it."

"Look, I'm sorry it's still botherin' ya, but I'll be in real trouble if I'm caught even talking to …"

"It's called a night mare, and I think I know how to catch it."

Beto felt his heart start to race. "That sounds really dangerous, Laura. I don't want …"

"Just come by my house tonight after dark."

He turned and looked at her, frowning.

"You owe me this. At the very least, come by and hear me out."

"A week ago, you hated me. You said I'm a creep. Honestly, I can't blame ya. You're right. I was pretty bad to you. And now you want me to come to your house?"

He thought about it for a minute. "Why do I feel like this is a setup?"

"It's not. I swear."

He studied her, watching as her eyes went to the ground.

"Best I can do is I'll think about it. Okay?"

She looked up at him and smiled, but Beto could see the tears in her eyes. He nodded to her and then turned and walked away from her. He didn't stop until he was far away from the courthouse. He stopped at a small park near a creek and sat down on a bench to think.

She was right, he thought. He did owe it to her to help her. It was the least he could do to make up for what he had already put her through. If he did go to her house, however, and something happened and he was caught, he risked ending up in jail for a really, really long time. Both the judge and the prosecutor said as much. On the other hand, he realized no one was going to believe her. He had firsthand knowledge of this when everyone thought he was crazy. He had to lie to keep from getting thrown into a mental hospital.

Hours later that day, at 10 at night, Beto paused in the shadows in the backyard of Laura's house.

"This is so dumb," he mumbled as he slowly crept up to the glass sliding door at the back of the woman's house. He could see her sitting at the table in her kitchen. She was looking at her phone and sipping from a tea cup. He took a deep breath and walked to the door, but before he could knock, she jumped out of the chair and threw open the door.

"You came," she started to shout but caught herself, looking around the backyard as if she could see anything in the darkness.

"Yeah," he said. "It's the least I could do, I guess."

He could see she was not smiling. She stepped to the side, inviting him in, but he hesitated. He could see her looking at him, trying to read his face.

"I thought a lot about what I was going to tell you tonight," she said. "I want to say I don't trust you. Everything screams this is the worst idea, but I don't think I have a choice.

She paused for a moment then added, "Other than to say, if you mess with me, I'll fight back."

"I'm not gonna do anything," he said as he looked down at the ground. He looked up at her and continued: "I'm really sorry about what I did. I own it, and I'll be going to prison soon."

He met her eyes. "I know I don't deserve any forgiveness, and that's why I decided to come tonight. You're right. I owe you this. No matter what happens to me. I just wanted you to know."

He stepped inside the house. "So you said you know what to do with this thing?"

She smiled at him and then looked away at the table. "Right," she said. "Over here." She walked to the table, sat down, and picked up her iPad. "I was looking for images for 'creepy things that watch you while you sleep,' and I came across this picture."

She showed the screen to Beto. On it was an image of a painting depicting a small creature sitting on top of a sleeping woman. It looked just like the thing he saw in her bedroom.

"This is it, right?" she asked him.

He nodded in approval. "That's exactly what it looked like."

"They're called night mares," she said. "They come from way up in Scandinavia."

She put the iPad down on the table, closing the flap on it with a click. "From what I've read, a witch is usually hired by someone – like an angry wife who caught her husband cheating – and wants to curse him with one. The mare then torments the guy until he goes crazy or dies."

Beto watched her. It all sounded pretty bonkers to him. Had he not seen the creature with his own eyes he wouldn't have believed her either.

"But that doesn't explain why it's here," she said. "I don't have a husband or even a boyfriend, so I don't know why it's come after me."

She wiped her eyes with her hand and sat back hard in her chair.

"You said you know how to catch it?"

"Yeah," she said. "Hang on." She picked up the iPad again and turned it on. "Read this."

Beto took it from her and began to read the open page in the browser. It was English, but there were all kinds of weird names and words he didn't understand. He looked up at Laura, confusion clear on his face. "I don't understand."

She huffed out her nose and took the iPad back from him. She went on to explain that, according to this story, mares use knots in old trees as a way to travel across great distances. They can jump from tree to tree in the woods using this way, or they can use them to appear in homes that have old furniture with some knots in them. She looked at Beto. "I inherited a wood bed frame from my grandparents after they passed away. It's really old. I think that's how it's getting into my house."

Beto thought for a moment. "Why don't you just throw the bed away?"

"I thought of that, but I'm worried it'll just piss it off and it'll start using my woods to torture me at night. Or it'll go after my neighbors."

"So what do you want to do?"

And that was how Beto found himself on the carpet underneath Laura's bed just before midnight.

He had been lying there for about a half hour when he heard her whisper to him, "You okay down there?"

"More comfortable than the bed in my jail cell."

The only response he got to that was the sound of her rolling over in bed.

"You really think this thing is gonna show up?"

"I'm pretty sure it's been here every night since you saw it."

"Damn," he muttered. "You must be exhausted."

"Let's just say I'm not going to have any problem falling asleep tonight … even with you under my bed." She enunciated the word "you," drawing it out for emphasis.

"Well I won't bug you anymore then, so we can get on with this."

He heard the bed creak and the sheets rustle above him again.

It didn't take long before Beto heard the telltale sounds of Laura sleeping – the occasional soft wheeze and quiet snoring. He frowned, thinking back to what a creep he had been, hiding in the attic and violating such a nice woman. He shook his head back and forth, stifling the urge to punch himself in his own face for causing so much trouble. He was contemplating the prospects of turning back time when he heard grunting and scratching noises coming from the bed above him.

Beto said a silent prayer to himself and slid out from below the bed.

"Wake up, Laura," he shouted as he got to his feet and shined his flashlight on the creature.

When he looked at her on the bed, there it was in all its horror. The plump, little, naked night mare was sitting on her chest, its short, fat legs bent and pulled up to its body. Beto watched as its head swiveled to face him. It curled its top lip, showing darkly stained teeth, and it snarled at him, a low rumble that started in its chest.

"Laura, wake up!" he shouted again. "It's here!"

Laura's eyes shot open, and she sat up, sending the thing tumbling to the foot of the bed.

Beto ran to the baseboard and covered the one large knot that was on it. He shouted, "Now! Block the knots on the headboard!"

Laura shook her head and scrambled to place her hands over two spots on the front and the back of the headboard. The creature's head shot back and forth multiple times between Beto and Laura. Its dark eyes were wide, and, for the first time, Beto thought he saw fear on its face.

It stood up on the bed and hissed at Beto. Then it rocketed off the side, scrambling down the comforter, and onto the floor where it slipped under the bed.

"We know what you are," yelled Beto. "You're trapped. You have to make a deal with us."

Beto heard a noise come from under the bed, like something between a rasp scraping across dry wood and the huffing sounds a deer may make at night.

He looked at Laura, who he could see was still half asleep. "I think it's laughing."

Beto squatted down and shined his flashlight under the bed. His heart was racing. He moved it across the room, ever so slowly, until he found the creature at the top of the bed, squatting down against the wall, tucked in right next to Laura's nightstand.

"Talk to me, night mare," he said. "We know what you are, and we know how to trap you here. You have to make a deal."

It made that noise again. It was definitely laughing at them. Then it spoke. "You think you have me, human, but you don't know what you've caught and what I can do to you and the bitch."

It was small, barely three feet tall, but its voice was deep. It sounded more like a full-grown old man whose voice had been destroyed from years of pipe smoke. Beto shivered involuntarily and goosebumps popped up all over his arms.

"We know how to trap you," answered Beto, "And we can keep you here until the sun rises."

It was shielding its face from the flashlight with its hand, but Beto could still see it. He studied its reaction.

"You know what that means, don't you? What happens when the sun comes up?"

The night mare dropped its hand, hissed, and lunged at him, but, to his credit, Beto didn't even flinch.

"We blocked the knots," said Laura. "You only have power when I'm sleeping, and I'm awake. So who's the bitch now?"

"So let's deal, night mare," said Beto. "You agree to never physically or psychologically torment, harass, torture, or otherwise irritate Laura. If you're good with that, we will let you leave. But if you keep acting like an annoying little shit, then we will wait until the sun comes up, and you'll get crispy-fried."

He studied the night mare. "We got a deal?"

The night mare hissed again at Beto.

"Wait a second," interrupted Laura. "How do you know he'll honor the agreement?"

"It is our way, human," said the night mare. "Our word is bond enough."

It paused for a moment and then added, "We have a deal, humans."

"We good then, Laura?"

He didn't hear anything from Laura, but he didn't want to take his eyes off the creature. "Laura … We good here?"

"Yeah, yeah," she answered. "We're good. Let it go."

Beto lifted his hand off the baseboard and took three steps back. He still had the flashlight positioned on the night mare and followed it as it walked toward him. When it got to the foot of the bed, it looked up and around, focusing on the knot in the wood, and, in a flash, it simply vanished from the room.

Beto let out a breath and slumped to the floor. He saw Laura crawl to the nightstand and turn on the light. She looked over at him and smiled. "I guess I owe you now," she said to him.

"Nah," he answered. "As far as I'm concerned we're pretty much good."

She sat back against the headboard. "I think I need a strong drink. You want a strong drink?"

Beto shook his head. "I got to go, Laura. I can't be seen here."

He watched her look up at the ceiling. She looked back at him, and their eyes met.

"I guess I should get that crack fixed," she said, laughing.

Beto looked down at his feet. He shook his head, but he was smiling.

They did get that drink, and it went down a little too easy, and then Beto left right after that, but this time, Laura held the sliding glass door open for him as he disappeared into the dark woods right behind her house.

- End -